# MAIN CHARACTER ENERGY

NEW YORK TIMES BESTSELLING AUTHOR

# KENDALL RYAN

Editing by Guilana Gomez-Brown
Proofread by Virginia Tesi-Carey
Cover Design by KB Keane
Formatting by Alyssa Garcia

# ABOUT THE BOOK

*She's ice. He's fire. Watch them ignite.*

Andi Callahan prefers the quiet company of the dead.

As a morgue tech in a sleepy coastal town outside Boston, she lives for silence, predictability, and zero small talk.

Living people? Too loud. Too messy. Too nosy.

The dead don't interrupt her, meddle in her life, or flirt with her.

Cole Hartley does.

He's everything Andi avoids—charming, persistent, and entirely too good-looking for his own good.

The town's beloved firefighter-paramedic has a hero complex the size of Massachusetts and a dangerous talent for cracking Andi's ice-cold composure.

What starts as a harmless bet to make her smile turns into something neither of them saw coming.

Now Cole's determined to prove that life is worth the mess—and that love might be the riskiest, most rewarding thing of all.

Funny, heartfelt, and impossible to put down, this opposites-attract romance asks what happens when a woman who's made peace with solitude finally lets herself feel everything.

***Perfect for fans of quirky slow-burns, grumpy-***

*sunshine, spicy banter, enemies to lovers, and one very determined golden retriever in human form.*

# AUTHOR'S NOTE

Hey there,

First off, thank you for picking up *Main Character Energy*. I'm so excited (and slightly terrified) to share Andi and Cole's story with you.

This book has heart, heat, humor, and a few emotional moments along the way. It also touches on themes of grief and loss and includes some occupational hazards—our hero is a firefighter/paramedic, so there are references to dangerous situations and emergency calls.

Also? There's a 140-pound dog named Beef who shamelessly steals the spotlight every chance he gets.

Thank you for reading, and I hope you fall for these characters as much as I did.

With love and gratitude,

# 1

## MEET UGLY

*Andi*

Dead people don't waste my time. That's why I like them better.

They don't talk back. They don't ask stupid questions. They just lie there, still and quiet, while I do my job and keep the world from falling apart.

Which is more than I can say for the living.

I snap off my gloves, toss them into the bin, and stretch my neck until it pops. The morgue is hotter than hell today, the AC humming like it's trying but not really trying, and sweat is already prickling at the back of my neck.

I glance at the clock. Not even noon.

Figures.

I'm halfway through logging a transfer when Mikey strolls in like he has nothing better to do than annoy me. Which he doesn't, let's be honest.

"Morning, sunshine," he says, holding out a cup of hospital-grade sludge like it's a peace offering.

I eye it. "Is it poisoned?"

"You wish." He leans against the counter, grinning. "You look murderously hot today, by the way."

I don't dignify that with a response. He's not wrong—I know I look good. Fresh blowout, my favorite purple scrubs. Enough bracelets to strangle him with if necessary.

"Don't talk to me until you've tagged and bagged three bodies in ninety-degree heat," I quip instead.

"Damn, Andi. Buy me a drink first."

I snatch the cup, take a sip, and grimace. "This is disgusting."

"You're welcome." He wiggles his brows. "I bring the best to the best."

I don't respond. He'll take it as encouragement. Mikey's been here almost as long as I have, and while I'd never admit it out loud, he's tolerable—in small, heavily regulated doses.

He watches me for a beat, waiting.

"What now?" I sigh.

His grin stretches wider. "You heard about the auction?"

"What auction?"

"You're gonna love this—and by *love*, I mean you'll hate it with every fiber of your being."

I give him a side-eye. "Well?"

"This one's straight out of HR's worst ideas folder." He chuckles.

"Spit it out, Mikey."

"The hospital's doing a bachelor-bachelorette auction—for charity. All singles in the building are supposed to do it." He pauses for effect. "That means you."

I stare. "No."

"Yup."

"No chance in hell."

He chuckles. "Voluntold, Callahan. Our supervisor's already got your name on the list."

I slam my cup down, hard enough that coffee sloshes over the rim. "They can't make me."

"They can. They are. All proceeds go to the children's wing. You gonna fight sick kids?"

He's right. The fact that it's "for the kids" makes it even worse because how do you say no to charity without looking like a complete monster?

I sigh loudly. "This is the most manipulative bullshit I've ever heard."

Mikey is loving this. "Oh, it gets better. They're gonna print flyers to hang around the hospital. I'm helping pick your photo."

I point at him. "I will end you."

"You'll look great on a poster. Maybe we can

get you holding a scalpel□—"

"Get out."

He's gone, but the damage is done.

The morgue feels colder now. Or maybe it's just me— patience shot, my skin prickling with irritation that has nothing to do with the AC humming overhead.

It's been like this all week—tourist season—which means the town's population triples and so does my workload. More people, more accidents, more mess.

More reasons to lose it.

It's fine. Dead people are easy. They don't complain, don't make demands, don't need anything from me. That's exactly how I like it.

The living? Different story. They're messy, loud, and somehow always manage to make everything worse.

I grab the next file and skim it. Mid-sixties. Heart attack. Found in a rental cabin by his wife.

I heard she cried the whole time they worked on him—loud, raw, unrelenting.

Grief sucks.

Like I don't know that weight. It crushes your chest until breathing feels like a choice you're not sure you want to make anymore.

But it's the silence that follows—the stillness after the storm—that's where I do my best work.

I wash my hands, letting the water run hotter

than necessary, and glance at the clock. Only three hours left. I can survive three more hours.

Probably.

Maybe.

My phone buzzes in my pocket. I don't have to look to know who it is.

Shay.

I slide the phone out, answer, and tuck it between my ear and shoulder.

"Tell me something good," I say, reaching for the next file.

Her voice crackles through, bright and chaotic. "Two things. One, I just did the worst haircut of my career—on purpose—and two, your ex is still a flaming pile of trash."

I flip the page. "That's not new information."

"Yeah, but now he's trash with a new girlfriend. Guess who walked into my salon holding hands with a watered-down version of you?"

"Beef?" I deadpan.

She cackles. "Beef would never betray you like that."

My eyes flick to the corner where Beef is sprawled out, massive and snoring, like the world's most useless guard dog.

"Anyway," Shay continues, "you owe me dinner for that trauma. Or at least a drink."

"I'm working."

"You're always working."

"Dead people don't process themselves."

"If anyone could make that happen, it'd be you."

I smile, just barely. "I'll see what I can do," I mutter, ending the call before she gets too comfortable. Shay's great—in doses. But right now, I need focus. I need quiet. Three more hours until Beef and I are out of here.

Clock out. Go home. Pretend the living don't exist.

I'm halfway through the next file when I hear them.

Male. Too loud, too casual, echoing down the hall like they own the place.

I grit my teeth.

The paramedic team. Of course.

The doors swing open, and in they come, Brennan first—all swagger and noise, laughing at something that wasn't funny even before he said it. He's hit on me at least four times this month. I've given him exactly zero reasons to continue.

And then him.

The cute one.

I don't want to notice that he's cute. I really don't.

I've seen him before, once or twice, usually at night when I'm covering a late shift. New to this schedule. Cole, I think. Taller than Brennan, broader too. Lighter hair—messy, like he ran his hands through it.

They're still laughing, still talking like this room doesn't matter.

I close the file slowly and straighten my spine.

Let's see how fast I can ruin their day.

Brennan's halfway through a story about pulling a guy out of a kayak who couldn't swim. His voice bounces off the walls, filling the room with forced bravado I've been ignoring for months. But it's the other one—Cole—who speaks first. "Hey, got one for you," he says, too casual.

I don't look up. Don't need to.

"What's the name?" I ask, flipping to a fresh page.

"Timothy J. Ashton. Single-vehicle rollover. Highway 7."

There's something softer in his voice. I hear it, but I don't care. It's important to remain as detached as possible in this job. I learned that the hard way.

I step around the stretcher, check the tag, glance up—just once—and there he is again—closer this time.

Cole. Taller than I thought. Broad. Solid in his firefighter/EMT uniform. There's a smudge on his cheek—dirt or blood, I don't ask.

But it's his eyes that stop me cold. Hazel, with little gold flecks that have no business being that warm in a place this cold. And he's studying me, like I'm some equation he's trying to solve.

"You good?" His voice is deeper than I remember.

"I'm fine." I keep my tone flat. Professional. "This is my job. Are you?"

Something flickers across his face—amusement, maybe. He tilts his head, and I hate that I notice the line of his jaw, his mouth.

"Sure. I mean, I don't spend my days hanging out with corpses, but I manage."

Brennan barks out a laugh that echoes off the walls.

I let the silence stretch. One heartbeat. Two.

This place—my place—isn't just cold steel and chemical smell. It's sacred. The last stop for people who deserve dignity and respect. And I don't let anyone treat it like a comedy club.

"You're in the wrong room for jokes." The words come out sharper than intended as I snap the clipboard shut.

Brennan whistles low, already wheeling the stretcher into position.

Cole's almost smile dies. Just for a second, something else crosses his face before he locks it down.

"If you're done," I say, turning away, "I have actual work to do."

They hesitate. I can feel them exchanging looks behind me. Then Brennan claps Cole on the shoulder, steering him toward the door.

"Told you," Brennan stage-whispers. "Total ice queen."

The door swings shut, cutting off whatever Cole might've said.

I exhale. Slow. Controlled.

Coffee. That's what I need.

Not sleep. Not comfort. Just caffeine. Black, bitter, hot enough to scald my tongue and remind me I'm still standing.

I toss my gloves, grab my hoodie, and whistle for Beef. He doesn't move. Not even an ear twitch.

Figures.

Probably dreaming about a squirrel.

The hallway's cooler than the morgue. I keep walking until the cafeteria's hum hits me.

It's late enough that most people have cleared out, just a few stragglers grabbing whatever's left before the line closes. A couple of nurses laugh at a table like they haven't just pulled twelve-hour shifts.

I keep my head down, aiming for the counter. One goal: coffee. Maybe whatever pastry hasn't been assaulted by fingerprints. And then I see it.

The last breakfast burrito. Wrapped, golden, still under the heat lamp like a beacon.

I reach for it—so does someone else.

Our fingers brush.

I look up.

Cole.

"You've got to be kidding me," I mutter.

He grins, holding it up. "Guess we've got the same taste."

"In food, maybe."

He laughs—like it's funny. Like *I'm* funny.

The line cook calls out, "She finally speaking to you, Cole?"

"Barely," he says, chuckling. "But I'll take it."

I hate this. How everyone lights up around him.

The janitor waves. The nurse on the other side of the room smiles. The cashier calls him by name and cracks some joke I don't catch. I sip my coffee, bitter and hot.

"If you want it..." His eyes meet mine. "The burrito's yours."

"Keep it. Maybe you'll shut up while you eat it."

He steps closer, mouth lifting in a lazy grin. "You always this fun, or just with me?"

A slight tremor runs through me at the low sound of his voice—taunting, teasing.

I look up. "I don't do fun."

"Yeah." His eyes flicker. "I'm starting to get that."

I turn to leave, but he calls after me.

"You don't have to hate everyone who talks to you."

I pause. "And you don't have to charm everyone like it's your job."

His smile fades, just for a second.

Good.

The last thing I need is another man thinking he can fix me—or worse, make me feel something. Especially one who looks like that. He can take his broad shoulders, trim waist, and savior complex somewhere else. Preferably far, far away from me.

# 2

## FAMILY TIES AND FIRE DRILLS

*Cole*

The house is exactly the same as it's always been—one story, yellow siding, a porch that needs paint again, and the apartment above the garage I've called home since I moved back after college. It's not fancy, but it's comfortable. Familiar.

I let myself in and notice the smell of garlic bread and whatever magic my mom works with pasta sauce when she's in a good mood. I kick off my boots at the door, run a hand through my still-damp hair, and head for the kitchen.

"Hey, Ma," I call.

"In here," she replies, her voice warm, clinking dishes together as if she's been waiting for me.

The kitchen is small and cozy, there's too many photos on the fridge and a drawer that jams when it's humid. She's already got plates out, steam rising from the pot on the stove.

I live in the apartment above the garage now, but Tuesday night dinners? Those are non-negotiable.

She gives me a quick once-over, checking for damage. "Long shift?"

"Same as always," I say, dropping into my usual chair. "A couple of calls. Some idiot climbed a tree to rescue his drone and couldn't get down. Basic stuff."

She raises an eyebrow but doesn't press.

I don't tell her about the casualty on Highway 7 that we delivered to the morgue instead of the ER after working on him for almost forty minutes. No need to bring her down.

I've been back in town for a couple of years now. EMT/firefighter, just like I planned. Living above the garage until I figure out the next step—if there is one. I'm not in a rush. Dating? I haven't done much of it. Casual's fine. Easy. Hookups that don't ask for more than I'm willing to give.

I've got Brennan, Mom, and work that matters—it's all I need.

"Oh, and I kid you not, I actually got a call about someone's cat today. Really saved the day with that one."

Mom rolls her eyes, but she's smiling. "You love it."

"I like helping people. Doesn't mean I want to talk about it."

She sets a bowl down in front of me, still fussing like I'm twelve. "Did you eat today?"

"Yup. Hospital burrito."

She snorts. "You're impossible."

I grin, tearing into the bread. "You love me."

"Someone has to."

I chuckle.

"What else is going on?" she asks.

I reach for the salad, already starving. "Alright, how about this—did you hear about that ridiculous date auction the hospital's doing?"

Her eyebrows lift. "Auction?"

"A bachelor and bachelorette auction at the upcoming gala. All the proceeds will go to the children's wing, apparently."

"Are you going to do it?"

I shrug. "Probably. It's for a good cause." How can you say no to that?

Plus, apparently, everyone who's single is getting tossed into the lineup, so it's not like I have much choice.

She picks up her fork. "You know they're going to fight over you."

I bark a laugh. "Who, the nurses? Nah, I'm old news."

She gives me that look. The one that says I'm full of it. She's not wrong, but I don't need her boosting my ego. I do just fine on my own.

"What else happened today?" Mom asks.

I'm halfway through a bite when *she* pops into my head.

Andi Callahan.

Sharp tongue. Lavender hair. The kind of perfect ass you notice even when you're trying not to.

I've heard the rumors. That she keeps to herself, that she's cold, that no one's ever really gotten past her walls. People say she's a hard ass. Mean. Untouchable.

But standing across from her in the morgue today?

She didn't look mean.

She looked dangerous.

Delicate features that don't match her sharp tongue. Eyes that dare you to say something stupid. And that hair—soft, light, nothing like the rest of her.

"Cole?"

I blink. My mom's watching me, waiting.

"Sorry," I say quickly, stabbing at my food. "What were you saying?"

She narrows her eyes, but she lets it go. "You should do the auction. Maybe meet someone."

I snort. "Yeah, maybe."

She gives me that look—the one that's half motherly concern, half amusement. She knows I'm not looking for anything serious. She's asked before, more than once. I guess that's her job though.

I haven't dated anyone in a while. Haven't wanted to. Hookups are fine. They don't ask questions. Don't expect more. It works for me. For now, anyway.

My phone buzzes on the table, dragging me away from my thoughts.

> **Brennan: Beer at O'Malley's?**
> **20 mins.**

I scrub a hand down my face, standing. "I've got the kitchen, Mom. Thanks for dinner."

"No problem. Are you going out?" she asks.

"Yeah. Grabbing a drink with Bren."

"Be good."

"Always." I wink.

I load the dishwasher quickly and scrub down the counters. Twenty minutes later, I'm pulling into the parking lot of our favorite Irish pub downtown.

O'Malley's is loud, half-full, and smells like beer. I like it. It's familiar. Predictable.

Brennan's already at our usual table in the corner, two pints waiting, and his feet kicked up like he's got nowhere better to be.

"Took you long enough," he says, tossing a peanut at me as I sit.

"Had to eat real food first. You should try it sometime."

He grins, already raising his glass. "To surviving another day in the circus."

We clink, drink, and for a while, it's just the usual—trash talk about the Philly game we watched last night, who's the worst driver on the team (definitely still Mike), and whether or not Brennan could win an arm-wrestling contest against Janine from ER.

He couldn't. We both know it.

A few beers in, Brennan leans back, smirking. "So, you doing the auction thing?"

I shrug. "I guess. Why not?"

"Man, you're gonna rake in the bids. You've got, like, half the nurses waiting to throw cash at you."

"Right. Because that's why I do this job. For the glory."

Brennan laughs. "Nah, seriously. I'm thinking about it too."

"You? I thought you had that thing with—what's her name?"

He waves a hand. "It's casual."

Figures.

I'm about to let it drop when he glances sideways, all smug. "Wonder if that chick Andi will be in it."

I don't say anything.

Brennan keeps going. "Can you imagine? Someone actually bidding on her? Ice Queen Special, now with extra attitude."

I glance up, slowly. "She's not that bad."

Brennan snorts. "Please. She'd probably charge extra just to talk to you."

I don't laugh.

"She's solid at her job," I say, my tone flat. "Just because she doesn't fall over herself to be nice doesn't mean she's a bitch."

Brennan raises his eyebrows, caught. "Damn, alright. Didn't know you were a fan."

I shake my head, downing the rest of my beer. "Not a fan. Just not an asshole." Actually, I might be lying. So what if I am a fan?

Brennan watches me for a second, curious, but he lets it drop.

I lean back, letting the noise of the bar fill the space between us, but my mind's already somewhere else.

Her eyes, sharp and daring. The way she didn't flinch, didn't play.

She's gorgeous, even if all that venom does scare me a little. Not that I'd ever admit it.

# 3

## SILENCE, INTERRUPTED

*Andi*

I'm not heartless; I just don't have the energy for other people's nonsense.

And today? There had been a lot of it.

Mikey wouldn't shut up about the auction. The hot firefighter/EMT Cole wouldn't stop looking at me like I was some kind of challenge. Plus, let's not forget he stole my burrito.

Which was next-level annoying.

The pan hisses as I drop in a piece of chicken, the smell of garlic filling my tiny kitchen like it's trying to make up for the silence.

Beef stretches out near the door, his head resting on his paws, watching me with those lazy eyes as if he's judging my seasoning blend.

"This is why I don't go out," I mutter, flipping the chicken. "Everyone wants something."

He huffs, his tail thumping once.

It's not much of a dinner—just something to eat so I don't pass out tomorrow. But it's mine. The dishes clatter, the fan above the stove rattles, and everything feels quiet in that way I like best.

No noise. No people. No pretending.

I settle on the couch with my plate, and Beef's head nudges my knee, begging for a bite.

"Don't push it," I say, but I give him some anyway.

The TV's on, but I'm not watching. It's just background noise while I scroll through my phone. There are a couple of texts from Shay, begging me to come out.

Then I see it.

A message from Mikey.

> Mikey: Preview of your big debut. Tell me this doesn't scream SOLD.

I click.

It's a draft flyer. My name, bold and bright: Andrea Callahan. Some stock photo he must have pulled from my ID badge, showing me looking halfway to murder.

I stare at it, my fork paused halfway to my mouth.

This should piss me off more than it does.

But it's just... typical.

People deciding things for me. Mikey being Mikey. Annoying, is what it is.

I set my phone down and push my plate away. I'm not hungry anymore. Beef nudges closer, resting his massive head on my lap.

"I'm fine," I tell him, scratching behind his ear. "Completely fine."

He doesn't move, just breathes. Steady. Solid.

Unlike the rest of the world.

My phone buzzes again, and I check it.

Shay this time.

The thing about Shay is that she's never been good at taking no for an answer.

Not when we were fifteen, sneaking out to drink stolen wine coolers on her roof. Not when I tried to disappear after my parents died. And definitely not now.

She's loud, nosy, all fire and sharp edges—but she's all I've got.

The texts keep coming.

> Shay: You better be putting on makeup.

> Shay: Don't make me come over there.

> Shay: Okay, I'm coming over.

I groan, tipping my head back against the couch.

"Remind me again why I have friends?" I ask

Beef, who sighs as if he's over it too.

The knock isn't polite.

It's Shay, which means it's more like a threat.

*Bang-bang-bang-bang.* "Let's go, Callahan!"

"I swear, we should've gone into hiding," I tell Beef, who blinks at me like he's already halfway there.

I get up to answer the door, pushing a hundred and forty pounds of fur off me first.

I crack the door, already regretting it.

She's in leather pants, her eyes lined like she's ready for war. "You've had your alone time. Now it's my turn."

"I'm not in the mood."

"You never are. Doesn't mean you're getting out of it."

Shay doesn't care that I'm tired, or pissed, or that all I want is to stay in my little bubble where no one expects anything from me.

She cares that I don't disappear.

"I'm good right here," I try again, motioning to the couch, the dog, the half-eaten plate.

"Nope. You're getting dressed, you're putting on those black jeans that make your ass look illegal, and you're coming with me."

"Shay—"

"I brought tequila."

She waves a little flask at me like it's some kind of prize.

Beef lets out a low groan, as if he's tired of this already. *Same, buddy. Same.*

I sigh, knowing I've already lost the battle. "You owe me."

"Please, you'd do the same for me."

I wouldn't, but I don't say it.

I pull open the drawer where I keep my going-out clothes—what little I have—and grab the black jeans Shay loves to harass me about. They fit tight, high-waisted, and remind me that I might be five foot two, but I can still make people look twice. Small doesn't mean soft.

I throw on the jeans she insists are magic for my ass, add some ankle boots, and a basic white tee. A thousand chunky bracelets and some eyeliner later, I glance in my full-length mirror and turn slightly. Okay, so my ass *is* amazing, but that's beside the point. I run a hand through my hair, the lavender dye catching in the dim light. Just longer than my shoulders, slightly wavy, like it can't decide whether to behave.

That's as good as it's getting.

Big Don't Mess with Me energy, in a small package.

Beef watches me like he's judging every life choice I've ever made, and honestly, same.

"Bye, bubs," I say, patting his head.

Thirty minutes later, we're pushing through the doors of O'Malley's, and I'm already counting down the minutes until I can leave. Bras suck, and pants are overrated.

The place is packed. Music thumps in the background, the air thick with beer and bad decisions. Shay's in her element, pulling me toward the bar like she owns it.

"You look hot," she says, glancing over her shoulder. "Try to have fun."

I don't *do* fun. I just try to survive. That's enough for me most days.

I'm about to order something strong enough to make this night end faster when I hear him.

"Didn't peg you for the bar type."

I turn.

*Are you kidding me?*

Cole's here.

He leans against the bar like it was made for him, a beer in hand and forearms casually flexed. He's ditched the uniform, trading it for a dark T-shirt and jeans that fit just right—annoyingly right. His hair is still a mess, as if he ran his hands through it on the way over, and I hate that it works.

I arch an eyebrow. "Didn't peg you for a mind reader."

He grins, slow and easy. "Lucky guess."

I turn back to the bartender and order. Cole shifts closer—not enough to crowd me, just enough to make it clear he's not leaving.

"Rough night?" he asks.

"Every night's rough when people won't leave you alone."

"Ouch. That was almost personal."

"It's been a long week."

He nods and takes a sip. "Yeah. You could use some fun."

I shoot him a look. "I don't do fun."

"I've heard."

His eyes flicker, warm and amused, and for some stupid reason, it makes my chest feel tight.

Shay slides in next to me, two shots in hand, already glowing. Her eyes land on Cole, and she lets out a low whistle.

"Damn," she says. "I'd ride that ride."

My stomach drops. "Shay—"

"What? Look at him." She nudges me, not even trying to whisper. "Tell me you wouldn't climb that like a tree."

Brennan appears behind Cole, grinning like he's at a comedy show. "She's got a point."

Cole just laughs, unfazed. "Should I be flattered or file a complaint?"

"I'm mortified," I mutter, shooting Shay a death glare.

"Oh, relax. He knows he's hot."

Brennan raises his beer. "Cheers to that."

I should walk away. I should shut them all down.

But Cole's still looking at me, like he's waiting

for me to admit something.

I don't. I down my drink instead.

"I'm not interested," I say, more to myself than anyone.

He leans in, his voice low. "You sure about that?"

I meet his eyes, steady. "Positive."

But my pulse says otherwise.

Well, *that's* annoying.

Some people have resting bitch face. I have resting don't-talk-to-me energy. But Cole seems undeterred by that.

I try to focus on my drink, but he's still there—too calm, too steady. Like he's used to waiting people out.

"You always this difficult?" he asks, taking another slow sip.

"You always this nosy?" I shoot back.

"Only when I'm interested."

I snort, shaking my head. "Well, don't be."

"Too late."

His gaze doesn't waver, and for a second, I forget what I'm supposed to say. He's closer now, the crowd disappearing around us, making the room feel smaller than it is. I catch a whiff of his cologne—clean, something woodsy—and it's annoying how good it smells.

"How long have you been working at the hospital?" he asks, his voice casual.

"Long enough."

Shay suddenly leans into the conversation like she never left.

"Six years," she says, tossing back another shot. "She started right after school. Could've gone anywhere, but she stayed here."

I glare at her. "Thanks, Shay."

"What? It's not a secret."

Cole raises an eyebrow. "You like it?"

I shrug. "It's a job."

"She loves it," Shay cuts in again, ignoring the kick I send to her ankle. "She just doesn't like talking about it."

He smiles, clearly enjoying this.

"What about you?" Shay asks, turning the attention back to him. "You always wanted to run into burning buildings for fun?"

"Something like that." He sets his beer down and rolls his shoulders like it's no big deal. "Tried college first. Spent two years at Boston College."

"Ohh, smarty pants," Shay says.

"Anyway, I didn't like sitting at a desk, so I figured, why not?"

"Figures." I cross my arms. "Adrenaline junkie."

He grins. "You say that like it's a bad thing."

"It's not a compliment."

Another laugh, low and easy.

"Okay, your turn," he says, narrowing his eyes

slightly. "What do you do when you're not slicing people open?"

"None of your business."

"She reads true crime books and takes Beef for long walks in the park," Shay answers, way too cheerfully.

I choke on my drink. "Shay."

"What? He asked."

I'm going to kill her.

Cole's smile grows, but he doesn't push. "Beef's your dog?"

I nod, wiping my mouth. "Yeah."

"I like dogs."

Of course you do.

"Well, he hates all men, so… good luck with that." I force a grin.

I wait for a joke about how similar I am to my dog or something equally stupid, but he doesn't say anything for a second—just watches me. I shift my weight, suddenly too aware of everything—my clothes, my hair, the way his eyes flick to my lips when I breathe in.

Cole wraps one hand around his beer, eyes still on me. "So, what made you want to work in the morgue?"

I shrug. "Dead people are quiet."

Shay rolls her eyes. "And she likes being the smartest person in the room."

"What about fun? What's your idea of it?"

"Not this," I mutter.

Shay pipes up, because *of course* she does. "She bakes when she's mad. Pies, mostly."

Cole smiles like he likes this answer. He watches me even closer now, as if he's fully invested even though I've given him zero reason to be.

"You don't give up easily, do you?" I ask, trying to break whatever this is.

"Nope. And you're not very good at being chased."

I don't have a response for that.

But I wish I did.

# 4

## SMOKE SIGNALS

*Cole*

The firehouse is already buzzing by the time I get there.

The coffee's brewing, someone's in the kitchen cooking up bacon, and the guys are in the middle of arguing over which action movie to put on later when things quiet down. Typical.

This place? It's home.

It's loud. It smells like burnt toast, sweat, and old leather, and I wouldn't trade it for anything.

I have forty-eight hours on shift, and unless someone dies—which, for humanity's sake, I hope doesn't happen—I won't be seeing Andi Callahan.

But I kinda want to.

I shake off the thought and head straight for the kitchen, where Trey and Walker are already gearing up for breakfast like it's a competition.

"Took you long enough," Walker says, flipping something in a pan. "We thought maybe you got smart and called in."

"Tempting," I reply, grabbing a mug, "but then I'd miss your sparkling personality."

Trey grins and tosses me a strip of bacon. "You're stuck with us now. Welcome to hell."

Hell's not so bad, though.

We work together, eat together, and sweat through workouts in the garage gym until someone nearly pukes. These guys? They're family. Loud, annoying, but they've got your back when it counts.

I lean against the counter, sipping my coffee, but my brain won't stay still.

I keep thinking about last night.

About Andi. The way she looked—in those jeans that made my thoughts wander to places they shouldn't, those eyes sharp as ever, and that smart mouth that wouldn't quit.

She didn't smile much. But when she did?

Yeah.

"You good?" Trey asks, watching me like he knows something's up.

"Yeah," I lie. "Just tired."

He shrugs, unconvinced, and gets back to stirring eggs like he's about to win a prize.

I'll settle into the rhythm soon. We've got a long shift ahead, calls to respond to, drills to run.

It's always busy. It's always something.

I love it.

Well, most of it. I can't say I love the narrow bunks and the snoring that hits decibel levels no human should survive.

But even that? It's not so bad once you get used to it.

The radio crackles just as we finish cleaning up from breakfast.

"Engine 4, Medic 2, respond to a fall—elderly male, possible broken hip. 221 Briar Lane."

Trey's already moving, tossing me the keys. "You're up, Romeo."

I roll my eyes but grab my gear.

The rig is still warm from the last run, the usual smell of antiseptic and stale coffee clinging to the seats. Trey climbs in beside me, flipping on the lights as we pull out.

"Briar Lane," he mutters. "Didn't we just have a call there?"

"Last week. Kid with a peanut allergy."

"Right." He grins. "Bet this guy'll be more fun."

When we arrive, the scene's calm—neighbors milling around, pointing us toward the backyard where the patient's propped against a tree, wincing but breathing.

"Morning," I say, crouching beside him. "Heard you're trying out for the gymnastics team."

The old man huffs a laugh, eyes crinkling. "Damned ladder broke. My wife's gonna kill me."

"We'll keep you alive long enough to argue with her, I promise."

Trey's already checking vitals while I assess the leg—swollen, definitely broken, but nothing life-threatening. The guy's tough, cracking jokes while we splint him, even as the pain bites.

"You guys do this every day?" he asks, teeth gritted.

"More or less. You're making it easy."

"Good. I hate being a bother."

"You're not," I say, steadying myself as I lift him onto the stretcher with Trey's help. "But you're not getting out of a hospital visit."

He groans but doesn't fight us.

The ride's smooth, the usual chatter between Trey and the hospital radio. The old man keeps trying to tip us for "good service" with a crumpled twenty from his wallet.

"Save it for the nurses," I tell him. "They've got a harder job."

We wheel him in, straight through the sliding doors of the ER, where the familiar buzz hits—monitors beeping, voices layered over each other, the hum of organized chaos.

A nurse I know, Marissa, steps up with a tablet in hand, already eyeing our patient.

"What do we have?"

"Robert Davies," I say as we lock the stretcher in place. "He was trying out for a senior citizen's gymnastics team…"

Marissa eyes the elderly man, then swings her gaze back to me.

"Kidding. He took a dive off a ladder in his backyard and landed wrong. Suspected hip fracture, vitals are stable. He's been giving us hell about coming in."

Robert groans. "Don't let them cut me open."

Marissa smiles and pats his shoulder. "No promises, Robert. Let's get you checked out first."

"He tried to tip us," Trey adds, grinning. "Wanted to give Cole a twenty."

Marissa laughs. "You taking bribes now?"

"Only from the cute ones," I say, flashing her a grin.

She rolls her eyes, scribbling notes. "Alright, we'll take it from here. You two get lost."

I give Robert a nod. "Take care, man. Let the pros work their magic."

"Thanks, boys," he says, already being wheeled down the hall.

Trey claps me on the back. "Back to the rig?"

"In a sec."

He smirks, not even bothering to ask. "Tell her I said hi."

I wave him off, heading toward the stairs.

The guys like to joke with me that I could have

any single female here. There's always a hot nurse joke at the ready, and usually, I'm a good sport about it. But today, I'm in a hurry.

I don't head to the basement.

Not yet.

I head to the cafeteria and pick up a breakfast burrito—just like the one I stole from Andi yesterday.

I grab it, pay cash, and head down the hall.

Is this weird? Maybe. I could just leave, go back to the rig, get on with my day, but my feet don't get the message. Instead, I'm heading downstairs, taking the back stairwell, where the air shifts—cooler, heavier, quieter.

It's calmer down here. No rush. No noise. I guess I can see the draw, if you like that kind of thing. The place kinda weirds me out, to be honest.

I spot her before she sees me.

Clipboard in hand, focused, her lavender hair efficiently tucked behind one ear as she leans over a desk. Her scrubs are dark and fitted, and she looks so damn serious it almost stops me.

I should leave.

But I don't.

She still hasn't seen me.

Which is ridiculous because I'm standing here, holding a damn breakfast burrito like it's a peace offering—or a bribe. My palms are actually sweating.

I'm not nervous. I don't do nervous.

Except maybe now.

She shifts, turning slightly, and I clear my throat before I can chicken out.

Her head snaps up, eyes narrowing the second she sees me.

"You stalking me now?" she says, dry as ever.

"Nope," I say, stepping closer. "Just figured I owed you something."

I hold out the burrito. She eyes it like it might explode.

"You brought me food?"

"You seemed pissed about the last one. Thought I'd make it up to you."

Her gaze flicks from the burrito to my face, suspicious. "You didn't poison it, did you?"

I smile, shrugging. "Only a little."

She huffs, grabs it from my hand, and I swear her fingers linger just a second too long.

"I'm starving," she mutters, like she's annoyed about it.

I lean against the edge of the desk, watching her tear the wrapper open. She takes a bite, eyes closing for half a second, and it's almost enough to make me forget how hard she's shut me down.

Almost.

"Slow day?" I ask, trying to sound casual.

She chews, nodding. "For once. It won't last."

"Lucky me."

She shoots me a look, but there's no heat behind it—just tiredness, and maybe something else.

I've been shot down before, but not like this. Not by someone who makes me want to try again anyway.

I shove my hands in my pockets, suddenly restless.

"You're not as mean when you're eating," I say.

"You're not as annoying when you're leaving."

I laugh and step back.

"Later, Callahan."

She doesn't answer, but she doesn't tell me to get lost, either.

# 5

## BOOK CLUB AND BAD IDEAS

*Kate*

The house is quiet.

Too quiet. The restless sort that leaves you wondering what the hell to do with yourself.

Cole's on a forty-eight-hour shift, which means I have two whole days with the place to myself—a rare thing, even now. You'd think after twenty-five years of raising a kid, I'd be better at enjoying the silence. Turns out, I'm not so great at it.

I fluff the pillows on the couch for the third time, adjust the angle of the lampshade like it matters, and glance at the clock.

My book club is supposed to start in ten minutes.

I actually read the book this time. An Oprah pick—surprisingly good, even if half the plot made me roll my eyes. But it's not really about the book. It's about Helen and Margot, wine, and girl talk. An excuse to laugh too loud and pretend we're not all trying to figure out what the hell comes next in life.

I light a candle, mostly because the house smells like lemon cleaner, and pour the first glass of wine.

Cole's a good man. Better than I could've hoped for. I did my job.

Now what?

My therapist keeps telling me it's time to focus on me.

Margot's version of that is more fun—download a dating app, get laid, live a little.

Helen just nods and tells me the truth in that quiet way she does: You've earned more.

I don't disagree.

I just don't know what more looks like, even if I want to.

The doorbell rings, loud and insistent.

I open it to find Margot, holding a bottle of Chardonnay, and Helen, carrying the book like she's about to quiz me.

"We brought backup!" Margot declares, sweeping past me into the kitchen.

"Wine and moral support," Helen adds with a smile, giving me a quick hug before following her.

"You two are a hurricane," I say, shutting the

door behind them.

"You love it," Margot calls.

She's not wrong.

Margot is the first to kick off her shoes, already halfway to the kitchen. She's all legs and wild curls, wearing something boho that I'm sure she bought off a street vendor in a city I've never been to. She's never been married, never wanted to be, and lives like the rules were never written for her.

Helen's the opposite. Classic and polished. Her hair's always perfect, her clothes tailored just enough to say she's got it together—even when she doesn't. She's been widowed for five years now and somehow always knows the exact thing I need to hear—even when I don't want to hear it.

We've been friends since our kids started kindergarten, bonding over bad PTA meetings and worse coffee. They were the first ones there when my husband walked out, and I was the first one there when Helen lost Patrick. We've stuck together through everything.

I wouldn't survive without them, even if they drive me crazy sometimes.

They head for the couch like they own the place.

Margot pours a glass without asking. "Alright, let's get to it."

"To the book?" I ask, settling into the chair across from them.

"To your love life," Helen says, deadpan.

I choke on my wine. "What?"

Margot grins. "You thought we were here to talk about plot holes? No, honey. We're here to talk about your holes."

Helen nearly spits her wine.

"Margot!" I shoot her a look, but I'm laughing despite myself.

"What? When was the last time you got any? Be honest."

Helen shakes her head, wiping her mouth. "This is an intervention."

"It feels like one."

"Because it is," Margot says, smug. "I've had it with your excuses. Cole's grown. You're hot. And you're wasting prime years hiding behind a candle collection and book club."

"I'm not hiding."

Helen gives me *the look*.

"I'm... easing into it."

"Into what?" Margot shoots back. "Celibacy?"

I groan. "You're impossible."

"And you're downloading a dating app. Tonight."

Helen snatches my phone, already scrolling. "I've got three good ones. You can't argue."

I straighten my posture, ready to stand my ground. "I can absolutely argue."

"But you won't," Margot says, kicking her feet

up. "Because deep down, you know we're right."

I sip my wine, watching them, this whirlwind of truth and trouble.

Maybe they are.

Maybe it's time.

Margot's already got her legs tucked under her, scrolling through the phone like she's on a mission.

"I'm thinking something simple. Fun. Not too slutty."

"Please don't pick anything slutty," I say, eyeing her.

Helen smirks, holding up her own screen. "Hinge or Bumble?"

Margot leans over, peering. "Bumble. She gets to make the first move. Safer that way."

I laugh. "Safer for who?"

"For the poor souls you'd destroy with that teacher glare," Helen says, tapping away like it's already decided.

"Guys, I'm really not ready for this."

Margot looks up, her grin all teeth. "Kate. When was the last time you were ready for anything we've done?"

She's got me there.

I cross my arms, sinking deeper into the chair. "Fine. But no shirtless guys. Or fish pics."

"God, no," Helen says. "We have standards."

"Barely," I mutter, but they're already too deep into this.

Margot waves the phone like a wand. "Okay, give me your info. Age, location, favorite things, least favorite—"

"Favorite things? Wine, books, and not doing *this*."

"Cute," Helen says, typing. "We'll spin it."

Margot's fingers fly. "Hobbies? Cooking for your son doesn't count."

"I don't have hobbies."

"She bakes," Helen adds, without missing a beat.

I groan. "I bake when I'm stressed."

"Even better. Men love homemade pie; that's good."

Margot's cackling now, nearly spilling her wine.

"Oh my God, you're going to give me a heart attack."

"No, we're going to give you options," Helen corrects, handing me the phone. "There. Profile made. All you have to do is say yes."

I stare at it.

Kate. 45. Teacher. Wine, good books, bad TV, and better company. Looking for someone who can make me laugh harder than the two friends who made me create this profile.

"You're both insane."

"But you love us."

I do.

And maybe they're right.

I hit NEXT.

The screen shifts.

Welcome to Bumble.

Margot throws her arms up like we've won something. "Now let's see what Boston's got to offer."

Margot is fully horizontal now, one leg draped over the arm of the couch, wine glass balanced on her stomach, phone raised high like she's narrating a sporting event—or just because she's forgotten her reading glasses.

How is this my life now?

"Alright, contestant number one. Shirtless. Holding a fish. Immediate no."

Helen leans over. "Is it a big fish at least?"

Margot squints. "Honestly? Could be a trout. Either way—rejected."

I rub my temples. "I already regret this."

"Too late," Helen says cheerfully. "We're in it now."

"Next," Margot announces. "Firefighter. Muscles. Dog in his lap. Wait—is that a puppy? Oh hell, Kate, this man's a ten."

"No," I say automatically.

Margot grins. "Why not?"

"Because it's too obvious. He knows what he's doing."

"That's the point," Helen mutters, sipping her

wine.

Margot swipes. "Fine. We'll come back to puppy guy."

Plus, he's a firefighter—he could work with my son, and that's a scenario I very much want to avoid. I'm pretty sure Cole likes the idea that I'm celibate.

The next few come and go—one in a fedora, one with a weird selfie in a gym mirror, and one who says "sapiosexual" in his bio, which earns a collective groan from the couch.

"What does that even mean?" I ask.

"Means he thinks liking books makes him deep," Helen says. "Swipe left."

Margot throws her arm out. "Oh! Wait. This one. Mid-forties, salt-and-pepper hair, owns a bookstore, plays guitar."

"Too good to be true," I say.

"Or exactly what the universe is trying to send you," Helen counters.

I take a long sip of wine.

Margot turns the phone toward me. "What about this one? Not bad, right?"

I glance at the screen. My first thought is—wow, he's cute.

Jack. 43. SAR coordinator. Divorced. Says he prefers hiking to small talk and dogs to people. No fish, no fedora.

I raise an eyebrow. "What's SAR?"

"Search and Rescue," Helen says. "Could be hot."

"Sounds like the kind of guy who'd mansplain survival tactics," I mutter.

"Perfect," Margot fires back. "You need someone who can handle your attitude in the wild."

I give her a hard look. "He's probably the type who judges people for not having a compass."

Helen leans forward. "You could use some direction."

I snort. "Rude."

"You love it."

They both turn to me, expectant.

I hesitate. Then tap.

Matched.

Margot claps like we're at a graduation. "This is the beginning of your sexual renaissance."

"God, don't say that," I groan, sinking into the couch.

Helen's already topping off my wine. "To Kate."

"To questionable decisions," Margot adds.

"To getting laid before Christmas," Helen says with a smirk.

I clink glasses with them both and laugh until my stomach hurts.

Maybe I really do need this.

Or maybe it's just the wine.

Either way… I'm in trouble.

The house is still dark when I wake up.

It always is at this hour, and I move through the motions automatically. Ten minutes of yoga, shower, coffee, makeup in the hallway mirror that catches too much truth under fluorescent light.

I pull on a soft sweater, ankle boots, and my favorite pair of slacks that don't feel like they're trying too hard. I've got papers to grade and a room full of teenagers waiting to see if I'll let them off easy on this next essay. It's just another day.

Except it's not.

Because now I'm someone with a dating app on her phone.

I sip my coffee and immediately think about Margot and Helen, wine-drunk and cheering like I'd just won *The Bachelor*. It was fun—God, it was fun. I hadn't laughed like that in a while. I know they love me and care about me.

But also... what the hell did I do?

I glance toward the kitchen counter, where my phone is still sitting, facedown.

No rush. Probably just more spam emails and calendar reminders. Nothing important.

I pick it up anyway.

The screen lights up.

1 New Notification – Jack.

My stomach tightens.

Oh no.

Oh no, no.

He messaged me.

I stare at it, thumb hovering over the app. My heart kicks up like I've just been caught doing something I shouldn't.

I could ignore it. Pretend it never happened. Delete the app, blame it on the wine, and tell Margot and Helen the universe sent a sign.

Or...

Am I really going to do this?

My thumb twitches.

I haven't even opened it yet, and still, somehow, everything feels different.

I close my eyes.

Take a breath.

And tap the screen.

# 6

## DEEP WATERS

*Jack*

The water's cold. The kind that sinks into your bones and settles there—biting and heavy.

I adjust my mask and kick down another few feet. Visibility's trash, but I know these waters, know what I'm doing. We've been out here since first light. A drowning victim—a young guy in his early twenties. His kayak was found yesterday afternoon, bobbing against the shoreline. No sign of him since. His family is up there now, waiting—silent. The worst kind of quiet. I've seen it before. I'll see it again. It doesn't make it any easier.

This is the part no one talks about—the part where the search stops being about saving someone and starts being about finding them, bringing them home, giving someone answers. Closure. That's the only thing I care about. I don't crack jokes or try to lighten the mood. Walt does enough of that for both of us. That's his thing. I don't need to be the guy who offers sad smiles through this. I need to be the one who finishes it.

The radio in my ear crackles. "Anything?" Walt asks, his voice easy—too easy.

"Not yet," I answer. "Pushing west."

"Copy that."

I surface long enough to adjust my gear and get my bearings. The current is moving along at a pretty good clip. I'm guessing he got pushed further than we're expecting.

I go under again. There's comfort in the rhythm: breath, dive, scan, resurface, repeat. I've been doing this for fifteen years now. Five years in the Army taught me how to keep moving when things get dark. This job taught me how to live with it. I wouldn't know who I was without it.

But lately… something's off. Not with the work, but with me.

I'm good at this—being steady, being the one people count on. But outside of it? I don't know. The hours feel longer. The house feels emptier. It's been over ten years since the divorce—ten years of being fine on my own. Until I wasn't.

Which is why I signed up for that damn dating app.

It still feels ridiculous. I spent half an hour convincing myself it was stupid, that it wasn't real—

that people are supposed to meet the old-fashioned way: at bars, bookstores, or while reaching for the same ripe avocado in the produce aisle.

Except apparently that only happens in movies. And when you spend all your time working, training, and buying protein powder on autopilot, you don't exactly bump into anyone new.

So yeah, I signed up. I picked a picture where I didn't look like I was about to arrest someone, wrote a line about dogs, hiking, and coffee, and swiped a little before bed. I thought maybe I'd delete it in the morning.

And then there she was—Kate. Cute smile, kind eyes, a teacher. She looked like someone who doesn't take shit from anyone, which, apparently, is my type.

I matched with her.

Didn't expect that.

I messaged her last night. Nothing wild—just something real. And now… now I'm wondering if she answered.

But I don't check. Not yet.

Because there's still work to do.

I resurface again, haul myself back into the boat, soaking and sore. Walt hands me a towel. "You good?" he asks. I nod. He doesn't ask more.

My phone's in my bag, tucked beneath my gear.

I could look.

But I don't.

Not while someone's still waiting onshore.

Not until I've done what I came here to do.

"Let's move west," I say, and Walt agrees, as does our team lead, starting up the boat and pointing us in that direction.

Walt's been around longer than most. He retired two years ago—officially, anyway. It didn't take. He's still here, volunteering like he never left. Says it keeps him sane. I think he just doesn't know how to stop.

He was the first one who showed me the ropes when I joined the team fifteen years ago. Taught me how to read a scene, how to know when it's time to push and when to pull back. I was younger then, angrier—thought I could carry it all.

Walt's the only one who knows I still try to.

He doesn't say much unless it matters. But when he does, I listen.

Most of the time.

I fiddle with my gear on the short ride over and check my air supply. I drop in when we stop and head back under. It should feel eerie; instead, it's second nature.

I spot him just past the drop-off, caught in the rocks. His jacket's torn, and the kayak paddle is still floating a few feet away. I don't pause or think; I just move. It's not shock anymore, not sadness— it's just work. I radio up, my voice flat. "Found him."

Walt responds, quick and sharp. "Copy. We're ready topside."

I haul the body up, careful and respectful. It's not about who they were to me; it's who they were to someone else—that's all that matters. We get him bagged, strapped, and secured. Walt handles the gear, quieter than usual. He knows I don't talk much after.

As we reach the shore, the family's waiting. The mother's face crumples. The father just nods, stiff, like his chest might cave in.

I take it in. Let myself feel it. Let it sit heavy.

It's supposed to.

Walt squeezes my shoulder. "You did what you could."

"I know."

The ambulance pulls up, doors already open. Two EMTs hop out—I recognize one of them, Cole.

I'm good with names—always have been. And he's not someone I'd forget even if I weren't.

He's got that look—easy, calm, like he's here to help but isn't crushed under it like the rest of us. He nods at me as they approach.

"Rough one," Cole says, glancing at the scene.

"No shit," I reply.

Brennan starts loading the stretcher while Cole lingers, hands on his hips.

"You good, man?" he asks.

"Fine."

Cole gestures at the family, his voice a little softer. "You handled it. That's something."

I turn to him, my jaw tight. "You think I do this for a pat on the back?"

His eyebrows lift, surprised. "No, I just meant—"

"Don't. Don't try to make it light. There's nothing light about this."

Cole backs off, hands raised. "Alright. Got it."

Brennan watches us, eyebrows raised but smart enough not to say anything.

Walt steps between us, his voice low. "Jack."

I shake my head, walking toward the truck. "We're done here."

Walt falls in step beside me. "What's with you and the EMT kid?"

"Nothing."

Except for the fact that the kid annoys the crap out of me—young, yet thinks he knows everything. Confident to a fault. And trying to lighten the mood with his easy humor? Not the time or place.

"Didn't sound like nothing."

I toss the gear in the back, slamming the hatch. "He doesn't get it."

"Maybe not. Or maybe you've been more on edge lately."

I don't answer.

But he's not wrong.

As we head back, Walt fills the silence. "You remember when we started? How we used to think we'd save everyone?"

I nod. Barely. It seems like forever ago.

"Now we just bring them home."

That hits harder than I want it to.

Walt's voice is quiet. "You ever think about what else there is, Jack? Outside of this?"

"Like what?"

He shrugs. "Like someone to come home to."

My grip tightens on the wheel.

"Drop it, okay?"

"Roger that," Walt says.

# 7

## OPERATION MELT THE ICE QUEEN

*Cole*

We're chilling in the engine bay, enjoying a brief reprieve from the day's action when Brennan rolls in for his shift.

When he spots me, he grins like he's been waiting all day for this moment.

"You recover yet?" he asks, kicking his boots up on the bench across from me.

I don't look up from my phone. "From what?"

He smirks. "From getting your ass handed to you by that chick Andi at O'Malley's."

Trey straightens, wiping his hands on a rag. "Who?"

Brennan leans in, eyes wide, mock-whispering like it's a secret. "Andi Callahan. Cute girl who works in the cooler at Memorial. Purple hair. Five feet of pure rage."

"Oh," Trey says, nodding. "Her. Yeah, she's smokin' hot."

"Yeah." Brennan laughs. "And she hates our man here."

Trey looks at me, one eyebrow raised. "Is that right?"

"She doesn't *hate* me," I say, slipping my phone into my pocket. "She just hasn't experienced my charms yet."

"She's experienced enough to want none of it," Brennan fires back.

I shrug, leaning back. "Give me time."

Brennan cackles, turning to Trey. "You should've seen it. The look she gave him? Man, I thought she was gonna throw a drink in his face."

"She didn't, though."

Trey shakes his head. "You give off golden retriever; she gives off rottweiler. Why do you gotta go for the scary ones?"

"Nah," I say, but my grin's already there. "She's not scary; she's just... *misunderstood*."

Brennan snorts. "She works with dead bodies all day. She's a little scary."

None of us like that part of the job. I can't imagine making it my career. That part is curious. But hey, I like the mystery—like peeling back the layers of an onion.

"She's like a wounded bird," Trey adds.

"Well, not to me. She seems cool—a little

guarded, obviously, but I bet she's great once you get to know her."

"Like that'll ever happen," Brennan scoffs.

"Not worried," I counter. "I like a challenge."

"Or," Brennan drawls, "you could go for her friend instead. The one who said she'd ride your ride."

I roll my eyes. "Shay? Please. I prefer a little less fire hazard in my life."

"She seemed into you."

"She's into anyone breathing."

Trey laughs, tossing the rag aside. "So what's the play, lover boy?"

"Simple," I say, stretching my arms over my head. "I'll get her to go out with me."

Brennan perks up. "You really think she'll say yes?"

"I know she will."

"Wanna bet?"

I pause, grinning. We basically bet on everything around here. "What's at stake?"

"If you lose, you're on the Wall. Full photo, glitter border, we pick the pose."

Trey's already laughing. "Oh, hell yes."

The Wall.

Every station's got one. Ours just happens to be legendary.

A whole section of the back hallway, plastered with photos of every idiotic move, every failed bet, and every prank gone wrong in the last ten years. Some are harmless—guys caught napping with their mouths open, a Sharpie penis drawn on their cheek, food disasters, rookie mistakes. One guy caught napping with a stuffed animal? Up there for life.

Trey's up there twice. Once in a tutu, thanks to a lost fantasy football league. Once in a photo where he's holding a sign that says "I'm not allowed to make chili anymore" after the great firehouse chili incident of 2022.

Brennan's got a spot too. Shirtless, covered in glitter, holding a birthday cake he dropped before it ever left the counter.

It's not just the photo; it's the story that comes with it. Every time someone walks past, they ask. Every time someone new joins, they hear about it.

And glitter? That means they're really gonna make it hurt.

"And if I win?" I ask.

Trey leans back, cocky. "If you win, Brennan has to wear something ridiculous on a call... I'm thinking a banana suit? And I'll throw in a week's worth of chores at the station—no cooking, no cleaning."

Not a bad deal.

I stand, already feeling the adrenaline kick in. "Deal."

"Poor bastard doesn't know what he's in for,"

Trey mutters.

But I do.

And I'm not backing down.

Trey returns from the office with a marker and a piece of cardboard. "Alright, gentlemen," he says, slapping the cardboard onto the table like it's sacred. "Let's make history."

Brennan leans over, eyes wide. "We need levels. Like a real challenge."

I sigh and lean back in my chair, arms crossed. "You're both idiots."

"Correct," Trey says, grinning. "Stage one: She smiles. Genuine smile. No pity, no sarcasm."

"Generous," Brennan says, laughing. "Fine. Stage two: She talks to him for more than five minutes without telling him to get lost."

"Smiles at me?" I ask. "That's it? Easy."

"Oh, he's cocky now," Trey says, scribbling it down. "Stage three: She gives him her number. Real number. No fake digits. And not for anything work-related."

Brennan chuckles, agreeing. "Next level—what's stage four?"

Trey leans in, deadly serious. "She agrees to go out with him. Coffee, drinks, I don't care. He asks. She says yes."

"Stage five," Brennan says, rubbing his hands together. "She shows up."

I laugh. "You think she'd bail?"

"Man, she *hates* you," Brennan says. "We're just being realistic."

Trey taps the marker. "Stage six: She initiates something. A text. A call. She makes the move."

"Oh, that's bold," Brennan says. "I like it."

"Stage seven," Trey adds. "First kiss."

The room erupts. A couple of guys walking in pause, eyeing the board.

"What's this?" Walker asks, heading for the coffee.

"Cole's gonna crash and burn trying to win over the girl who works in the cooler at Memorial," Brennan says, waving him over.

"Purple hair?" Walker asks. We nod. "She's hot. Put me down for five bucks he doesn't make it past level two."

"Deal."

Trey adds names to the side of the board, a list of bets forming faster than I thought possible.

"Stage eight," Brennan says, eyes sparkling. "She admits she likes him. Full on. Says it."

I just shake my head, watching them like they've all lost their minds. "You're idiots."

"True," Trey says, tossing me the marker. "But are you in?"

I grin slowly. "Oh, I'm in."

And there's no way I'm losing.

The laughter fades a little as the guys head off, already plotting what kind of glitter they're gonna use when I lose. I shake my head, pull out my phone, and lean back against the lockers.

Two missed calls from Mom.

I scroll, thumb hovering over her name.

She always calls during her planning period just to check in. Nothing urgent, nothing heavy. She doesn't want to be the mom who hovers, but she still is.

I hit call.

She picks up on the second ring. "Hey, sweetheart."

"Hey. Sorry I missed you earlier. Things were nuts."

"It's okay, I figured. How's your shift?"

"Good. Long."

"You eating?"

I smile. "Mom."

"Someone's gotta ask."

I lean against the lockers, closing my eyes for a second. "I'm good. I promise."

She hums, like she half-believes me. "Alright. I just wanted to hear your voice. I'm heading into class now. Call me later?"

"Yeah. Love you."

"Love you more."

She hangs up, and for a second, the noise around me fades out.

She's tough—stronger than she gives herself credit for. But sometimes I worry. She's been on her own for so long, always putting me first and making sure I was okay.

And now? It's just her.

I wonder if she ever gets tired of the quiet. If the house feels too big, too empty. She never says it, but sometimes, when I stop by and catch her just sitting there, staring at the TV like she's not watching... I know.

I wish there were more I could do for her.

But she's proud. Stubborn.

A lot like Andi, actually.

I shake the thought off, pushing my phone back into my pocket.

I've got enough on my plate without turning into one of those guys who starts psychoanalyzing every woman he meets.

Still.

I'd give anything to see my mom laugh like she used to.

# 8

## TERMS AND CONDITIONS MAY APPLY

*Andi*

There's nothing like the smell of bleach and bad decisions to start my morning off right.

I'm catching up on administrative work at my desk when I hear it—the door creaking open, followed by the distinct sound of someone who doesn't belong trying to walk in like they do.

I don't even look up.

"Unless you've got a body or a reason, turn around."

Silence.

Then his voice.

"I've got a reason."

I sigh, hard.

Cole.

I glance up, and there he is, leaning in the doorway like he's got all the time in the world, a stupid grin plastered across his face, and something tucked under his arm.

"What is that?" I ask, already annoyed.

He steps inside, holding it up. A piece of cardboard, messy handwriting scrawled across it in thick marker.

"Your future."

I blink. "Excuse me?"

He walks over, sets the cardboard on the desk in front of me with way too much pride.

THE ANDI BRACKET.

In subtext below it, *"Will Cole get Andi to go out with him?"*

My eyebrows shoot up.

"You're joking."

"Nope."

I scan the levels—talk for five minutes, smile, give him my number, go out with him, blah blah blah—all the way down to *kiss him* (not happening) and *admits she likes him*. (Um, never?)

Someone's overconfident.

At the bottom, someone's used markers to scrawl out the words—*Operation: Melt the Ice Queen.*

"What the hell is this?"

He looks down, almost bashful, for just a second. "I might have mentioned to the guys at the station about my raging crush on a certain morgue tech… and they did what they usually do... which is to take things too far."

"I… see that." I'm still reading over the bracket; it's shockingly detailed. I finish reading and look up at him, deadpan. "You actually think I'm gonna fall for this?"

He shrugs, easy. "I figured I'd give you a heads-up. Let you know exactly how I plan to win you over."

"Win me over?" I repeat, eyebrows raised.

He leans in, resting his hands on the desk. "Most people play hard to get. You're just hard. Period."

I narrow my eyes. "And most people take the hint."

"Yeah, but most people aren't me."

I should tell him to get lost. Should tell him this is pathetic. But instead, I'm staring at this dumb bracket, and all I can think is… no one's ever tried this hard to get close to me.

Most people want to get away.

He's doing overtime to get in.

I hate it, but I respect it.

And damn it, it *is* kind of cute. If I were one of *those* girls. The kind who flirted and enjoyed flings with hunky firemen. Thank goodness I'm not, because that sounds exhausting, and I'm sure it only ends in disaster anyway. Much better to just save myself the trouble.

"You know I'm not going to make this easy," I

say, crossing my arms.

His eyes don't leave mine. "I wouldn't expect you to."

There's something in his voice—steady, sure—and it does something weird to my chest.

I glance down, hoping he doesn't see it.

"And what happens when you lose?" I ask.

"I won't."

"You're that sure?"

He smiles, slow. "I notice things, Callahan. Like how you're still talking to me."

I roll my eyes, but it's weaker than it should be.

And worse—I notice things too.

The way his hair's a mess again, like he's been running his hands through it. The stubble on his jaw, just enough to make him look more like trouble. The way his arms stretch the sleeves of that uniform like it was made for him.

I hate that I notice.

"Go home, Cole."

"I will. After you smile."

"Get out."

He laughs, backing away, hands raised. "I'll be back. Bracket's not going to win itself."

I shake my head, but when he's gone, I'm still staring at it.

And damn it, now I'm smiling.

I'm still staring at the bracket, fighting the urge to burn it, when Mikey walks in, whistling like he's got no concept of personal space—or silence.

"Callahan, tell me you've got coffee because—"

He stops dead, eyes locked on the cardboard disaster still sitting on my desk.

"What the hell is that?"

I sigh, pushing it away like it might bite. "Don't ask."

His grin spreads instantly. "Oh, I'm asking."

He steps closer, squinting at it.

"Operation: Melt the Ice Queen?" He snorts, shaking his head. "Wow. Bold."

I glare. "It's Cole's latest dumbass idea."

"Figures. Guy's got a death wish."

He picks it up, scanning the levels, laughing harder with each one. "Stage seven: First kiss? Damn, he's ambitious."

"Stage eight's better," I mutter.

Mikey reads it out loud, gasping between laughs. "She *admits she likes him*? Oh no. Oh no, no, no. This is gold. I'm framing this."

I snatch it back, stuffing it under a pile of folders. "Not a chance."

"You're no fun."

"I'm plenty of fun. Just not for him."

Mikey wiggles his eyebrows. "Not yet."

"Do you want to get punched?"

He holds up his hands, still grinning. "Fine, fine. I'll back off. For now." He plops down in the chair across from me, stretching like he owns the place. "Anyway, you hear the latest about the gala?"

I groan. "What now?"

"They finalized the auction list. Guess who's still in?"

"Don't say it."

"You."

I drop my head onto the desk.

"And," he continues, way too happy, "they're making flyers this week. Public flyers. Your face, front and center."

"I'm quitting."

"You say that every week."

"This time I mean it."

Mikey just laughs, kicking his feet up. "Better pick a good outfit. You're gonna make someone's night."

I lift my head, glaring. "Over my dead body."

He shrugs. "Hey, maybe Cole will bid on you. Win himself an actual date."

I throw a pen at him. He ducks, still laughing.

When Mikey finally leaves—still laughing, still talking about how "this is going to be your year, Callahan"—the room feels quieter than before. Too quiet.

I stare at the files on my desk, suddenly unmotivated. My hand finds the edge of the bracket again, fingertips brushing the stupid cardboard.

I shove it in a drawer.

It's just noise. All of it.

I check the clock. Still two hours to go.

Outside the morgue, I can hear voices, someone pushing a cart, the low hum of the hospital moving on like nothing ever stops it.

But me?

I'm stuck.

It sneaks up on me every year. Right around this time. The day everything I knew slammed into a guardrail on a highway three towns over. Fast. Brutal. Final. The anniversary of the day I lost my parents.

Seven years.

You'd think it'd get easier.

It doesn't.

People like to say grief is a wave. Something that rises and falls. But no one tells you about the undertow—the way it can pull you under, even when you think you're standing strong. You look fine on the surface, and underneath, you're drowning.

I still remember the call. The way everything slowed down. The way no one could look me in the eye. I was about to graduate from high school, and then suddenly, I was planning funerals.

Since then, I've been fine. Or whatever version of fine works when you decide needing people just isn't worth it anymore.

No one sticks.

No one stays.

Except Beef. And maybe Shay.

And now this idiot with a bracket and a death wish... I don't have it in me to care.

I pull open the drawer again, staring at the mess of levels.

He doesn't get it. He doesn't know.

And he won't.

Not if I can help it.

It's dark by the time I slide into the booth at Rita's Diner. It's a place that hasn't changed since the seventies and probably never will. Vinyl seats that squeak, fluorescent lights that hum, and a waitress who knows your order before you open your mouth.

I like it here. It's predictable.

I tug off my hoodie, leaning back as the door swings open.

Jack walks in, solid and steady like he always is, a man who takes up space without trying to. He nods to the waitress, barely glancing around, then heads straight for me.

"You're late," I say, just to poke.

He grunts, sliding into the seat across from me. "Traffic."

That's it. No apology. No excuse. Just Jack.

We've known each other since I was a kid. He was my dad's best friend—back before the accident, before everything changed. After they died, he didn't say much, didn't push, but he checked in. Always has.

A text here. A call there. The occasional fix-it job when something breaks and I refuse to call a real repair guy.

He's not warm, not someone who asks how you're feeling. But he shows up. And sometimes, that's enough. "You eat yet?" he asks, flipping open the menu even though he always gets the same thing.

"Not really."

"Good."

The waitress appears, sets down two waters. "The usual?"

My usual is a milkshake.

Jack nods. "Yeah. And she'll have the grilled cheese."

I roll my eyes. "You ordering for me now?"

"You need to eat something."

I don't argue.

He leans back, watching me like he's trying to figure something out. He's got gray at his temples now, more lines around his eyes than I remember from when I was younger. Still tough. And sharp and incredibly fit. Probably more like me than I want to admit.

"That sink in your downstairs bathroom still giving you trouble?"

I snort. "I fixed it."

"Sure you did."

I sip my water, hiding the smile. "Beef would've called you if it wasn't working."

"Speaking of." He tilts his head. "You let him out?"

"Yeah, before I left. He's probably ripping apart my couch cushion."

Jack shakes his head. "That dog hates everything."

"Except me."

"And me."

I can't argue that. Beef loves Jack. Always has. The only man he doesn't bark at, doesn't growl at, doesn't try to scare off.

It's weird. But then again, Jack's always been the exception.

The food shows up fast—vanilla milkshake and a grilled cheese for me, steak and eggs for him, just like always.

We eat in silence for a minute, the clink of silverware filling the space.

Then he says it. "So, you dating anyone?"

I nearly choke on my sandwich.

"God, no."

Jack doesn't react, just cuts into his steak.

"Good."

I raise an eyebrow. "What about you?"

He shakes his head. "Nah."

I smirk. "No? Figured you'd at least be on one of those dating apps by now. Isn't that what old people do?"

He grunts. "I'm not that desperate."

I laugh, sipping my water.

But something shifts in his expression. Just a flicker.

"What?" I ask, narrowing my eyes.

He shrugs. "Got talked into trying it."

I sit up straighter. "You? On a dating app?"

"Don't start."

"Jack, that's... wow. I'm impressed."

"It's stupid."

"Anyone bite?"

His jaw twitches, like he doesn't want to answer. "Maybe."

I grin. "What's her name?"

"Kate." He smiles when he says it. Okay, that's new.

"She's either a saint to put up with you or just blind."

Jack snorts, his eyes crinkling in the corners. "I'll let you know."

I go back to my sandwich, still smiling. It's weird. Jack dating. But kinda good, too.

He nods toward me. "You sure about the no

dating thing?"

I roll my eyes. "Positive. Got some idiot EMT stalking me lately."

He pauses, fork halfway up. "Stalking?"

"Not literally. Just… persistent. It's dumb."

"What's his name?"

"Cole."

Jack frowns, like he's heard it before.

"You know him?"

"Yeah. A little."

"Well, you can tell him to back off."

He doesn't answer right away.

And now I'm wondering why.

# 9

## EMERGENCY PIE PROTOCOL

*Andi*

Tourist season means two things: more work, more bodies, and more idiots who don't know how to stay alive.

I'm fine.

No, really. I am.

It's just been one of those days where everything feels like sandpaper—rough, scratchy, and grating until there's nothing left but raw, frayed nerve endings.

First, there was the car accident victim who should've made it, but didn't. Too young. Too fast. And yeah, I know they're not my responsibility anymore by the time they get to me, but still. It stung.

Bad.

I had to take a few minutes to compose myself—which doesn't often happen.

Then Mikey decided to crank up the auction talk again, like I haven't already threatened to set fire to every flyer in this building.

And now, I've got paperwork coming out of my ears and a headache that won't quit.

But I'm fine.

Because that's what I do. I show up, do the job, go home. No complaints. No breaks. No nonsense.

The morgue is cooler than usual today, which should help, but it doesn't. I'm already tense, chewing on the end of my pen while I stare at a report I've read three times but still haven't processed.

Mikey's gone somewhere on his break, thank God. Left me in peace for once.

I don't even notice it at first—the small white container sitting on the corner of my desk. Styrofoam, the type that usually holds something greasy and bad for you. I swear it wasn't there ten minutes ago. I frown and reach for it.

There's a sticky note on top, scrawled in handwriting that's too neat to be Mikey's.

*In case of emergency. Pie usually helps.*

I freeze and read it again.

There's no name. No clue where it came from.

Did the universe know I needed pie to keep from having a complete and total panic attack?

I peel back the lid slowly, like it might be a trap. Inside? A perfect slice of cherry pie. Still warm, somehow. Flaky crust, red filling, a little messy like it's been cut in a hurry.

My stomach growls, loud and obnoxious.

Of course it does.

I glance around, half-expecting someone to jump out and claim it, but there's no one.

Just me, the pie, and a note that feels... weirdly personal.

I haven't told anyone that cherry's my favorite.

I pick up the fork tucked beneath the container, still wary, still braced for some kind of prank. But the smell alone is enough to make me cave.

One bite.

Just one.

The sweetness hits, and my eyes close for half a second because it's good. Too good.

It shouldn't feel like anything, but it does. A little like being seen. A little like being cared about.

Which is ridiculous.

I'm halfway through when Mikey walks in, pausing mid-step when he sees me.

"Is that... is that a smile?"

I freeze.

"Shut up."

"No way. Callahan's smiling. Someone call the press."

"It's pie," I mutter. "It's basic biology."

He cackles, moving closer like he's discovered a new species. "Nah, this is monumental. Hold still, I'm gonna document this."

"Touch your phone and I'll kill you."

He leans over, peeking at the container. "Where'd that come from?"

"No idea."

He raises an eyebrow, but before he can say more, the door creaks open again.

It's Cole.

I don't know how he does it, but he strolls in like he owns the place—casual and confident, and—heaven help me—looking way too good for someone I plan to keep rejecting.

His eyes land on me, then the pie, then the note still sitting beside it.

And he grins.

"Level one. Complete."

I blink, the fork pausing mid-air. "What?"

He taps the desk like it's obvious. "You smiled. That's level one."

My jaw drops. "This was you?"

"Guilty."

I stare at him, then back at the pie. "You... how did you even know?"

He shrugs, leaning against the wall like he's not the most irritating man alive. "I notice things."

Mikey whistles low. "Damn, he's good."

"Don't encourage him," I snap, but the heat in my cheeks betrays me.

Cole's still watching me, like he's waiting for

me to throw something—or kiss him. I'm not sure which.

"Just pie," he says, holding up his hands. "No strings. Unless you count the bracket."

I groan. "I'm going to burn that thing."

He approaches and grabs it from the corner of my desk. "You'll have to catch me first."

I glare. "Get out of here, EMT."

He pushes off the wall, heading for the door, but not before throwing me one last look over his shoulder.

"You're welcome, Callahan."

And just like that, he's gone.

Mikey's grinning like a kid on Christmas. "I'm telling everyone."

"Do it and die."

He laughs. "You hate everyone today or just the cute EMT?"

I glance down at the pie, then the note, then the door.

It's just pie.

But it's the best damn pie I've had in a long time. On a day when I especially needed comfort.

"Not sure yet," I admit. "But the day's still young."

The last bite of pie is halfway to my mouth when Mikey strolls in from the hallway, smug like he just won something.

"Still smiling?" he asks, dropping into the chair

across from me.

I scowl, wiping my mouth. "It's gone."

"Too late. I saw it." He leans forward, elbows on the desk. "Level one achieved. Should we pop champagne or wait till he gets your number?"

"You're insufferable."

He grins. "You love it."

"No, I tolerate it."

I'm about to kick him out when he pulls something from behind his back—folded, glossy, and already pissing me off.

"Speaking of things you love," he says, sliding it across the desk. "Ta-da."

I unfold it.

It's worse than I thought.

The auction flyer.

Front and center—my face, scowling like I've just been asked to babysit a pack of toddlers. The photo's from my ID badge because apparently HR has zero standards when it comes to public humiliation.

Andrea Callahan. Morgue Technician. Single. Fierce.

"What the hell is this?" My voice is sharp, rising with every word.

Mikey's practically vibrating with excitement. "They're going up today. Gala's three weeks out. You're officially famous."

I slam the flyer down. "I didn't agree to this."

"It doesn't matter. Voluntold, remember?"

"No." I push back from the desk, standing. "No, no, no. This is not happening."

Mikey laughs, holding up his hands. "Hey, don't shoot the messenger."

I pace, blood boiling. "I'm not doing it."

"It's for charity."

"Screw charity."

Mikey whistles. "The kids would be so disappointed."

I glare. "Not even pie can save this shitshow."

He chuckles, already backing toward the door. "Better pick out something hot to wear. I hear scrubs don't sell well."

"Out."

"I'm going, I'm going. But hey—if Cole bids on you, just take the win."

The door shuts before I can throw something at him.

I sit back down, breathing hard, staring at the flyer like it's personally out to ruin my life.

This is not how today was supposed to go.

Not even close.

# 10

## BET ON IT

*Cole*

I grab the thick black marker off Trey's desk and stride straight to the wall, still holding the bracket. I proudly tack it up on the wall. The guys are lounging in the bay, waiting for the next call—or for me to fail.

Not today.

In bold, dramatic strokes, I scrawl "COMPLETE" next to Level One: Make her smile.

Trey whistles low. "No way."

Brennan leans over my shoulder, eyebrows raised. "Witnesses?"

I don't flinch.

They both groan like I've just broken every code of betting etiquette.

"Nope, doesn't count without confirmation," Trey says, flopping into the nearest chair. "You could be lying."

I turn, deadpan. "Call Mikey. Her coworker was there. He saw it."

Brennan pauses. "Wait. That guy with the red hair?"

"Yup."

Trey grabs his phone, grinning. "Let's go. I want to hear this from the source."

I roll my eyes and head for the fridge. I've already won this one, but fine, let them have their fun. I crack open a water and sip while listening to Trey's side of the conversation.

"Mikey! Yeah, man, it's Trey. Listen—we're running a very important investigation here. Did Cole, or did Cole not, make the Ice Queen smile today?"

A pause.

Then laughter from Trey—full and obnoxious.

"Confirmed," he announces, tossing his phone onto the table like it's a mic drop. "Mikey says she smiled and ate a slice of pie he brought her like it was a religious experience."

Brennan grins. "Damn. Okay. Level One, official."

I head back over, capping the marker and tossing it onto the desk.

"Next up?" I ask.

Trey checks the board. "Level Two: She talks to him for more than five minutes without telling him to get lost."

"Great." I lean against the wall, sipping my drink. "Any tips?"

"Don't be yourself," Brennan says, dead serious.

I flip him off, but it's all noise now.

Truth is? I feel a little stupid. Not about the bracket. That's just fun. But about why I'm even bothering.

Most girls? I could flirt, throw a smile, maybe grab a drink. Easy. And if it progresses, great—if not, no hard feelings. Plenty of fish in the sea.

Andi?

She's not a game. She's not someone who plays by the rules or gives a shit about my charm. She's tough, sharp, all hard lines and don't-fuck-with-me energy.

But there's something else. Something beneath all that.

I want to know what it is.

Maybe I'm just wired to like a challenge. Maybe I'm tired of easy.

Or maybe… maybe I like her.

And she doesn't scare me.

Not one bit.

I finish my water and toss the bottle, watching it bounce off the wall and land perfectly in the bin.

Trey claps once. "Alright, Romeo. What's the plan for Level Two?"

I shrug, heading for the door. "We'll see."

But in my head?

I'm already thinking of ways to crack that armor of hers.

Because I'm all in now.

And I'm not backing down.

The morning sun is starting to heat up when I pull into the driveway, headlights cutting across the familiar yellow siding of the house. My body's wrecked—forty-eight hours of nonstop calls, adrenaline highs, and caffeine lows. All I want is a shower, something greasy to eat, and maybe eight hours of sleep without dreaming about sirens.

I kill the engine of my truck and step out. My apartment above the garage is calling my name, but first, I head toward the house to grab the leftovers Mom always insists on making when I'm on shift. Not that I'll ever complain about that.

The front door is unlocked, as usual, and I step inside, already unzipping my jacket. The smell hits me first—not garlic bread or baked pasta this time, but something lighter. Floral, almost. Perfume?

"Ma?" I call, dropping my keys into the dish by the door.

"Kitchen!" she yells back, her voice a little too cheerful for grading papers—which is what I usually find her doing on a Saturday.

I walk in and stop dead.

She's at the counter, dressed in jeans and a soft pink sweater, her hair curled like she's heading somewhere that isn't the grocery store. Lipstick. Earrings. The whole nine.

"What's going on?" I ask, eyeing the scene. Maybe she's having her girlfriends over? But even then, they're usually all casual.

She glances up, flushed but smiling. "Oh—hey, sweetheart. Didn't think you'd be back this early."

I lean against the doorway, arms crossed. "What's going on?"

She laughs, brushing past me to grab her purse. "I've got plans."

"Plans?" I echo, my eyes narrowing.

"Brunch. With a friend."

I raise a brow. "A friend?"

She sighs, but she's smiling. "Fine. A date."

I blink. "Wait, what?"

She looks at me, calm and casual like she didn't just drop a bomb. "I signed up for one of those dating app things. Figured I'd give it a try."

Confusion rushes through me. I open my mouth, close it, then open it again. "Since when?"

"Since Margot and Helen staged an intervention." She shrugs like this is normal. "You're not the only one who gets to have a life."

"I didn't say that," I mutter, still trying to catch

up.

"You're thinking it." She nudges me, grinning now. "Relax. It's just coffee. I've got pepper spray and a fully charged phone."

I rake a hand through my hair. "You met this guy online?"

"Yes, and his name's Jack. He's normal, I promise."

I shake my head, laughing despite myself. "You're really doing this?"

She softens. "Yeah. I think I need to."

I don't argue. Can't. She deserves this. Hell, I want her to have it. But still.

"Alright," I say, pushing off the doorframe. "Just—be smart, okay? Meet in public, don't leave your drink unattended, and text me when you get there."

She rolls her eyes. "Don't be a worrywart."

"Better than ending up as a news headline."

She chuckles, grabbing her keys. "I'll be fine, Cole."

I follow her to the door, still uneasy but letting it go. "Have fun."

She kisses my cheek on her way out. "Love you."

"Love you too."

I watch her get into her car, rubbing the back of my neck.

Great. Now I get to wonder what kind of guy

thinks he's good enough for my mom.

# 11

## SWIPE RIGHT FOR TROUBLE

*Kate*

I stare at my reflection in the rearview mirror and question all my life choices.

What am I doing?

I run my hands down the front of my sweater for the third time, smoothing out wrinkles that don't exist, and check my phone again. Ten minutes. I'm supposed to leave in ten minutes.

I could cancel.

I *should* cancel.

Why the hell did I think this was a good idea?

I grab my phone, already halfway through typing a polite excuse when Margot's name lights up the screen. Of course.

"Not now," I mutter, but I answer anyway.

"You're not bailing, are you?" she says without preamble.

"I'm not... *not* bailing."

"Kate."

"I'm serious, Margot. This was stupid. I haven't been on a date in decades. What if I say something ridiculous? What if he's awful? What if□—"

"What if you just went and had coffee?"

I let out a slow breath, my heart pounding. "I don't even know this guy."

"That's the point. You're supposed to get to know him."

"Margot—"

"No. No, ma'am. You are not talking yourself out of this. One date. That's all. One cup of coffee, and you get to say you tried."

I press a hand to my chest, trying to slow my racing thoughts. "I don't want Cole to see me like this."

"You've had a successful career. You raised a great son. You've done everything right. It's your turn. Time to have some fun."

I close my eyes, breathing through it. "You call this fun?"

"Go," she says, softer now. "You can do this."

I nod, even though she can't see me. "Okay."

"Good. Text me when you're done. And if he's terrible, I'll buy you dinner and wine."

"Deal." I flip closed the mirror on my car's visor and start the car before I can change my mind.

The drive is a blur, my thoughts stuck in a loop of what-ifs, but somehow I make it to the café without turning around. It's cute—small and warm, with the smell of fresh bread and something sweet baking in the back.

I pause just inside the door, scanning the room.

And then I see him.

Jack.

Oh dear God.

He's standing near the counter, taller than I would have figured from his photos, broad shoulders filling out a dark jacket, salt-and-pepper hair slightly tousled. There's something about the way he holds himself—solid, sure—that makes my stomach twist in a way I haven't felt in years.

He has what Margot would call Big Dick Energy.

I blush just *thinking* it.

He turns, and our eyes meet.

There's a beat of silence, and then he smiles—just a little, just enough to make my breath catch.

Okay.

I can do this.

I think.

He walks toward me, each step measured, confident, like he's exactly where he's supposed to be. Like this isn't weird or nerve-wracking or completely out of left field.

"Kate?" he says, stopping just close enough.

I nod, my voice temporarily missing. "Hi."

*Get it together.*

He offers a hand, and I take it—his grip is firm, warm, and just rough enough to remind me he's not one of those guys who spends all day behind a desk.

He looks younger than his age—43, according to his profile. Then again, whenever I look in the mirror, I'm still a little surprised I don't look as old as I sometimes feel. Aches in my back, my knees aren't great these days... I sleep like crap. Sometimes I'm surprised I don't look worse. I don't get carded as much as I used to, but still. Maybe there's a chance Jack's thinking the same thing about me. Let's hope.

"I'm glad you came," he says.

"Me too," I manage, though it's half a lie. I'm glad now, maybe, but fifteen minutes ago I was considering faking an illness to get out of this.

He gestures toward a corner table. "You want to sit?"

"Yes, please." I almost trip over my own feet getting there. Smooth, Kate. Very smooth.

We settle in, and the waitress appears like magic. I'm grateful for the distraction.

"I'll just have a coffee," I say quickly, not trusting myself with anything more complicated.

"Black," Jack adds, like it's obvious.

Of course, he drinks his coffee black.

She leaves, and then it's just us, sitting there, the weight of first impressions pressing down.

He's even more attractive up close. There's a quiet intensity about him, one that doesn't need to fill silence with noise. His jaw is defined with the faintest hint of stubble along it, and when his eyes meet mine—steady, warm—I feel a flicker of heat low in my stomach. I wasn't expecting that. I wasn't expecting any of this.

"So," I start, my hands fidgeting with the edge of a napkin, "this is... nice."

Nice? Really? That's the best you've got?!

Jack's mouth twitches, like he's holding back a smile. "It is."

Silence stretches, but not in a bad way. More like he's waiting to see if I'll settle.

Spoiler: I won't.

"So," I try again, "how long have you been... doing what you do? Search and Rescue?"

"Fifteen years," he says, leaning back, arms resting on the table like he's carved from calm. "Started right after the Army."

I nod, impressed despite myself. "That's... intense."

"Sometimes."

I'd googled it last night—believe me, compared to teaching tenth-grade English, it's very intense.

The coffee arrives, and I take a sip, grateful for something to do.

"And you?" he asks, voice low and steady. "Teaching?"

"Almost twenty years." I pause. "God, that sounds ancient when I say it out loud."

He chuckles, and something in me loosens just a little.

"What made you want to teach?" he asks.

I shrug. "I always liked books. Stories. Thought maybe I could help kids figure themselves out through them. Turns out, mostly I help them figure out how to plagiarize less creatively."

He laughs, deep and genuine. "You don't strike me as someone who lets things slide."

"Not much."

There's a pause, and I realize I'm not nearly as nervous now. I'm not sure when that happened. His eyes are on me, but not in that way some men do—measuring, waiting. He's just... here. Present.

I set my cup down, fingers brushing the rim. "This is easier than I expected."

Jack raises an eyebrow. "You expected hard?"

I shrug, smiling despite myself. "I didn't ex-pect smooth."

"Good." He leans in slightly, just enough to make my pulse jump. "Because I'm not here to make things complicated."

"Just coffee," I say, half-teasing.

"Just coffee."

But something about the way he says it tells me

this isn't *just* anything.

And I'm okay with that.

Even if it terrifies me.

Because so far? Jack is really cute, normal, and nice.

Go, me!

Jack leans in a little. "So, you mentioned you had a son? Grown now?"

For a second, I almost panic. Is he stalking me? How did he know that? Then I remember I'd mentioned I had a son during our online chat. I breathe again.

"Too grown," I say, smiling. "I keep waiting for him to need me again, but so far, he's managing just fine."

Jack smiles too. "That's how you know you did your job right."

"Do you have kids?"

Jack shakes his head. "Nope. Never had the chance. Thought I would, once."

He's quiet for a beat, and I'm not sure what to make of that. Regret, maybe?

We've all got a few.

Jack leans back in his chair. "You're not as nervous as I thought you'd be."

I let out a breathy laugh. "Oh, I'm nervous. I'm just good at faking it."

He grins, easy. "That so?"

I nod, still playing with the napkin. "Alright,

your turn. When you're not diving into rivers or chasing down lost hikers, what do you actually enjoy?"

His mouth twitches as if the question caught him off guard in a good way. "I don't have a ton of free time, but... I like fixing things. Building stuff. It's... quiet."

"Let me guess," I tease, "power tools relax you?"

Jack chuckles. "Only when they cooperate."

"That's a dangerous answer. Next thing you know, I'll be asking you to fix my leaky sink."

"I'd be happy to anytime," he says, and it feels less like flirting and more like a promise.

He takes a sip of his coffee, studying me over the rim. "Hiking, camping, anything outdoors—how do you feel about that stuff?"

I groan, exaggerated. "I feel like bugs should stay outside, and I should stay inside."

That laugh again—low and warm—washes over me.

"Fair enough," he says. "We'll stick to indoor activities then."

My eyes widen, and I realize exactly how that sounded. "That's not what I meant," I stammer.

Jack doesn't miss a beat; he just lifts an eyebrow like he's daring me to backpedal. "Didn't say it was."

I flush, shaking my head. "You're trouble."

"Only if you want me to be."

Just wait until he finds out how long it's been since I've had sex. Oh, God… do I even remember how? Questionable.

I grin to myself when I realize Margot would probably be more than happy to remind me. In graphic detail.

I don't know how long we sit there, trading questions and laughing over answers more than I expected. It's easy—so much easier than I thought it would be. The kind of conversation that flows without effort, no awkward silences or forced small talk. Just... nice.

I glance at my phone, surprised. "Wow. We've been here over an hour."

Jack looks up, a little surprised too. "Didn't feel like it."

"No, it didn't."

He catches the waitress's eye, signaling for the check. When it comes, he slides a few bills onto the tray before I can even think about arguing.

"I could've paid," I say, half-hearted.

"You can get the next one," he replies, standing.

The next one. Like it's already decided.

I like the idea of it more than I expected to.

I grab my purse, suddenly aware of how stupid I was earlier. The nerves, the panic, the little bottle of pepper spray I tucked inside my purse like I was about to meet a serial killer instead of... this. A man who made me laugh, who listened more than he talked, who didn't once make me feel like I had to be anything other than myself.

"I'll walk you to your car," Jack says, already a step ahead.

"You don't have to."

"I want to."

It's not a question. Not a courtesy. Just a simple truth.

I guess there are still gentlemen in this world.

Outside, the air is warmer, a soft breeze stirring the early afternoon. We walk side by side, the easy silence stretching between us, and for once, it doesn't feel like something I need to fill.

When we reach my car, I turn to face him, keys in hand, not sure what to say now that the date's over.

"This was... really nice," I admit, my voice softer than I expected.

Jack nods, that same calm, steady look in his eyes. "Yeah. It was."

There's a pause, and then, "Can we do it again sometime?"

I don't hesitate. "I'd like that."

He steps closer, just enough that I can feel the warmth of him, and wraps his arms around me in a hug that's nothing like I expected. Strong, solid, protective. A hug that says you don't have to be tough right now. And for a second, I melt into it, just breathing him in.

"Have a good day, Kate," he says, low in my ear.

"Thank you for the coffee."

He waits until I'm in the car, door shut, before he steps back. I watch him in the rearview as I pull away, my heart a little lighter, my nerves completely forgotten.

One date.

And maybe, just maybe... it wasn't so foolish after all.

# 12

## BUILT FOR MORE

*Jack*

It's close to dinnertime by the time I make it home. After my date, I ran some errands and swung by the grocery store.

The house is too quiet when I get home.

It always is.

I toss my keys onto the table by the door, the metal clinking louder than it should. I shrug out of my jacket, drop it on the back of the same chair I always use, and stand there for a moment. Just... standing.

There's no one waiting. No one asking how it went. No one filling the silence.

I'm used to that. I've built a life around it. But tonight?

Tonight, it feels a little heavier.

I head for the kitchen, not really hungry—just

needing something to do with my hands. The fridge hums when I open it—leftover takeout, a beer or two, nothing worth the effort. I close it again.

She was worth the effort.

Kate.

She was nervous. I could see it the moment she walked into that café, eyes darting around like she wasn't sure she belonged there. But damn, she lit up the second she started talking. Her laugh? I didn't expect that. Didn't expect to want more of it.

I rub a hand over my jaw, pacing.

The date was supposed to be simple: one hour, coffee, no pressure. But she made it easy. She made me forget about everything else for a while—work, the kid we pulled from the water, the way the job sticks to you even when you scrub your hands raw.

For the first time in a long time, it felt good to talk about something other than rescue stats and gear maintenance.

And now I'm standing in my kitchen like an idiot, replaying it all.

I grab a bottle of water, twist off the cap, and lean against the counter. The clock on the stove blinks 4:32 PM—too early to call it a night, too late to call anyone else.

I take a long pull from the bottle, letting the quiet settle. The thing about being alone is that it gives you time to think. Too much time, sometimes.

Kate's different. Strong, like she's held the

world up for too long but hasn't let it crush her. She reminds me of someone.

Andi.

Stubborn as hell, once self-reliant, but underneath it... there's something more. I've known her since she was a kid. I've watched her turn into a force of nature who doesn't take shit from anyone. She's like me in that way—built walls so high that no one bothers to climb them.

I get it. I do.

But now? I don't know. Maybe it's seeing her like this—grown, on her own, carrying that same weight I've been carrying—and realizing I have more to give than just a check-in now and then.

She's not my kid. But part of me still wants to protect her like she is.

I drain the rest of the water and set the bottle down with a quiet thud.

This used to be enough: work, routine, silence.

Now?

Now I'm not so sure.

I glance at my phone. No messages. No calls. Just the same blank screen waiting.

I swipe it open anyway. No new notifications from Kate, but I scroll back to our last message, my thumb hovering as if maybe, if I stare at it long enough, it'll change something.

It doesn't.

I put the phone down and run a hand through

my hair.

Yeah. It's going to take more than one date to figure this out.

But for the first time in a while, I want to try.

# 13

## I WANNA DANCE WITH SOMEBODY

*Andi*

The morgue is quieter than usual. Normally I'd welcome it. But today, it feels too still, as if everything is holding its breath. Even me.

My meetup with Jack the other night keeps circling in my head, like a song I can't turn off. He's always been a constant—steady and predictable—but something about him felt different this time. Tired, maybe. Or distracted. And I hate that I noticed. I hate that it stuck.

Because noticing means feeling.

And I don't have time for that.

I snap on a pair of gloves and reach for the next file, but the words blur a little. My fingers tighten, and I focus harder.

Just get through the shift. That's all. Like always.

I'm not fine, but no one needs to know that.

Especially not Cole.

The thought of him pulls at something I don't want to name. He's still out there, somewhere in this building, probably plotting his next ridiculous move. The bracket's burned into my brain now, every stupid stage daring me to react.

Smile? Done.

Talk for five minutes? Not happening.

I won't play his game.

Except... I already am.

"Earth to Callahan."

I blink and glance up. Mikey's leaning in the doorway, a smug look on his face, holding up a fresh cup of coffee like he's Saint Starbucks or something.

"Got you something," he says, setting it on my desk. "Thought you might need a refill before your next emotional shutdown."

I snort. "You're hilarious."

"I'm a treasure," he agrees, dropping into the chair across from me without an invitation. "So... how's lover boy?"

I groan. "Don't start."

"Too late. He's making progress, I hear."

"You've got ears everywhere, don't you?"

He grins, stretching like he owns the place. "The pie was a nice touch. Thought I was your work husband, but apparently, I've been replaced."

I roll my eyes, but the mention of the pie makes something tight in my chest loosen, just a little. I haven't let myself think about it too much. Haven't let myself think about why it mattered.

"It was just pie," I say, focusing on my screen.

"Sure," Mikey says, eyes twinkling. "And I'm just a humble civil servant."

I push back from the desk and stand up. "Don't you have something to do?"

"Yeah," he says, rising as well, still watching me too closely. "Like making sure you don't drown in all that broody energy. Seriously, Andi. Lighten up a little."

I stiffen, something sharp piercing my chest. "Not everyone gets to just... lighten up."

He frowns, but I'm already brushing past him, coffee in hand, pretending I didn't let too much show.

The hallway is cooler and quieter, but I can still feel it—the weight. Grief season. Jack's visit. Cole's attention. It's all piling up, and I don't know what to do with it.

I'm fine. I'm always fine.

But today? I'm not so sure.

I'm finishing my final report of the day, trying to focus when the door creaks open.

"You've got to be kidding me," I mutter without looking.

"Miss me?"

I glance up, and sure enough, there he is.

Cole.

Not in uniform this time—just a soft-looking T-shirt that clings in all the right places, dark jeans, that same stupid grin.

"What are you doing here?" I ask, narrowing my eyes.

He steps forward, hands behind his back like he's hiding something. "I brought you something."

"Your pie didn't work," I say, glancing at him.

He grins. "Didn't it?"

"Nope."

"Liar."

I narrow my eyes. "Do you ever give up?"

"Not when I'm winning."

"You're not."

"We'll see."

"Fine," I relent. "What'd you bring me?" *More pie?* My stomach gives a hopeful lurch.

He shrugs, pulls out a small pink pastry box, and sets it on my desk.

I stare at the box. It's not from the cafeteria; it looks more like something from a fancy boutique bakery. "You really don't have anything better to do?"

I realize that's an odd way to say thank you, but the last thing I want to do is encourage him.

"I have today off." He shrugs.

That explains why he's not in uniform.

"Then why aren't you somewhere else? Any-where else?"

"Maybe I wanted to see you."

My pulse quickens, but I keep my face still. I don't do this—whatever this is.

I tell myself not to read into it. He's just messing around. It's just a game. It's probably just more of his charm.

But for a moment... it doesn't feel like nothing.

I open the box slowly—inside is a cupcake, an adorable, perfect white cupcake with pink frosting topped with a slice of fresh strawberry. It's practically Instagram-worthy.

I don't thank him; I just lift it from the box, partially unwrap it, and take a bite. It's perfect—creamy frosting that's not too sweet paired with fluffy cake.

He leans against the counter, arms crossed, watching me like I'm a puzzle he can't wait to solve.

"You know, you're not as cold as people say."

I swallow slowly. "Don't get used to it."

He smiles like he already has.

"Are you off for the day?" he asks, eyeing my laptop bag and keys on my desk, along with the fact that I've removed my lab coat.

I nod and put my cupcake back in its box.

"I'll walk you out."

"No need."

"Too late."

I roll my eyes, but I don't fight him. I'll let him play gentleman if it makes him feel good. I grab my shoulder bag and my prized dessert, and we head for the doors.

We step into the lot, the sun dipping low, that golden-hour glow making everything softer—even him. I reach for my keys, hit the unlock button, and nothing.

Great.

I try again.

Nothing.

"You've got to be kidding me," I mutter.

"Problem?" he asks, already moving closer.

"Dead battery, I think."

"Pop the hood."

"I can handle it."

"I know," he says, stepping in anyway. "But you don't have to do it alone."

It's stupid, but that hits something I'm not ready for.

Five minutes later, we're both staring at the engine like it's personally insulted us. It wouldn't even turn over when I tried to start it.

"You need a jump," he says, "or a ride."

I groan. "I'll call someone."

"Or," he says, dangling his keys, "you can let me take you."

I hesitate—just long enough.

Cole smiles. "It's just a ride home, not a marriage proposal."

"Fine."

His truck's parked a few spots down, clean and sturdy, smelling like cedar and something that might be cologne. I slide in, arms crossed, still fuming.

"Where to?" he asks, starting it up.

I rattle off my street, then stare out the window, trying not to think about how weirdly nice this is.

He pulls out of the employee parking lot, and it's quiet except for the low hum of the engine and the soft, familiar beat of a song I haven't heard in years.

"I Wanna Dance with Somebody" filters through the speakers like it belongs there, as if it was playing even before I stepped inside.

I glance sideways, raising an eyebrow. "Are you listening to Whitney Houston?"

Cole doesn't flinch. He just grins, hands relaxed on the wheel. "I grew up with a single mom. Whitney's my girl."

I smirk, impressed. "Respect."

He taps the volume knob, nudging it up a bit. "This is her in her peak pop diva era."

"Absolutely," I agree, leaning back into the seat and letting the rhythm wrap around me. "Don't even get me started on *The Bodyguard* soundtrack…"

"Legendary," he cuts in, grinning wider. "I had

the CD in my mom's car growing up. Pretty sure I knew every word by the time I was eight."

I laugh under my breath, nodding. "Same. We used to play it on repeat in the kitchen. I'd dance around like an idiot while she cooked." The words spill out before I can stop them, and just like that, something shifts inside me—something warm and soft… and painful.

The memory feels like a lifetime ago: me singing into a spatula microphone while Mom laughed and encouraged me, Dad snapping photos on his phone. It was another life.

Cole doesn't say anything right away; he just lets the song play. The beat washes over me.

I clear my throat, my eyes fixed on the windshield. "She died when I was seventeen."

Still, there's no rush. No sympathy dripping off him like it does with most people. No fake condolences.

"Shit," he says, glancing over at me as if he's seeing me for the first time.

I nod, swallowing hard. "Car accident. Both my parents." My voice doesn't even shake. It's been years; I don't let it shake anymore.

"Damn, Andi." His jaw tightens, hands gripping the wheel a little harder. "That's... that's fucking horrible." He glances at me, eyes sharp, no bullshit. "How the hell did you even get through that?"

I shrug, my eyes fixed on the window. "You just do." My voice is quieter than I intended. "There's no magic trick. You wake up, and you get through the next hour. Then the one after that." I pause, swallowing hard. "Some days, that's all it is."

"Yeah," he replies, his voice low. "I get that." He drums his fingers lightly on the steering wheel, as if deep in thought. "Still... for what it's worth, I'm glad you did. Get through it, I mean."

"Are you okay… with the music?" he asks softly.

"Yeah." And weirdly, I am. I take a breath and let it out slowly. "It's strange, you know? Some days I barely think about it. Others..." I trail off, shrugging. "Songs like this— they just hit."

He nods, something flickering in his expression. "It's funny how the smallest things can bring it all back."

I glance at him, studying his profile in the glow of the dashboard. He's not just humoring me; he *gets* it.

"You ever lose someone?"

He is quiet for a moment longer. "My dad. Heart attack when I was fifteen."

"Oh." It's my turn to pause. "I'm sorry."

"Yeah." He shrugs, but there's weight behind it. "It's different, though; he wasn't really a part of my life, but... I get it. The way it sticks. We'll never get a do-over or a chance for a relationship."

His gaze remains steady—focused on the road—when he asks, "So what made you go into this line of work?"

I shrug. "Eh. The dead are easy. They don't expect small talk."

He glances over briefly. "Still, working with the deceased must be hard."

I shift in my seat. "My life has been full of challenges, and working with dead bodies? Not even in the top ten."

"Wow. Okay. Got it."

A comfortable silence falls between us for a moment, surprising me with how easy this feels.

"What about you? Firefighter-paramedic. Not exactly a walk in the park."

He drums his fingers on the steering wheel, the corner of his mouth lifting. "Just wanted to do my civic duty. Give back to the community."

I snort softly and give him a hard look. "That's the best you've got?"

He laughs, his eyes sparkling as he takes a slow turn. "What, you don't believe in noble causes?"

I shrug. He really is a golden retriever.

The rest of the drive is somehow easier. Not lighter, but... easier.

We pull up to my house—small, a little weathered, with white trim and blue shutters that could use a fresh coat of paint. The porch light is on, casting a warm glow on the steps. I like it that way. It feels lived in.

Cole throws the truck into park and turns to me, one hand still on the wheel. He's smiling—not the cocky, smug smile I've come to expect, but a softer, more genuine one.

"What?" I ask, arching a brow.

"Don't kill me," he says, holding up both hands, "but I'm pretty sure we just completed level two."

I groan and drop my head back against the seat. "You've got to be kidding me."

"Yeah. We talked for more than five minutes, and you didn't tell me to get lost." He's practically glowing now.

"Uh, you're right," I mutter, unbuckling my seatbelt. "Well, the fun ends now. I need to let my dog out, and he has a serious thing against men. Especially cocky ones."

Cole chuckles, not moving. "I'll take my chances."

I hop out, making my way up the porch steps with my keys in hand. "He's actually harmless, but he acts tough. I think something happened to him at the shelter. He doesn't trust easily. He'll probably bark his head off at you."

"Sounds familiar," Cole murmurs, following me.

Before I can respond, the door swings open— and there he is. Beef.

One hundred and forty pounds of pure fluff barrels out like a missile. I brace for the usual—growling, barking, the whole routine—but instead, Beef makes a beeline straight for Cole.

"Beef—wait!" I start, but it's too late.

Beef's tail is wagging, his body wiggling, and his nose is pressed into Cole's leg as if they've been best friends for years.

Cole kneels, scratching behind Beef's ears like it's nothing. "My best boy Beef," he says, grinning. "Why'd she have to name you like that, huh? You're a damn marshmallow."

I'm dumbfounded—my mouth is open, and words aren't forming. Where is the venom? The pure hatred? Doesn't Beef understand Cole is male? And why is Cole talking to him like he's a human?

Cole looks up, smirking. "You were saying?"

I blink. "He's never done that before."

"Dogs love me."

"Must be a fluke."

He stands, brushing off his hands, his eyes still sparkling. "So... how about you give me your number so we can move on to level three?"

I cross my arms and shake my head. "Not going to make it *that* easy on you."

"I know," he replies, taking a step back with his hands in his pockets. "But can you blame a guy for trying?"

"Bye, Cole."

"Bye, Andi."

I watch him walk away, Beef still wagging like he's found a new best friend, and for the first time in a long time, I don't know what to make of anything.

# 14

## LEVELING UP, THANKS TO SHAY

*Andi*

**S**hay and I slide into a high-top table at O'Malley's, the same bar she dragged me to last week, like it's some kind of therapy. It's late, but the place is still buzzing, full of people I don't want to talk to, music I barely like, and her—grinning like she's got plans I won't survive.

"I'm just saying," she starts, dropping her purse with a dramatic sigh, "the jeans were a good choice."

I tug at the waistband. "I wasn't dressing for anyone."

"Uh huh. And I drink tequila for the taste."

I shoot her a look, but the waitress is already there, so I order a drink strong enough to make this conversation fade into background noise. Shay orders something pink and dangerous, leaning in like we're plotting a crime.

"Alright," she says, eyes sharp. "Give me the latest."

"There's nothing to tell."

She raises her eyebrows.

"Shay."

She leans back, waiting.

I sigh. "Fine. He brought me dessert. Again."

"Pie?"

I shake my head. "A cupcake this time. With pink frosting."

She grins like I just told her we won the lottery. "Oh for the love. The hot firefighter's feeding you now?"

"It's not like that."

"Is he hand-feeding you?"

"Shay."

"Because if he is, I'm gonna need video."

I groan, but she's not letting up.

"You're smiling right now."

"I'm not."

"You are." She points, victorious. "Admit it."

I take a long sip of my drink instead.

Confidence is a hell of a drug. That's the only explanation for why I'm still thinking about Cole long after our encounter with the cupcake.

The most delicious cupcake.

But that's beside the point.

I surprised myself by opening up about my parents. It had felt natural at the time. Then again, I never took him for a Whitney fan. How random. I can't tell Shay all of that, though, or she'll never let me hear the end of it.

"Come on, Andi. What's the worst that could happen? You smile too much? Maybe enjoy yourself for once?"

"I don't do that."

She rolls her eyes. "Yeah, because you're allergic to fun. I forgot."

I glance down at my glass, swirling the ice. "It's not just fun, Shay. He's... I don't know. He doesn't back off."

"And you hate that?"

I open my mouth. Close it. "I don't know."

She watches me, her voice softer now. "When's the last time you even let someone in like this?"

The answer hangs there, heavy.

"Since... never," I admit, throat tight.

Shay doesn't gloat this time. She just nods, like she knew that all along.

"And Jack's been texting me more lately, too—just checking in, asking how I'm doing. It's... weird. He's never been this, like, involved before."

She sets her drink down. "Jack's always been there for you when you needed it."

"Yes, but it was always more out of obligation—his loyalty to my parents. This feels like something different. I almost get the sense he's lonely or something."

Shay shrugs.

My phone buzzes on the table, and I snatch it up before she can get a look.

> Cole: Question—if a guy brings you three pieces of pie, does that guarantee he gets bumped to level 3? Asking for a friend.

I bite my lip, but the laugh still slips out.

Shay leans in, eyes narrowing. "That better not be him."

I shove my phone facedown. "It's not important."

She grins, all teeth. "It's totally him. Told you he's hooked."

"Wait—how does he even have my number?" I ask, suddenly realizing I never gave it to him.

She shrugs, way too casual. "Oh, I gave it to him."

I blink. "You *what*?"

"You weren't gonna, and I was tired of watching you play hard to get without even giving the poor guy a chance."

I gape at her, half mortified, half ready to strangle her. "Shay."

"You're welcome," she says sweetly, taking another sip of her cocktail.

I lock my screen. "That was very uncool."

Her grin is pure evil. "You like him."

"I do not."

"You so do."

"Do not."

But my stomach's still flipping, and the smile won't leave my face.

Dammit.

I sip my drink, trying to wipe the stupid grin off my face, but it's no use. She's already clocked me. I need to put a stop to this before it gets out of hand.

"Honestly though, Shay. What do we even really know about this guy?"

She leans in, eyes gleaming, like she's about to expose something criminal. "I did some digging."

I groan. "Of course you did."

She pulls out her phone, tapping away. "Look, you don't trust anyone. I get it. So, I did the heavy lifting."

"Seriously?"

She ignores me, scrolling. "Okay, listen to this. Cole Everett Hartley. Twenty-five years old. Born and raised here, except for college. Boston College dropout, two years. Switched to Fire Academy. Been with the department for—wait—four years now."

I blink. "You've got his résumé?"

A determined grin lifts her mouth. "Public records, baby. Also, I may have bribed one of the ER nurses with coffee."

I shake my head. "That's insane."

"You're welcome." She flashes her phone at me. "He's clean. No criminal record. No baby mamas. No weird political rants on Facebook."

I laugh. "That's the bar now?"

"Hell yes. Oh, and he's got, like, zero social media. Which is either hot or suspicious."

"Suspicious," I mutter, but it's half-hearted, because I don't have social media either.

"Or," she grins, "he's just not into oversharing."

"Still. What do we even know about him?" I press, trying to find solid ground. "This could all be for show."

She leans back, arms crossed. "And what's he showing, huh? That he likes you? That he's trying?"

I hate how that lands. Square in the chest.

"He's not the only one who's tried, Shay."

"No," she says, gentler now. "But he might be the first one worth it."

I go quiet, fingers tracing the rim of my glass.

"You're a walking conundrum, girly." She eyes me, chuckling. "Dead people? *Easy*. Living, breathing firefighter? *Total nightmare*."

I shoot her a look that hopefully gets my point across.

Shay reaches over, nudging me. "You don't have to decide tonight. But maybe don't shut him out just because you're scared."

"I'm not *scared*."

"Right."

I glance at my phone again, still lit with that dumb text. My fingers hover.

"Maybe," I say slowly, "he's not a complete idiot."

She grins. "Progress."

"Don't push it."

She raises her glass. "To maybe."

"To maybe," I echo, barely a whisper.

# 15

## CAREER DAY CURVEBALL

*Cole*

The bracket's blown up.

What started as a stupid joke between me, Trey, and Brennan has officially taken over the whole damn firehouse. There's a new poster—clean lines, fresh markers, and about seven more names betting on how far I'm gonna get with Andi. Trey even added a bonus round: if I get a second date, they're all chipping in for steaks.

Bunch of idiots with nothing better to do.

I stare at it and run a hand through my hair. There's something about seeing her name up there—bold, underlined, next to mine—that doesn't sit right. Not in a bad way, just... I don't know. This isn't some stupid game to me.

"Dude," Brennan says, dropping into the chair beside me, "you've got them all watching now. It's like the playoffs."

Trey laughs from across the room, waving his phone. "They're taking side bets. Marissa from ER put money on you crashing and burning by level four."

"Good to know," I mutter.

Brennan elbows me. "You're not chickening out, are you?"

"No." I shake my head. "I'm just—this was supposed to be fun."

"It *is* fun." He grins. "You just don't like that you're catching feelings."

I shoot him a look, but he's not wrong.

Andi was supposed to be a challenge, a little spark in an otherwise predictable routine. But it's more than that now. The more time I spend with her—the real her, not just the one who glares and throws out one-liners—the more I want to know. Like why she looks tired sometimes, not just physically, but soul-deep. Or why her dog, Beef, trusted me when he clearly doesn't trust anyone else.

She's complicated, with sharp edges and soft spots, and I can't stop thinking about her.

Trey tosses a stress ball at my head. "You're up, lover boy."

I blink. "Up?"

"Did you forget? Career day. Your mom roped you in, remember?"

Shit.

I glance at the clock. I've got twenty minutes to get over to the high school.

"Right. Thanks."

Brennan's already laughing. "Bet you a donut he makes the kids cry."

"Bet you two he doesn't even know what to say."

I flip them both off as I grab my gear. "I'll be back before you can miss me."

The high school's only ten minutes from the station, but the parking lot's a nightmare. Kids everywhere, teachers directing traffic like it's a war zone. I finally squeeze into a spot, adjust my shirt, and head inside. The place hasn't changed since I was here—same hallways, same crappy lockers, same smell of teenage body spray and anxiety.

I spot my mom near the front office, and she's in full teacher mode, clipboard in hand, directing volunteers where to go.

"Hey, Ma."

She turns, brightening. "You made it! I was starting to wonder."

I kiss her cheek. "Wouldn't miss it."

"Classroom 3B," she says, waving toward the hallway. "You're up after the medical technician. She's already in there."

I nod, about to head that way—when she adds, way too casually, "Oh, and Cole? Eyes on the students, not the pretty guest speaker."

I pause mid-step. "What?"

She smirks and waves me off. "You'll see."

I narrow my eyes, but she's already gone, herding some latecomer toward another room.

I head down the hall, rounding the corner—and there she is.

Andi.

Standing at the front of the classroom, totally composed, totally *not* noticing me. She's talking about her job like it's no big deal, like she's not the most captivating person in the entire room.

Her lavender hair's pulled back in a neat, low bun, but a few pieces have escaped around her face. She looks gorgeous. Sharp. Confident. These kids don't scare her. She's fielding questions like she's done this a hundred times, even the dumb ones about zombies and whether bodies can sit up on their own. She's got them laughing, even as she deadpans about rigor mortis and cause of death investigations.

She's good at this.

Really good.

And I'm frozen in the doorway, watching her like an idiot.

"Cole Hartley?" a teacher calls from behind me, breaking the spell. "You're next."

Right. Focus.

I shake it off, step inside, and nod politely. Andi's still mid-answer, but her eyes flick to mine—

just for a second—and something shifts. She doesn't react. Doesn't smile. But I swear there's a flicker of something.

I slide into the back while she wraps up. The teacher thanks her, the kids clap, and then it's my turn.

I step up front, clearing my throat. "Alright, be honest—who's here just to get out of class?"

A dozen hands shoot up.

"Yeah, I don't blame you," I say, grinning. "But since you're stuck with me for the next ten minutes, I'll make it worth your while."

I launch into the usual—fire safety, cool calls I can actually talk about, how I got started. I toss in a joke about saving cats from trees and the time Brennan locked himself out of the rig during a donut run. The kids eat it up.

But I'm not at my best. Not really.

Because every time I glance left, I see her. Leaning against the wall, arms crossed, watching me. She's trying to look bored, I know she is—but I catch the corners of her mouth twitching when I talk about some of our more ridiculous calls.

I wrap up, the class clapping again as the teacher steps forward.

"Let's thank Mr. Hartley and Ms. Callahan for visiting us today!"

They all cheer, and I back away, grabbing my jacket.

"Hey," she says, suddenly at my side. Her voice is low, unreadable.

I turn. "Hey."

"You stalking me now?" she asks, one eyebrow raised.

I grin. "I could ask you the same thing."

"I was invited."

"So was I."

We stand there for a beat, the classroom clearing out around us.

"You were good," she says, almost reluctantly.

"You weren't so bad yourself."

Another beat.

Then I nod toward the door. "Coffee?"

She doesn't answer.

Yet.

"I should get back to the hospital."

I nod. And I should get back to the station, but ten minutes never hurt anyone. "There's a Starbucks on the way. I'll make it worth your while…" I grin.

I fully expect her to shoot me down.

"Okay," she relents.

*Damn. Okay then.*

The coffee shop's crowded, but not too loud—just enough noise to keep things easy, casual. I hold the door for her as we step inside; the smell of roasted coffee beans hits instantly.

I hold the door, smirking. "I'll try not to make

this the worst ten minutes of your day.”

She chuckles but rolls her eyes.

We hit the counter, and I glance at her. “So, what’ll it be? Let me guess—black coffee, no room, no soul?”

She shrugs. “Why mess with perfection?”

I turn to the barista. “One heartless brew, and a vanilla latte for me.”

She scoffs. “Vanilla? Really?”

I shoot her a grin. “What, no respect for the classics?”

The barista laughs as I hand over the cash, and Andi shakes her head. “You’re impossible.”

“Yet here you are.”

After we get our drinks, we find a high-top table near the window with barstools that wobble just enough to keep you on edge. She slides into one, tucking her hair behind her ear, and my pulse kicks up. Not because she’s glaring at me, but because she’s *not*. And she looks exceptionally hot today in her skirt and blouse combo.

“So,” I start, resting my elbow on the table. “Any plans after your shift, or just the usual— avoid human interaction at all costs?”

She sips her coffee, and something about the way she leans in, half-daring, half-curious, makes me forget every line I’d practiced in my head.

“Maybe I’m rethinking my stance on people,” she says, deadpan.

"Big day," I murmur, smiling into my cup. "So, besides your obvious distaste for human interaction, what's your thing?"

She raises a brow. "My thing?"

"Yeah. What makes you... you?"

She pauses, like she's not used to being asked. "I don't know. I like quiet. Dogs. Not this." She gestures between us.

"Not flirting with a very charming firefighter-paramedic?"

"Exactly."

I grin. "Noted. But you didn't leave yet."

"I'm weighing my options." She takes a sip, and I swear she's hiding a smile. "I guess one of my *things* is that I'm allergic to bullshit. I'd rather save myself the hassle."

"Lucky for you, I'm pure charm."

She lifts an eyebrow. "That so?"

I nod, dead serious. "It's exhausting, honestly. Carrying all this charisma."

She finally laughs—really laughs—and it hits me right in the chest.

"You're relentless," she groans.

"You like it."

"Don't push it."

We sip in silence for a beat, but it's not tense. Just... easy.

Her gaze sharpens, but she doesn't pull back.

"Why?" she asks, voice lower. "Why me?"

I lean back, rolling the cup between my hands. "Because you don't fall for the easy stuff. You make people work for it."

"And you like working for it?"

"I like working for you."

That gets her. She shifts, uncomfortable but not in a bad way.

I change the subject before she bolts. "Alright, what's something I don't know about you?"

She pauses, considering. "I hate mornings."

"Same."

"And I bake when I'm mad."

I grin. "Interesting. What kind of baking?"

"Pies are my favorite. Peach. Apple. Whatever."

"Good to know for if I ever piss you off."

"You mean *when*?" she teases.

I laugh. "Fair."

We finish our drinks, talking about nothing and everything—stupid bets at the firehouse, the way people always assume Beef is part wolf. Time slips by faster than I want it to.

Eventually, she checks her phone, sighing. "I really do have to get back."

I nod, grabbing our cups. "I'll walk you out."

Outside, it's warm, but she doesn't rush to her car. We linger by the curb, neither of us quite ready to call it.

"Thanks for the coffee," she says, pulling her

keys from her pocket.

"Thanks for not running."

She smirks. "Yet."

I take a step back, hands in my pockets. "See you around, Callahan."

She opens her car door but pauses. "Cole?"

"Yeah?"

She tilts her head, eyes narrowing. "You're not what I expected."

"Good or bad?"

She slips inside, shutting the door. Doesn't answer.

But the smile on her face?

I'll take it.

# 16

## PAUL BUNION STRIKES AGAIN

*Kate*

Cole's been pacing the hallway for the past ten minutes, fussing with his bow tie like it personally offended him.

"You know, it's supposed to go under the collar," I say, setting out wine glasses on the coffee table.

He groans, stopping in front of the mirror again. "This tux is a torture device."

I glance up—and yeah, he looks good. Too good. The black tux fits perfectly, crisp white shirt, polished shoes. His hair's still damp from the shower, pushed back in that way that always makes him look older, sharper. Like a man who's about to break hearts and pretend he doesn't notice.

"You look very handsome," I tell him, softening. "Now stop fidgeting."

He turns, smirking. "You sure you don't want to come to this thing with me? We could trade—I'll do book club, you come to the gala."

"As tempting as that is," I say, crossing my arms, "I'll take wine and gossip over a room full of people I don't know, thank you very much."

He chuckles, grabbing his jacket off the back of the couch just as the doorbell rings.

"That'll be Margot and Helen," I say, moving toward the door.

Cole gives me a mock look of panic. "Should I run now?"

I laugh. "Too late."

I open the door and Margot breezes in first, wrapped in a colorful shawl, eyes immediately locking on Cole.

"Holy hell," she says, fanning herself. "If I was twenty years younger, I'd jump your son."

"Margot!" I gasp.

"Please," Helen deadpans, following behind her, "you're still considering it."

Margot winks. "Just keeping my options open."

Cole's ears go red as he grabs his keys, grinning despite himself. "Nice seeing you both. I'm heading out before this gets worse."

"Have fun," I call, shooing him toward the door.

"Don't do anything I wouldn't do!" Margot yells after him.

"Which leaves him a lot of options," Helen adds.

The door clicks shut and the house feels instantly lighter—full of laughter and the familiar chaos only these two can bring.

Margot flops onto the couch, kicking off her shoes. "Alright, pour me something strong. We've got books to pretend to discuss."

Helen settles in beside her, already pulling out her copy. "I actually read it this time."

I smile, heading for the kitchen. "Me too."

Margot grins. "Well then, let's ruin it with wine and bad advice."

And just like that, book club begins.

Margot takes a generous sip of her wine, legs already tucked under her like she's moved in for the night. "So, what did we think of the book? Personally, I think it was a little too heavy on the metaphors and not heavy enough on the shirtless scenes."

Helen raises an eyebrow. "You mean the emotional rollercoaster disguised as literature?"

"Exactly. A tasteful abs moment wouldn't have killed anyone."

I laugh, curling into my chair. "I actually liked it. The writing was really beautiful."

Margot waves a hand. "Sure, sure. But no one fell into bed screaming, and honestly, that's just unrealistic."

Helen smirks, but she's already toeing off her shoes to get more comfortable. "I give it three stars. One of them's just for the dog."

Margot points. "Now that, I agree with. More dogs, less emotional repression."

We all take a sip, pretending like we're about to dig deeper—but then Helen shifts, rubbing her foot absently, and Margot groans.

"Oh no. Don't do it."

"What?" Helen blinks, all innocence.

"Don't start with Paul Bunion again."

I nearly spit out my wine. "Paul?"

Margot nods, deadly serious. "Her bunion. It's got its own personality at this point."

Helen shrugs, deadpan. "It's a medical condition. I'm not going to apologize."

"You've made us apologize to it," Margot shoots back.

"One time," Helen mutters.

"You made me toast it with champagne on your birthday," Margot says, eyes wide.

"Because it's part of me," Helen replies, taking a slow, deliberate sip of her wine.

We dissolve into laughter that shakes our shoulders and makes it impossible to stop. I wipe my eyes, still giggling. "Okay, okay. No more about Paul."

Margot grins, leaning forward. "Fine. We'll switch topics."

Her eyes gleam, and I know exactly what's coming before she even opens her mouth.

"So… tell us about this Jack."

I freeze, mid-sip. "What?"

Helen perks up, instantly alert. "Oh yes. Let's. We need the full update."

Margot's already practically vibrating. "You've been holding out on us. We need details." She rubs her hands together, more than ready for some juicy gossip.

I set my glass down, feeling my cheeks heat. "There's nothing to tell. We've just… been talking."

"Texting," Helen corrects, arching a brow.

"Every day," Margot adds, sing-song.

I groan, sinking lower in my chair. "It's new. But it's… exciting. He's—" I stop, fumbling for words.

Helen leans in, softer now. "He's what?"

"He's kind," I say, almost surprised by it myself. "And steady. Like, really steady. I didn't expect that."

Margot grins like she's won something. "You like him."

"I do," I admit, heart thudding.

"Have you seen him since your date?" Helen asks.

"Not yet." I shrug. "We've both been busy, but talking to him has been nice. The getting to know you stuff. It's just easy, you know?"

Margot beams. "I knew it. I knew you needed to get out there more. Get laid, ideally."

Helen laughs. "*Margot.*"

"What? I'm happy for her."

I cover my face, laughing despite myself. "You two are impossible."

Margot raises her glass. "To Jack. And to new things."

Helen clinks hers against mine. "And to never hearing about Paul again."

We all laugh, the wine making me warm, and the night just starting.

And for the first time in a long time, I feel like maybe, just maybe, something good is starting too.

# 17

## GOING ONCE, GOING TWICE, MINE

*Andi*

I don't do nervous.

Not for autopsies, not for small talk, and definitely not for dressing up.

And yet—here I am, standing in front of my mirror, holding my breath while Shay zips up a dress that might actually kill someone if I breathe too hard.

"Holy crap." Shay steps back, hands on her hips, eyes wide with something bordering on religious awe. "You look like the sexiest disco ball I've ever seen."

I roll my eyes, but even I have to admit… damn. The silver sequins catch every bit of light, hugging my body as if this thing were stitched by angels—or at least a team of very determined saleswomen at Nordstrom.

"This is too much," I mutter, smoothing the fabric down my hips.

"It's exactly enough," Shay fires back, already reaching for the curling wand like she's prepping me for battle. "Now sit. I'm not done."

I obey, mostly because I'm afraid of what she'll do if I don't. She's got that look—the one that says she won't stop until I'm fully transformed into some kind of glittering goddess.

It's slightly terrifying.

"Fancy underwear?" she asks, already rifling through the drawer where I keep the stuff I never wear.

"Shay."

"You didn't shave your legs for nothing," she sing-songs, tossing a lacy black set my way.

I groan but change anyway—sliding off my preferred boy shorts and tugging on some torture device that Shay insists won't create panty lines.

An hour later, my hair's curled, my makeup's flawless, and my heels are—well, dangerous. I catch my reflection again, and for a second, I almost don't recognize myself.

Not because of the sequins or the lipstick, but because I'm actually… excited.

What is wrong with me?

Mikey would have a field day if he knew. I'd never hear the end of it.

I look like trouble. The fun kind—wavy hair,

perfect makeup, a figure-hugging dress, and killer shoes.

"Okay, final touch." Shay swipes a tube of lipstick from her bag and hands it over. "Red. For maximum impact."

I apply, blot, and glance in the mirror one last time. My heart's doing something weird—something I don't like.

Hopeful.

"Crazy," I whisper.

Beef lifts his head from the couch, huffs like he agrees, then flops back down dramatically.

"Don't look at me like that," I tell him. "It's just a party."

Shay grins. "Sure. And Cole's just a guy."

I narrow my eyes, but she's not wrong.

I'm not doing this for him.

…But if he likes it?

I won't hate that.

I should've stayed home.

That's the first thought that hits me as I step into the gala, all glitter and glass, surrounded by people who look like they belong in magazines, not real life. The air smells like money—expensive perfume, polished wood, and something vaguely floral that probably costs more than my rent.

My heels click too loudly against the marble floor, each step echoing like a warning: You do not belong here.

I fidget with the strap of my clutch, scanning the room. Bigwigs. Donors. Hospital board members who wouldn't know a scalpel from a butter knife. Fancy hors d'oeuvres float by on silver trays—tiny things I can't pronounce that look like they'd taste like pretension. People laugh into tall champagne flutes, their teeth too white, their suits too perfect.

And me? I'm one wrong move away from bolting.

This is not my scene. Not even close. I'm a sweatpants-on-the-couch kind of girl, not someone who knows how to schmooze with people who use "summer" as a verb.

I tug at my dress—Shay's idea of "perfection"—and try not to think about how my underwear feels like it's trying to strangle me from the inside out. Glittery silver sequins catch the light, hugging my body in a way that demands attention, which is exactly what I *don't* want. My heels pinch, my lips are dry, and I swear if one more person bumps into me with their tiny plate of foie gras or whatever-the-hell, I'm going home.

Then I see him.

And just like that, the whole damn world stops spinning.

Cole.

He's standing near the bar, laughing at something one of his buddies said. Black tuxedo. Clean-shaven. Hair styled in that neat, polished way that makes him look like he just stepped out of a James Bond movie and into my personal space. He's deadly like this—tall, confident, stupidly gorgeous—and for a second, I forget how to breathe.

This? This is worth every stray eyebrow Shay plucked. Worth the glitter in places glitter shouldn't be. Worth the shoes, the dress, the literal torture chamber of a bra. Because seeing him like this? Holy out-of-body experience.

And then he spots me.

His eyes light up, slow and warm, like he's been waiting just to see me.

He crosses the room in a few long strides, weaving past the crowd like none of them matter. His gaze never leaves mine, and my heart? It's pounding against my ribs like it has something to prove.

"Hey," he says, and damn if his voice isn't lower and smoother than usual—like silk mixed with something dangerous.

"Hey," I manage, because words are apparently hard now.

He leans in, grinning. "Is it just me, or did it get way hotter in here?" He pauses, still grinning. "Oh wait, never mind—it's you."

I laugh—sharp and quick—and it feels like all

the air comes rushing back. Instant relief. Instant calm.

This? I can do this.

"That was the cheesiest line I've ever heard," I shoot back, lifting my chin.

His eyes roam slowly but respectfully before landing back on mine. "I know. Seriously, though, you look incredible."

I blush, hating that I do, but not caring enough to hide it. I let my eyes take their fill of him too—this is a very different look from his polyester fire-fighter uniform or his jeans-and-T-shirt combo.

"You don't look so bad yourself."

"Careful, Callahan. You keep looking at me like that, and I'm gonna think you like me."

I clear my throat. "Shut up, Cole."

He chuckles, then offers me his arm—classic and easy. "Ready to survive this circus?"

I hesitate. Just for a second. Then I loop my hand through his, trying not to melt at how solid he feels. *Holy biceps, Batman!* I let him lead me through the madness, and for the first time tonight, I believe I might just make it.

I'm still reeling when he leans in, his voice low and warm.

"By the way, if you're trying to kill me, you're doing a damn good job."

It hits me right in the chest—sharp, quick, and totally unfair.

"Shut up," I mutter, heat rising to my cheeks. But I can't stop the grin, not when he's looking at me like that—like I'm the only person in this crowded, fancy room who matters.

"You want a drink?" he asks.

"Definitely."

The bar's tucked in the corner, all sleek lines and polished wood. A waiter is already handing out champagne as if everyone here is used to it, but Cole orders me something stronger—bourbon, neat. I raise an eyebrow.

"What, no sweet vanilla latte this time?"

He shrugs, handing me the glass. "Thought you might need the hard stuff tonight."

He's not wrong.

The drink burns in a good way, and I'm just starting to relax when chaos hits.

"Andi Callahan?" A woman in a sleek black dress and headset materializes out of nowhere, clipboard in hand. There's too much energy in her voice. "We need you backstage. It's almost time." Her gaze swings over to Cole. "And Cole Hartley. Yep, you too."

My heart plummets. "Time for what?"

"The auction!" She beams. "You're up after Cole."

Cole freezes mid-sip. "Wait, *you're* in the auction?"

I glare. "Apparently."

He's fighting a smile. "Didn't peg you for the bachelorette type."

"I'm not," I mutter, setting my glass down harder than intended. "I was tricked."

"Voluntold?" he teases.

"You have no idea."

She's already tugging at my arm. "Let's go. You'll love it, I promise!"

I shoot Cole one last look—part panic, part *if I survive this, I'm killing someone*—and let her herd me backstage. Cole follows closely behind.

The noise backstage is overwhelming. It's too bright, too loud. People mill about in designer dresses and tuxes, some fidgeting like me, others looking way too excited. I'm definitely not in my element. I'm more of a *pjs and crime documentaries* kind of girl. Not… *this*. Whatever this spectacle is—a complete and total horror show.

Cole appears next to me a second later, all casual, as if we're not about to be paraded in front of every bigwig and donor this town has.

"You good?" he asks, nudging me gently.

"Right now? No. I'm questioning all of my life choices," I admit.

"Yeah." He laughs softly. "Same."

And then—boom.

"Let's keep things rolling with our next bachelor," the emcee announces, his voice all smiles and hype from beyond the curtain. "You've seen him around town, you've probably been saved by him once or twice, those biceps… that smile… and rumor has it he makes a killer breakfast burrito... give it up for COLE HARTLEY!"

Cole smirks. "That's me."

I watch, almost in slow motion, as he straightens his jacket and walks through the curtain like it's nothing. Cool. Confident. Deadly.

*Rude!*

I peek around the side of the heavy curtain, heart racing, and holy hell.

He owns that stage.

The lights catch the sharp lines of his tux, his clean-shaven jaw, and that perfectly messy hair he somehow managed to style just right. He waves, smiles, and says something to the emcee that makes the crowd laugh.

I'm frozen. Spellbound.

This is *so* not fair.

"And let's start the bidding at one hundred dollars!"

Hands fly up.

"Two hundred!"

"Three!"

My chest tightens.

The numbers climb quickly. He's grinning easily, as if this is just another day at the office. The emcee shares more about him—how he volunteers, how he once saved a cat from a sewer, how he's *single and ready to mingle.* The crowd eats it up.

"Four-fifty!"

"Five hundred!"

Cole flexes on stage and somehow makes it funny, not cringey.

My eyes narrow as I spot her. Blonde. Tall. One of the ER nurses—I've seen her flirt with him before. She waves her bid card like she's been waiting all night for this.

"Six hundred!" she shouts.

Cole glances at her, then—*damn him*—right at me.

The hammer slams.

"Sold! To Marissa from ER!"

Cole steps down, still grinning, while the nurse looks like she just won the lottery.

And me?

I should not care.

I should *not* care.

And yet…I'm a mess of jealousy and confusion.

Because what is even happening right now!?

I barely have time to process the ridiculous knot in my chest before someone touches my arm.

"You're up," the clipboard woman says, smiling like this is *fun.*

I swallow hard; my legs feel like concrete. "Do I have to?"

"Yep." She's already steering me toward the

curtain. "Smile!"

The lights hit me like a punch in the face.

Too bright. Too hot. Too much.

I squint, trying to make out the crowd, but all I see are silhouettes and champagne flutes. My heart's in my throat, my palms are sweaty, and the sequined death trap Shay made me wear feels too tight.

"And now, one of Memorial's finest," the emcee booms. "She's smart, she's strong, she's not here for your bullshit—put your hands together for ANDI CALLAHAN!"

I step out. Barely.

The crowd claps, polite but hesitant. I don't blame them. I'm not exactly bachelorette material. I'm not all smiles and sparkles. I'm the girl who works with dead people and has a don't-mess-with-me attitude.

"She's a morgue tech, loves dogs, and makes a mean pie—just don't get on her bad side," the emcee jokes.

A small laugh comes from somewhere in the crowd. Then a cough. Then total silence.

I already regret every decision that led to this moment.

"Alright, let's start the bidding at one hundred!"

More silence.

My stomach drops.

"One hundred, anyone?"

A hand goes up. I squint. It's... an elderly woman? Great. A pity bid.

"One-fifty?"

Crickets.

Okay, now this is just mortifying.

Then—

"Two hundred," a deep voice calls.

My head snaps up.

Cole.

He's standing near the back, jacket off now, sleeves rolled to his elbows like he's here to work. His eyes are locked on mine, daring me to say something.

"Two-fifty!" some old guy yells, winking at me.

I nearly gag.

"Three hundred," Cole fires back, smooth.

"Three-fifty!"

"Four."

The emcee's loving this. "We've got a bidding war, folks!"

Do we?

Because one's an ancient creeper and the other's the only man who's ever made me laugh at my own expense.

"Four-fifty!" the old man shouts, his voice cracking.

Cole doesn't blink. "Five."

The man hesitates, looking me over like I'm a

damn steak.

I shoot him my best death glare.

"Going once," the emcee grins.

The old man frowns.

"Going twice—"

"Sold! To Cole Hartley!"

I stand there frozen, smile plastered on like I'm in one of those dreams where you show up to work naked and everyone applauds.

Cole's grin is too smug, too sure. He gives me a slow, infuriating wink as the emcee claps him on the back like he's just solved world hunger.

"Congratulations to our lucky bachelor!" the emcee crows. "And to his date—don't look so terrified, sweetheart, he doesn't bite."

The crowd laughs. I don't.

Cole mouths something toward the stage—*maybe later*—and I swear my eye twitches so hard I might need medical attention.

Mikey's grinning from the from the back of the room, of course.

I glare in his direction, then step off the stage before I can do something violent with my sequin heels. Cole's waiting near the steps, hands in his pockets like he didn't just publicly purchase my evening.

"You didn't have to—"

"Sure I did," he cuts in easily. "You looked like you were about to bolt."

"I was."

He smiles, that slow, steady kind that probably melts other women. "Then I saved you. Again. You're welcome."

I cross my arms. "You're ridiculous."

"Maybe. But now you owe me a date."

"I owe you nothing."

"Pretty sure that's not how auctions work."

"Pretty sure this isn't a charity fundraiser for your ego."

Someone brushes past us carrying champagne, and Cole reaches out automatically, his hand on my elbow to steady me. It's casual—gentle even—but it sparks something inconveniently warm.

He lowers his voice. "Relax, Callahan. It's just dinner. You pick the place. I'll even let you bring a chaperone. Beef, maybe."

That gets me. My mouth twitches before I can stop it. "He'd eat your face off."

"Nah, Beef loves me."

I hate that I laugh. Just once. Quick and quiet.

Cole catches it like it's gold. His grin softens. "See? Not that hard."

I shake my head, brushing past him toward the bar. "You are exhausting."

He calls after me, low enough for only me to hear. "Worth it, though."

And damn him—he kind of is.

# 18

## NO GOING BACK

*Cole*

I was planning to bid on her the second they announced her name.

Didn't care how high it went—I'd already decided she was mine for the night.

But I didn't expect it to feel like this.

Now she's standing next to me, radiating fury in sequins. My pulse is still kicking from the adrenaline of it all—half pride, half disbelief. I expected I'd have to go higher—way higher.

She keeps her arms crossed, trying to look unmoved, but the color in her cheeks gives her away. She's flustered. Beautifully so.

The emcee's voice fades into background noise. People clap me on the shoulder, laugh, tell me I'm a brave man. Maybe I am. Or maybe I just like doing stupid things that feel good.

Because right now? Winning her feels *so damn good.*

She says something under her breath—probably an insult—but I'm too busy watching the way the light catches in her lavender hair, how her pulse jumps at her throat. The part of me that runs into burning buildings thinks this is the same kind of rush. Only more intense. Because it's personal.

Andi Callahan. The woman who never flinches, even at death, now glaring at me like she's rattled and doesn't know what to do about it.

If this is what losing control feels like, I'll take it.

"You okay?" I ask.

She narrows her eyes. "Are you insane?"

I grin. "Debatable."

She huffs, crossing her arms. "You didn't have to do that."

"I think the words you're looking for are—*thank you, Cole.*"

Her mouth opens, then shuts again. She's still flushed, her eyes wide, and honestly? I can't stop staring. The sequins on her dress catch the light just right, and her hair's slipped a little from whatever fancy twist she tried for—but it just makes her look more like her. Gorgeous. Real.

"Come on," I say, nodding toward the side door. "Let's get out of here for a bit."

She hesitates, but curiosity wins.

"Where are we going?"

"Somewhere better."

I guide her through the hotel, past the catering staff and guests still buzzing from the auction, until we reach the back hallway. She shoots me a look.

"This better not be a broom closet."

"Trust me."

I head toward the old lounge—the one that's been waiting almost a decade for a remodel. It's half-hidden behind the main ballroom. But before we can enter, one of the waiters spots me and grins. "Cole? That you?"

"Hey, Mark." I clap him on the shoulder. "Think you can hook us up? We need to hide out for a bit."

He winks. "For you? Always."

Then I push open the door and usher Andi in. It's just like I remember it. Cozy, dimly lit, and partially used for storage—with scattered tables on one side and big mismatched armchairs on the other. A fireplace that's just for show, but it's quiet.

"How'd you find this?" she asks, looking around.

I shrug. "Used to valet here in high school. Spent a lot of time figuring out where to hide during breaks."

She chuckles, shaking her head. "Of course you did."

Five minutes later, we're sunk into armchairs, a bottle of champagne in an ice bucket and two glasses in front of us. Mark even brought us a slice of tiramisu—the fancy kind.

She eyes me over the rim of her glass. "You really do know everyone."

"Perks of small-town life."

The banter is easy and light, but there's something heavier underneath. Her shoulders are still tense, like she's waiting for the other shoe to drop.

Speaking of shoes—she's kicked off her high heels, and damn—even her feet are cute, delicate and perfect, as if the rest of her isn't already driving me crazy.

"So," she says, setting her glass down, "what's your deal?"

"My deal?"

"Yeah. You. This. Why are you still here? Why not chase after one of those nurses who bid on you? You could probably get lucky tonight if you played your cards right."

"Yeah?" I lean in slightly, elbows on my knees. "I don't gamble when I already know what I want."

That gets her. Her breath catches, just enough for me to notice.

"Besides, I don't want any of them."

She swallows hard but doesn't look away.

"I want to know *you*, Andi."

"You don't know what you're asking." Her voice is low.

"Maybe. But I'm not scared of whatever it is

you're hiding."

She goes quiet, tracing the edge of her glass with her finger.

"You should be," she says softly. Her eyes lift to mine, searching.

The room feels smaller now. Warmer.

She's driving me insane.

Her long legs are tucked beside her, bare feet curled under the hem of that glittering dress—and for some reason, all I can think about is how goddamn cute her feet are. Delicate, with toes painted some dark color I can't quite see in the low light. I'm not a foot guy, but for her? I might reconsider.

And her mouth.

Don't even get me started on her mouth.

Full and soft, it tugs into a smirk every time she throws something sharp my way. I want to feel it. Taste it. I'm losing my grip, fast.

"Alright." I grin, trying to lighten the mood before I spontaneously combust. "What was your first impression of me?"

She snorts, turning toward me. "You really want to know?"

"Absolutely. Hit me."

She takes a sip of wine. "Big. Dumb. In the way."

I clutch my chest, mock-wounded. "Ouch."

She laughs, the sound soft and genuine. "Also the most tolerable of all the EMTs. And…" she hesitates, glancing at me. "Kind of cute. Or whatever."

My smile grows, but I keep it cool. "Or whatever. I'll take it."

"What about me?" she challenges. "First impression?"

I don't even have to think. "Sharp as hell. Brilliant. Didn't want anyone to know how soft you really are."

Her eyes narrow. "Excuse me?"

I lean in closer. "You act like you don't give a shit, but you do. You care more than most people. You just don't want anyone to find out."

Her breath catches, and her eyes flick away, then back to mine.

I keep going, my voice low. "But you still show up. Still take care of people in your own way. You're tough, Andi. But you're also good."

Silence stretches, thick with tension. Her gaze drops to my mouth for just a second, and that's all I need.

I move in slowly, giving her every chance to stop me.

She doesn't. Until we're both leaning close—inches apart.

Our mouths meet, and it's downright electric. The kind of kiss that rewrites every kiss that came before it. Her hand curls into the front of my shirt, pulling me closer, and my pulse jumps.

Her lips are soft, but there's nothing gentle about the way we devour each other. It's raw, hungry, like we've been waiting for this since the first second we met.

And maybe we have.

I break away just enough to catch my breath, resting my forehead against hers.

"Told you," I whisper. "You're not scary."

She smiles, eyes still closed.

"Shut up, Cole."

Then she pulls me right back in.

I kiss her like I've been starving for it.

But then—she pulls back. Barely.

Her lips brush mine, breath shaky. "You're still wrong, you know."

I blink, dazed. "About what?"

"Every time—" she kisses me again, quick, yet soft "—you brought me dessert, it made it harder to ignore you."

My heart stutters. She leans in again.

"And every time you—" another kiss "—smiled at me like that, it pissed me off."

I'm grinning now, can't help it, because she's melting and I'm gone. I kiss her again—a slow press of my mouth to hers.

She pulls back. "And every time," she whispers, "you looked at me like I was someone worth the trouble—"

I kiss her before she can finish.

"And I should have been mad—" she kisses me again—"that you got my number from Shay—" another quick kiss—"but I would have given it to you anyway."

I grin and press my mouth to hers.

But then—

"Hey! I thought these doors were locked."

We break apart like guilty teenagers. A hotel worker in his mid-fifties stands frozen, holding a clipboard, his eyebrow raised.

"Shit," Andi mutters.

I don't think, just grab her hand. "Run."

We're laughing as we bolt past him, her heels dangling from her fingers, the two of us darting down a side hall as if we're escaping from more than just a fancy gala.

We don't stop until we hit a quiet back hallway, breathless and hearts pounding.

"Damn," she gasps. "That's the most fun I've had in a long time."

She leans against the wall to catch her breath, and I kneel down in front of her.

"What are you—?"

"Let me help." I take one of her shoes, holding it steady.

She braces a hand on my shoulder as she slips her foot in, the other heel still dangling. Her grip tightens on my shoulder.

I lift her second foot, sliding the heel on slowly,

my fingers brushing her ankle. "Perfect," I murmur, rising to my feet.

And then I'm kissing her. Hard. Deep.

Not the careful kind from before. This is something else entirely—raw, urgent, like I've been starving for this. Her back hits the wall with a soft thud, and she makes a sound, a little gasp that shoots straight through me. Her hands slip beneath my jacket, fingers digging into my shirt as if she needs something solid to hold onto.

The kiss is all heat and desperation. Her tongue against mine sends electricity down my spine, and I can't think, can't breathe, can't do anything but press closer. My body molds to hers, every inch of me aware of her, and the ache against my zipper is almost painful.

A groan escapes me—rough, needy—and my hands find her waist, gripping her tightly as if I'm afraid she'll disappear if I let go.

When we finally break apart, we're both gasping. My chest heaves against hers as I drop my forehead to rest against her temple, trying to remember how lungs work.

"Andi." Her name comes out rough, wrecked.

She blinks up at me, her eyes wide and dazed, lips swollen and parted. For once—miracle of miracles—Andi Callahan has absolutely nothing to say.

I brush my thumb along her cheekbone, feeling the heat there. "We should, uh... probably head back before someone comes looking."

She nods, still looking slightly shell-shocked. It's adorable.

A laugh rumbles in my chest as I ease back, putting some much-needed distance between us. "Gonna need a minute though."

Her gaze drops automatically, then snaps back up as understanding dawns. The pink in her cheeks deepens to crimson. "Oh. Oh! Yeah, that's—yeah."

I shift uncomfortably, adjusting myself, and mutter a curse under my breath while she presses her lips together, clearly fighting a giggle. The sound escapes anyway—bright and delighted—and she shakes her head at me.

"Stop looking so pleased with yourself," I grumble, but there's no heat in it.

"Can't help it." She smooths down her dress, still grinning. "You should see your face right now."

"My face? You're the one who—"

"Who what?" She arches an eyebrow, all sass again, and there's my girl. Back to normal. Well, our new normal anyway.

Best damn night of my life.

# 19

## DENIAL IS A FULL-TIME JOB

*Andi*

The sunlight is rude.

Like, offensively bright. Blinding. And I can't even blame a hangover, because I only had one glass of champagne last night. Maybe a sip or two of bourbon. Definitely not enough to explain why my head feels like a blender on low speed and my chest is doing that stupid tight thing where breathing feels like work.

I groan, bury my face in the pillow, and will the memories to stop bombarding me.

But they won't leave.

Cole's mouth.

Cole's hands.

The way he looked at me like I was the only person in the room, like he'd been waiting forever just to kiss me and finally got permission.

Damn him.

Beef jumps on the bed like he owns the place, flopping down with a huff and a wet nose shoved into my arm. I peek one eye open and catch him judging me.

"I know," I mutter, pushing myself up. "I'm a disaster."

He yawns in agreement.

I pad into the kitchen, barefoot, still wearing the oversized T-shirt and sweats I yanked on after stripping out of that sparkly death-trap dress. My hair's a mess, makeup half-smudged because I was too distracted to take it off last night.

I blame Cole for that too.

Coffee. I need coffee. Maybe caffeine can re-boot my brain. Make everything make sense again.

As the machine sputters to life, I grab Beef's leash and he charges for the front door.

While I wait with Beef outside, my brain re-plays every second from last night. The gala, the auction, the way Cole didn't hesitate to bid on me. Like I was a prize worth winning.

And that kiss.

God, that kiss.

My fingers twitch, like they remember exactly where they were tangled in his shirt, pulling him closer, needing more.

This is bad. Really bad.

I don't do this. I don't get wrapped up. I don't

feel... whatever this is. Especially not for guys who show up at galas in tuxedos and steal kisses in stairwells like they've been waiting for me all along. It's like a sappy rom-com.

Except this is my real life.

Beef finishes and we head back inside. I hang up the leash just in time for the coffee machine to beep. I pour myself a cup with shaky hands.

I can't. I won't.

This isn't me.

I'm halfway through my first sip when my phone buzzes.

Shay.

Shay: SOOOOOO???

I groan, thumb hovering over the keyboard.

Me: What do you want?

She responds instantly.

Shay: DETAILS. NOW.

Me: It was fine.

Shay: Girl. Try again.

I stare at the screen. How do I even begin to explain?

That I didn't just kiss Cole—I melted for him. That I wanted more. That I didn't stop thinking about him the whole damn night. That I'm still not thinking straight.

Before I can type, the phone buzzes again.

Shay: He kissed you, didn't he? 😉

I toss the phone on the couch like it's betrayed me.

Beef watches with zero sympathy.

I collapse next to him, sipping my coffee, heart racing.

I don't know what this is, but I do know I'm in trouble.

Because for the first time in a long time... I want more.

I ignore the incoming texts from Shay, sip my coffee, and try to pretend last night didn't just flip my entire universe inside out. It doesn't work.

A few minutes later, the front door bangs open.

"Rise and shine, bitch!"

Beef barks once—joyfully—and launches himself down the hallway.

I groan, dropping my head into my hands. "Shay, I swear to God—"

"I brought donuts, calm your tits," she calls, already making herself at home.

Beef's tail is thudding against the floor like a drum solo, and I hear her cooing at him. Great. Now they're both hyped.

"Get in here!" she yells. "We have things to discuss."

I shuffle toward the kitchen, coffee clutched like a lifeline. "You're not subtle."

She's already at the table, tossing a bakery bag down, grinning like a maniac. "And you're glowing."

"I am not."

"You are *absolutely* post-makeout-glowing. Spill. Everything. Now."

I plop into the chair across from her, scowling. "I don't want to talk about it."

She leans in, eyes wide. "And yet, here I am."

I rip open the donut bag just to avoid her face. "It wasn't a big deal."

"Bullshit." She grins. "I saw your face last night before you left. That wasn't 'not a big deal' energy."

I bite into a glazed donut, chewing like maybe I can escape through sugar.

She waits, patient as hell, drumming her nails on the table.

I sigh, mouth full. "Fine. We kissed. Happy?"

Her scream is violent. Beef barks again, totally jazzed by the drama. *Traitor*.

"You *kissed* him?!" She's already halfway out of her seat. "You little liar. You said you weren't into him!"

"I said I didn't know," I groan. "Now I'm more

confused."

She drops back into her chair, grinning like she just won a prize. "Tell me everything. And don't you dare leave out any details."

I give her a look. "Details?"

"When. Where. His hands, his mouth, the whole damn thing."

"You're insane."

"I'm invested." She grins. "There's a difference."

I shake my head, but the blush creeping up my neck gives me away.

Shay gasps. "Oh my word, it was *that* good."

I take another bite, refusing to confirm or deny.

She snatches my phone off the table. "Has he texted?"

"Give me that!"

"You haven't heard from him?" Her eyes go wide. "Oh, hell no."

I grab it back, glaring. But she's right. I'm more rattled by that than I should be. I swallow the donut, which takes more effort than it should. "He's probably at work."

"Or he's a dumbass. But don't worry, I'll text him *for* you."

"Shay—"

She leans back, arms crossed. "You liked it. Like him. Admit it."

I stare at my donut like it might save me. "Maybe."

"Maybe, my ass. What's the worst that could happen?"

I don't answer.

She softens. "Look, I get it. You don't let people in. But this guy? He's breaking through."

Yeah, whether I like it or not.

"I haven't let anyone in like this since..." I stop.

Shay nods. "I know."

We sit in silence for a beat.

Then my phone buzzes on the table.

I snatch it up before she can, heart in my throat.

> Cole: Morning. Hope your feet survived last night. You left your smile in the stairwell. I'll return it if you want.

Shay watches my face and groans. "That better be him."

I bite my lip, but it doesn't stop the stupid grin.

"Yeah," I say softly. "It's him."

I stuff the phone into the pocket of my sweatpants. There's no guarantee she won't wrestle me for it, but a girl's gotta try.

Shay finally gives up with a groan, tossing her hands in the air. "You're impossible."

I smile and take another sip of my coffee.

"Well, I've gotta work today," Shay says, grabbing a donut for the road. "Thanks for being a jerk."

"Love you too," I mutter, holding the door open.

"Text me if you decide to stop being emotionally constipated."

"Bye, Shay."

She leaves with a dramatic huff, and I'm left standing in the quiet.

Alone.

Good. This is better.

I grab my phone, stare at the last text from Cole—and type fast before I can stop myself.

> **Andi: Last night was a mistake. I'm not into this. Don't make it a thing.**

Send.

Done.

I toss the phone onto the couch like it's cursed and head for the bathroom.

It's over.

It's what I wanted.

Hot water scalds my skin, but it doesn't wash anything away. My head's still a mess, spinning with flashes of his mouth, his hands, the way he looked at me like I was something he'd been waiting for.

I scrub harder. Crank the water hotter.

When I'm done, I towel off, throw on some shorts, and start drying my hair—fast, like if I move quick enough, I can blow-dry the regret out of me too.

Then my phone buzzes.

I freeze.

I pick it up and stare.

**Cole: I'm coming over.**

I stare at the screen.

I reread it.

I reread it again.

*I'm coming over.*

*What the actual hell?*

I type out a reply.

Delete it.

Try again.

Backspace, curse under my breath, and finish drying my hair. I get dressed in case he was serious, pulling on leggings and a T-shirt.

And before long, there's a knock at my door.

You've got to be kidding me.

Beef barks from the other room, already pacing like he's been waiting for this moment. Great. Now I've got a lousy guard dog and a boy problem.

I fling open the door, mouth dry, brain scrambled, and Cole's standing there.

Hands in his pockets.

Looking way too calm.

Way too sure of himself.

"This is not happening," I say, leaning on the

doorframe.

"It is," he says. "Move."

"Excuse me?"

"I'm not going away, Andi. So unless you plan on calling the cops—who I work with, by the way—you're letting me in."

He's serious.

And I'm... jeez, I'm a mess.

I cross my arms, glare, but I step back.

Beef trots over, tail wagging, because of course he loves this idiot.

Cole closes the door behind him, eyes locked on mine.

"You don't get to kiss me like that," he says, voice low, "and then send some bullshit text telling me you're not into this."

"It's not bullshit," I snap. "It's me telling you to leave me alone."

"Liar."

I blink.

"What?"

"You want me here. You just don't know how to deal with it."

*And just like that, I'm on fire again.* Why is him calling me on my shit hot?

I clear my throat, stepping back. "Do you need a water? I need a water."

I don't wait for him to answer. I just turn and head for the kitchen, needing space, air—something.

The cold tile under my feet grounds me as I grab a glass from the cabinet. My hands shake a little as I fill it, the sound of the faucet loud in the silence behind me.

I take a sip. Then another.

Breathe, Andi.

I can feel him in the other room, still standing there, watching me. Waiting. Not pushing.

My therapist's voice comes back, uninvited. Something about how I run when things feel good because I'm convinced I don't deserve them. That if I expect disappointment, it won't hurt as much when it comes. That trust isn't about knowing someone won't hurt you—it's about being okay not knowing.

I hate all of it.

Absolutely hate it.

I grip the counter tighter.

I can't do this.

You can, a voice that sounds a lot like Shay's says somewhere inside me.

I release a slow breath and set down my water glass. When I return to the living room, Cole's on one knee, scratching Beef's exposed belly.

When he spots me, he stands.

"You always do that?" His voice is low, but steady. "Push people away the second they get close?"

I stiffen, gaze roaming his. "Excuse me?"

"You heard me," he says, eyes locked on mine, hands in his pockets like he's holding back. "You're scared, I get it. But you don't get to tell me how I feel."

"You don't know how I feel," I shoot back, heat rising.

"Then tell me." He steps closer, not crowding me, just there. Solid. Unshakeable. "Or at least stop pretending last night didn't mean something."

I look away. My heart's pounding so loud I'm sure he can hear it.

"It's easier if I don't," I whisper.

He nods slowly, his jaw working. "For you, maybe. Not for me."

I swallow hard, and before I can think, I'm moving. My hands reach for him, pulling him in. His mouth crashes to mine, and suddenly we're tangled again—heat, hands, hearts racing.

His lips are perfect—insistent and sure, but not taking more than I can give.

But he pulls back first, breathless. His forehead rests against mine.

"I have to get to work," he murmurs, voice rough.

"Okay," I breathe, not letting go.

"We'll talk later, alright? I'm not going anywhere."

My throat tightens. "Okay."

He kisses me once more, softer this time, and then steps away, like it's the hardest thing he's ever done.

The door clicks shut behind him, and I'm left clutching the counter again, shaking.

Needing someone terrifies me.

But the idea of that someone being Cole?

It kills me.

Because it might be worth it.

# 20

## SOFT SPOTS & SHARP EDGES

*Cole*

**T**he marker squeaks as I drag it across the board.

COMPLETE. COMPLETE.

Then again—bolder, harder—as I skip ahead. *First kiss. COMPLETE.*

"Jeez, man, leave some ink for the rest of us." Trey laughs, watching me like I'm the headliner in a comedy show.

Brennan whistles low, grinning like he just won a bet. "That's what—three levels in a week?"

"Four," I mutter.

The room erupts.

Trey jumps up, fake clapping like we're at the Oscars. "Four levels! Four levels! Someone get this guy a medal!"

"Or a cold shower," Brennan adds, tossing a towel at me.

I drop the marker on the desk and step back, but I'm not smiling. Not even close.

Because all I can think about is her face this morning. That stiff smile. That "I'm fine" lie she keeps trying to sell me.

And it pisses me off.

Not at her. Never at her.

But at everything—and everyone—that made her believe she has to carry shit alone. That made her think love is a trap, not a safe place. That got her so used to holding people at arm's length she doesn't even realize she's bleeding out inside.

I want to fix it, make it all better, but I know sometimes life doesn't work that way. Sometimes there are no easy fixes.

Trey's still laughing, but it fades when he sees my face. "Uh... Cole? You good?"

Brennan eyes me too. "Yeah, why aren't you celebrating? You're the MVP of this bracket, man."

I shrug, grabbing a bottle of water from the fridge and twisting the cap off like it's done something wrong.

"This isn't a game for me. You know that, right?"

Silence.

Trey frowns. "I mean, it started as one."

"Not for me," I say again, sharper now. "Not when it's her."

Brennan exchanges a glance with Trey, then steps closer, lowering his voice. "Alright, look. Maybe slow down, yeah? She's cool, but... she's got walls, man. Thick ones."

"I know that," I snap.

"Do you?" he presses. "I'm just saying—you don't have to get dragged into it if it's too messy."

I look at him, dead in the eye. "She's not messy."

"Fine," Brennan backs off, holding his hands up. "But don't say we didn't warn you."

Trey tries to lighten it, tossing me a grin. "Or you could just win level five and retire a legend."

But I'm not listening.

Because yeah, I could walk away. I could chalk it up to bad timing, a girl who's not ready, whatever.

But the idea of leaving her behind?

It guts me.

I don't want easy.

I want *her*.

And just as I'm about to open my mouth—say something, anything—the station alarm blares to life.

"Any available units, report to Camp Brown trailhead—missing hiker located, severe lower leg injury with extraction required."

Adrenaline kicks in.

"Let's go," I bark, already moving.

Trey and Brennan are right behind me, the weight of our conversation shoved aside for now.

Because someone out there needs saving.

And right now, that's all I can think about.

The drive to the trailhead is quick, but my head's still back at the station—replaying everything.

Andi. Her walls. Her stupid "I'm fine" when she's clearly anything but.

By the time we pull in, I'm coiled tight, ready for action—or a fight.

"Looks like Search and Rescue's already here," Brennan says, nodding toward the group of people gathered near the trail entrance.

Great.

We jump out, grab the stretcher and medical gear. One of the rangers waves us over.

"About a mile in," he says. "Big guy. Slipped, landed hard, looks like a broken tibia. We need help carrying him out."

"No problem," I mutter, adjusting the straps on my gear.

Then I see him.

Jack.

*Great.* The guy was an asshole last time we worked a job together. And I'm not in the mood.

He's standing at the edge of the clearing, talking to another rescue worker like he owns the place.

He turns when he hears us coming, eyes locking on mine.

"Cole." He nods.

"Jack," I say, tight.

Trey and Brennan exchange a look, already bracing.

We follow the group into the woods, and every step feels heavier than it should.

When we reach the hiker, it's as bad as they said. The guy's huge, wincing in pain, leg at an angle it shouldn't be. We get to work fast—splinting, stabilizing, prepping for the carry-out.

But Jack? He's too close. Too in my way.

And I'm in no mood for his bullshit.

"You good there?" he asks, like he doesn't already know I'm one spark away from lighting up.

"Fine," I snap.

Trey's eyes flick up. "Cole."

I ignore him.

Jack moves to help lift, and I shift just enough to block him. "I got it."

He sighs. "This isn't about you, man. We're here for him."

"No shit," I bite back. "But maybe don't act like you're everyone's savior."

Jack straightens, eyes hard. "You got a problem, say it."

"Maybe I do."

"Cole," Brennan warns.

But I'm not done.

"You wanna check in on people, fine. You wanna play hero, go ahead. But don't think I don't see through it."

Jack steps closer. "You don't know shit about me."

"I know enough."

The hiker groans, shifting, and the ranger snaps, "Hey! Focus. We've got a carry-out to finish."

Trey cuts between us, pushing me back. "Not the time, not the place."

Brennan grabs Jack's arm. "You two settle your beef later. Right now, we've got work to do."

Silence.

Heavy.

I exhale hard, backing off. "Let's move."

We lift, together, because we have to.

But every muscle in my body's still tight.

And as we haul the guy down the trail, I can feel Jack's stare on me.

Whatever. Despite what Andi might think of me, it's not like I have to be friends with everyone.

# 21
## READING THE SIGNS

*Andi*

The grass is damp beneath my sneakers as I walk between the headstones, hands stuffed in the pockets of my hoodie. I come here when I need to breathe. When I need to remember that I'm not as alone as I sometimes feel.

Their names are etched into the granite, familiar and foreign all at once.

James and Clara Callahan.

I sink to a crouch, brushing away a few stray leaves, my throat tight. "Hey," I murmur. "It's been a while."

I brush my fingers over the smooth stone, tracing the dates I know by heart. "I don't even know what you'd say if you were here," I whisper. "Would you be proud of me? Or tell me to stop being such a pain in the ass?"

I try to laugh, but it comes out weak. "It's been a tough year. I keep thinking it'll get easier, but it's like… the more time passes, the harder it is…"

I pick at the hem of my sleeve. "Anyways, things are changing. I'm not sure I'm ready, but they are. I met someone. Well, not met. He's been around. And he's... not what I expected."

I shake my head, a tiny smile tugging at my lips. "You'd like him. He's stubborn as hell, but he makes me laugh. And he doesn't scare easy."

The smile fades, replaced by that familiar tightness in my chest. "I don't know if I can do this. Let someone in. I've spent so long just... surviving. Being fine."

The tears come, quiet but steady. "I wish you were here. I wish I didn't have to figure this out without you."

I sit there for a minute longer, letting the wind whip at my hair, the silence settle around me.

But then I hear footsteps behind me, and everything shifts.

I turn, and it's Jack.

He's standing a few feet away, hat in hand, expression surprised—and then soft.

"Hey, Andi."

I stand slowly. "What are you doing here?"

"Visiting," he says simply, nodding toward a different section of the cemetery. "Old friends of mine."

I nod, not sure what else to say.

"You come here often?" he asks.

I shrug. "Sometimes. When things get… heavy."

He walks closer, not crowding me, just there. Present.

I look down at the headstone again, eyes tracing the curves of their names. "I don't usually see anyone else out here."

"Guess we both needed something today," he says.

Silence stretches between us, but it's not uncomfortable. Just weighty.

After a minute, Jack clears his throat. "How've you been, kid?"

"Okay," I say. "Busy with work. The usual."

He nods. "Can I give you some advice?"

I glance at him, wary. "That depends."

He gives me a half-smile, but his eyes are serious. "Don't do what I did. Don't spend your whole life thinking you don't need anyone."

I freeze.

This is so out of the ordinary that I'm not sure what to say. Jack has never once given me a touching speech like this. Made sure I've eaten? Sure. Helped me change a flat tire? Yeah. But not…this.

He looks out over the cemetery, voice low. "It's easy, right? Telling yourself you're fine. That you've got it handled. But one day, you look up, and it's just… quiet. Too quiet."

My chest tightens. "I'm not—"

"I know," he cuts in gently. "But don't end up like me, Andi. Your parents wouldn't want that for you."

It hits like a punch.

I swallow hard, blinking fast. "Jack, don't—"

"But it's true."

A tear slips down my cheek before I can stop it. I swipe at it angrily, but he doesn't comment. Just lets me have the space.

After a minute, I draw a shaky breath. "You're not eighty, you know. You could still meet someone."

He huffs a laugh, the tension breaking just a little. "Yeah?"

I nod. "I mean, I wouldn't date you, but someone might."

He chuckles, the lines around his eyes softening. "Thanks for that."

I nudge him lightly. "I'm serious. You've got time."

Something shifts in his expression, something lighter. "I might've… met someone."

I blink. That's unexpected. "Wait, really? Who?"

Jack rubs the back of his neck, suddenly shy. "Her name's Kate."

I raise my eyebrows. "Kate?"

He nods, looking like he's trying not to smile too hard. "Yeah. She's smart. Funny. Doesn't put up with my crap."

I stare at him, stunned. "I've never seen you like this."

"Like what?"

"Like... this." I gesture vaguely. "Soft."

He shrugs, but there's color in his cheeks. "She's worth it."

I let out a breath, surprised at the warmth blooming in my chest. "Good. I'm glad."

Jack gives me a long look. "Me too. And I want the same for you, kid."

I nod, still processing, still hurting—but I'm listening—for once.

# 22

## WARNING: FEELINGS AHEAD

*Kate*

I'm stirring the sauce for the third time in five minutes, not because it needs it—but because I do. The kitchen smells like garlic and fresh herbs, the table's set, the wine is breathing, and my heart is on the verge of jumping out of my chest.

"This is stupid, right?" I turn to Margot and Helen, who are already halfway through the first bottle of Pinot like this is just any other Thursday.

Margot leans against the kitchen counter, swirling the wine in her glass. "What's stupid?"

"This." I wave the wooden spoon in the air. "Me. Cooking for a man. Giddy like some teenager. I mean, look at me."

Helen raises a brow. "You look great."

"Great and desperate."

Margot laughs. "Sweetheart, you're not desperate, you're glowing. Which, frankly, is kind of annoying."

I groan and wipe my hands on a towel. "It's just been so long. I don't even remember how to be with a man. What if I've forgotten how to—"

"Please don't finish that sentence," Helen cuts in, smirking.

Margot doesn't miss a beat. "Honey, it's like riding a bike."

I gape at her. "Margot!"

She shrugs. "Am I wrong?"

"You're incorrigible."

Helen grins into her wine. "You love her for it."

"I'm serious!" I lean against the counter, my nerves crawling under my skin. "Things are moving fast. We've been out a few times, and I feel like I barely know him, but also—like I've known him forever? Does that make any sense?"

"Actually, yeah," Helen says quietly.

Margot nods. "When you're older, you don't waste time. You know what you want."

"Do I?"

They both just look at me.

I sigh, heart thumping. "I really like him."

Margot's eyes gleam. "He should be here any minute."

"Not helping."

She grins, wicked. "We just need to meet him first. Make sure he's worthy."

"I'm still miffed I didn't get a say in that."

Helen clinks her glass with Margot's. "Obviously."

Before I can protest, there's a knock at the door.

My heart stops.

Margot's already up. "I'll get it."

"No—wait—" I rush to the door, smoothing my hair. "Behave."

Margot winks. "Define behave."

I shoot her a glare and open the door.

And there he is.

Jack.

Tall, calm, wearing a soft gray sweater and dark jeans, holding a bottle of wine like he doesn't have any idea he's just made my knees go weak.

"Hey," he says, smiling.

"Hi."

Margot's already behind me. "Well, well, well. Look at you."

Jack raises a brow, amused. "And you must be Margot."

Helen appears at my side. "And I'm Helen. We've heard things."

I groan. "Come in before they interrogate you in the doorway."

Jack steps in, and suddenly the house feels smaller, warmer, and I'm not sure if it's from the stove or the way he looks at me like I'm the only one here.

"Dinner smells amazing," he says.

"Thanks. I was aiming for edible."

He chuckles, eyes on mine.

*Dear God, he's cute.*

Margot's grinning like it's Christmas. "So, Jack, what are your intentions with our girl here?"

Jack glances at me, then at them, totally unbothered. "Treat her well. Keep her laughing. Try not to screw it up."

Helen whistles. "Smooth."

Margot raises her glass. "Alright, you pass. For now."

Jack laughs, handing me the wine. "This okay?"

"Perfect," I breathe, realizing I'm still holding a dishtowel.

And for the first time tonight, the nerves start to fade.

Maybe this is what it's supposed to feel like.

Margot drains the last sip from her glass and claps her hands together. "Well, we'll leave you lovebirds to it."

Helen rises, stretching with a little groan. "Remember, if he gets too handsy, just yell 'pineapple.'"

Margot winks. "Or don't. No judgment."

I roll my eyes, laughing. "Out. Both of you."

Jack chuckles as he opens the door for them. "It was nice meeting you."

Margot winks again. "Nice meeting you too,

Jack. Don't screw it up."

He smiles, easy. "I'll try not to."

Once the door shuts behind them, the house goes quiet, but not in a bad way. Just... us.

I turn, suddenly hyper-aware of everything— the way he's watching me, the hum in the air, the wine still on the counter.

"Sorry about them," I say, brushing my hands down my sides.

Jack steps closer, hands in his pockets, that calm energy wrapping around me. "Don't be. They're great."

He stops in front of me, close enough that I can feel the heat radiating off him.

"I've been wanting to do this since I got here," he murmurs.

Before I can ask what, his hand slides around my waist, pulling me in, and his lips are on mine— soft but certain, like he's been waiting for this just as long as I have.

I melt completely, my hands finding his chest, his heartbeat steady beneath my fingertips.

When he pulls back, I'm breathless.

"Sorry," he says, smiling. "I couldn't wait."

I shake my head, dizzy. "Don't apologize."

We stand there for a moment, just grinning like fools, before I manage to find my voice again. "Wine?"

He nods, stepping back just enough. "Please."

I pour two glasses, handing him one, trying not to spill it with how my hands are still shaking a little. "Want the tour?"

"Sure. Lead the way."

We wander through the house, stopping here and there—my favorite chair, the old bookcase I refuse to get rid of, the picture wall in the hallway. He listens, really listens, asking about little things most people wouldn't notice.

Then we reach the living room.

I point to a framed photo on the mantel—me and Cole on a fishing trip two years ago.

Jack's gaze lingers on Cole, something in his jaw tightening just for a second before he smooths it out.

"You okay?" I ask, frowning slightly.

He nods. "Yeah. Everything's great."

I smile softly.

Jack hums, setting his wine down. "Shall we eat?"

"Sure."

We head to the kitchen and fix our plates—pasta, garlic bread, a simple salad—and carry them out to the back patio. The sun's dipping low, casting everything in soft gold, and as we settle into the chairs, I realize I'm smiling again.

# 23

## WHEN IT CLICKS

*Cole*

She hates fancy. She hates pressure.

So, no candles. No reservations at some pretentious restaurant where the plates are the size of coasters and they charge extra for bread. She deserves something better. Something real. Something that feels like us. Most importantly, something that won't make her run for the hills.

That's why I'm here, blanket slung over one shoulder, pizza box in hand, waiting at the trailhead for her car to pull up.

As soon as I see those headlights, my chest tightens—nervous, like an idiot, but I can't help it.

The car door opens, and Andi steps out, wearing jeans, a sweatshirt that hangs off one shoulder, and her hair pulled back, like she didn't overthink it either. She's beautiful. Always.

"This better not involve bugs," she warns, eyeing me suspiciously.

I grin. "Promise—nothing that bites. Unless you count me."

She groans, but there's a hint of a smile. "Alright, what's the plan?"

"You'll see."

I lead her down the path, the woods quiet except for the hum of summer air, crickets, and the occasional rustle of leaves. It's not a long walk, just enough to clear our heads from the world behind us. Soon, we arrive at a small clearing, moonlight spilling through the trees, the sound of water trickling from the nearby creek.

I spread the blanket out and set the pizza down, pulling out two cold sodas from the cooler I'd stashed earlier.

"No candles?" she teases, sitting cross-legged.

"No candles."

She looks around, eyebrows raised. "This is… not terrible."

I laugh, settling beside her. "High praise."

She takes a bite of pizza, chewing thoughtfully. "Why this?"

I shrug. "Because I wanted something quiet. Just us."

She nods slowly, picking at the crust. "I don't do this."

"Picnics?"

She gives me a look. "Dating."

"I've noticed."

There's a beat of silence. Not uncomfortable, but heavy.

"I've never been good at it," she says, her voice lower now. "Letting people in. Every time I have, it's just—ended badly."

I reach over, brushing my thumb over her hand. "I'm not them."

She looks at me, really looks, and something softens.

"Oh," I say, suddenly remembering. "I threw away the bracket."

She props up on one elbow, surprised. "You did?"

"Yup."

"Did the guys kill you?"

I grin. "Almost. But I don't care."

She's quiet, processing that, and then she moves closer. "Good," she says.

We lounge there for a minute, the quiet stretching between us. A good quiet. One that feels like something is finally starting to click into place.

I glance over, watching as she chews and sets her slice down on a napkin. "What'd you do yesterday?"

She hesitates, then shrugs. "Went to visit my parents."

I turn toward her, propping myself up on an elbow. "Their grave?"

She nods, eyes fixed on the stars. "Yeah."

A pause.

"Tell me about them?" I ask.

She glances at me, surprised, like she didn't expect me to care. But I do. I really do.

She takes a breath. "My mom was loud. The good kind of loud—laughed too hard, sang off-key in the car, was always the first to make a joke. She never met a stranger. She could walk into a room and own it without even trying."

I smile, imagining it. "You get your fire from her."

"Maybe." She smiles too, but it's softer. "My dad was the quiet one. Solid. The guy you called when your tire blew or your dishwasher exploded. He always knew how to fix things. He hated attention, but he loved watching people he cared about shine."

"And you got your loyalty from him."

She looks at me again, eyes shining a little now. "Probably."

I reach for her hand, threading my fingers through hers.

"What else?"

She thinks for a second. "They were good together. Balanced. Like she made him come alive, and he grounded her when she needed it. They didn't make sense to anyone else, but they did to me."

I squeeze her hand. "Sounds like they were lucky."

"They were everything," she says quietly. "And losing them? That... wrecked me."

Her words hang there, heavier than silence. I can feel her retreating—just a little—like she's afraid she said too much.

I shift closer, brushing her hair back gently. "I wish I could've met them."

She swallows hard, but there's a small smile on her lips. "They would've liked you."

"Yeah?"

She nods. "My mom would've loved that you don't shut up. And my dad would've respected that you care enough to ask."

That hits me right in the chest.

"I'm glad you told me," I say. "Really."

She squeezes my hand back, eyes dropping to our fingers intertwined.

"Thanks for listening."

"Anytime."

And I mean it. Even if it's hard. Even if it hurts.

We stay like that, side by side, hands tangled together, watching the stars appear in the sky. I've gotta say—it's pretty damn perfect.

The following day, Mom's already got a booth when I walk into the diner. Same one she always picks, by the window, with a view of nothing but the parking lot and some half-dead bushes.

She's sipping iced tea, flipping through the menu when I slide into the seat across from her.

"Hey, sweetheart." She smiles.

"Hey, Ma." I grin, grabbing a menu even though I don't need it. "You getting the usual?"

"Thinking about it." She gives me a look, one of those loaded ones. "Thanks for coming."

"Of course," I say, raising an eyebrow. "What's up?"

She waves me off. "Let's order first."

Alright then.

The waitress—Betty, who's worked here since I was a kid—comes over, and I rattle off my usual. Mom gets her turkey club, extra pickles, and then we're alone again.

"So," I say, leaning back. "What's really going on?"

She fiddles with her straw. Classic stalling move.

"There's someone I've been seeing," she says, like she's ripping off a Band-Aid.

I blink. "Yeah, I figured."

She tilts her head. "And?"

"And what?" I shrug. "If you're happy, I'm happy."

"You're not weirded out?" she asks, genuinely surprised.

I laugh. "A little bit. But come on, Ma. I'm not twelve. You deserve to have a life."

She smiles, soft and touched, but I can see she's still bracing for something.

"What's he like?" I ask.

"His name's Jack. He's kind, smart, patient." She hesitates. "I wasn't sure I was ready for this, but... he's been easy to talk to."

"That's good." I nod, meaning it. "You feel safe with him?"

She nods. "I do."

I take a sip of water, thinking. Then I smirk. "Alright, ground rules."

She groans. "Cole—"

"Public places, at least for a bit longer," I say, counting off on my fingers. "No letting him in the house unless you're sure. Keep your phone on you."

"I'm not a teenager. And he's already been to the house."

"Well then that leads me to—" I point at her, grinning. "Safe sex, Mom. Don't make me have to explain condoms to you."

She nearly chokes on her tea, eyes wide. "Oh my God, Cole."

"What?" I laugh. "You think I don't know how this goes?"

She's bright red now, fanning herself with a napkin. "That's not something I need your advice on."

"Just looking out for you." I wink. "It's what you'd do."

She glares, but she's smiling too. "You're impossible."

"I'm the best son you've got."

"The *only* son I've got," she shoots back.

Betty drops off our food, and we dig in, the tension easing.

After a while, Mom sets her sandwich down, eyes soft. "You really mean it? You're okay with this?"

I nod. "I want you to be happy, Ma. And if he makes you smile like this? I'm good."

She reaches across the table, squeezing my hand. "Thank you."

"Just... don't tell me details, alright?"

She laughs. "Deal."

# 24

## LIGHTS OUT, WALLS DOWN

*Cole*

The sun is already beating down by the time I pull into the station's parking lot. Lawn chairs and pop-up tents dot the grassy field behind the building. Smoke curls from the grill, where Trey is manning it like his life depends on it, and the sounds of country music and laughter spill into the warm air.

It's the annual summer cookout—a tradition as old as the station itself. Usually, I'm all in. But today?

Today, I'm distracted.

Because today, I invited Andi.

And I don't know if she's going to show.

I climb out of my truck, grabbing the six-pack I promised to bring, and nod at a few of the guys setting up the cornhole boards. There are storms in the forecast, but so far, the weather has held.

"Look who finally showed up," Brennan calls, tossing me a beer from his cooler.

"Had to make an entrance." I grin, catching it one-handed. Even as I joke, my eyes scan the lot, hoping and waiting—

A familiar beat-up sedan pulls in, and my heart kicks up.

She came.

Andi steps out, sunglasses on, a tank top hugging her frame, jeans cuffed at the ankles, and a pair of sneakers that have definitely seen better days. Her hair is pulled up, loose strands catching the breeze, and she clutches a store-bought container of brownies like it's a shield.

I meet her halfway, trying to keep my grin under control.

"You came," I say, stopping just short of her.

"Don't act so surprised." She shifts, glancing around. "I almost turned around twice."

I reach for the brownies. "These for me?"

"Only if you earn them."

I laugh, stepping closer. "I like a challenge."

She rolls her eyes, but her mouth twitches like she's trying not to smile.

"Come on." I nod toward the back. "You hungry?"

"Starving."

I lead her through the yard, introducing her to

the guys as we go. Trey waves from the grill, apron on and tongs in hand.

"This her?" he calls.

"This is her," I confirm, nudging Andi gently. "Andi, meet Trey. Grill master and occasional idiot."

"Nice to meet you," she says, holding out a hand.

"Likewise." Trey grins, shaking it. "Hope you like burgers."

We grab plates, pile them with food, and find a spot under one of the tents. Brennan slides over to make room, and Andi sits stiffly at first, as if she's waiting for the other shoe to drop.

But it doesn't.

Instead, Trey cracks a joke about the last cookout and someone's disastrous attempt at karaoke. Brennan chimes in with a story about a rookie call gone wrong, and before long, Andi is relaxed, laughing, actually enjoying herself.

And damn, it's a sight.

She leans back in her chair, legs stretched out, beer in hand, and I can't stop watching her. The way the sun catches the strands of her hair, the curve of her smile, the way she snorts when Brennan makes a dumb pun about hot dogs.

"You're staring," she says without looking at me.

"Can't help it."

She flicks a piece of lettuce at me, but there's no heat in it.

After a while, someone suggests cornhole, and Andi perks up.

"I'm in."

"You sure?" I ask, standing with her.

She arches a brow. "What, you think I can't throw a beanbag?"

"Didn't say that."

"Good. Because I'm about to kick your ass."

Game on.

We team up—her against me—and the trash talk starts immediately.

"You know, it's cute that you think you have a chance," I say, lining up my shot.

"Just throw, pretty boy."

The beanbag hits the board and slides off the side.

She grins. "Lame."

Her turn. She steps up, focused, and nails it—right in the hole.

The guys cheer, and I groan. "Beginner's luck."

"Please." She smirks. "I've been hustling you since we got here."

We play a few rounds, and by the end, she's laughing, flushed, high-fiving Trey like they've known each other for years.

I'm watching her, heart full, when it happens.

A paramedic from another station—Jake, I

think—walks over, beer in hand.

"Hey, I haven't seen you around before," he says, all charm and easy confidence. "You one of Cole's sisters?"

Andi blinks. "Do I look like his sister?"

Jake laughs. "Guess not."

I stand, stepping closer, but I don't say anything yet.

"You work here?" she asks, cocking her head.

"Station 19." He nods. "I'd remember seeing you, though."

She gives him a tight smile, polite but cool. "I'm just here for the food."

"You should come by sometime," he offers. "We've got better beer."

"I'm good," she says, but her eyes flick to me, sharp.

Jake follows her gaze, finally noticing me.

"Oh. You two are—"

"Yup," I say, stepping beside her. "We're good here, man."

He raises his hands, chuckling. "Alright, alright. No harm done."

He walks off, and I exhale, forcing my fists to unclench.

Andi looks up at me, amused. "Cute."

"What?"

She shrugs. "You're cute when you're territorial."

"I wasn't—" I start, but she's already laughing.

"You were totally jealous."

"Maybe a little."

She grins, bumping her shoulder into mine. "Don't worry. I'm not into pretty boys with no game."

I wrap an arm around her waist, pulling her close. "Good. Because I've got enough game for both of us."

"Debatable," she teases.

But she stays there, leaning into me, and for the first time all day, I feel like I've won—even though I got my ass handed to me at cornhole.

The storm that was in the forecast today finally hits after sundown.

I'm halfway through folding laundry when the sky cracks open, thunder rolling so loud it shakes the damn windows. Rain slams against the roof, fast and relentless, and I glance at the clock—9:03 PM.

I drop the shirt I'm folding when I hear my phone.

**Andi: Power's out. Fantastic.**

I grin.

**Me: Come here. Mine's still on.**

No reply.

Another rumble of thunder.

I call her.

"Cole," she answers, her voice low and annoyed.

I laugh, grabbing my keys. "Come on, you can't sit in the dark all night."

"I'm fine."

"You hate storms."

"I don't hate them."

"Get your stuff; I'm five minutes away."

She huffs into the phone. "I don't need—"

"Not asking," I cut in, already heading for the door.

By the time I pull up to her place, the street's pitch black. I spot her in the doorway, phone flashlight on, a hoodie thrown over her tank top and leggings, and a duffel slung over her shoulder. Beef is on a leash beside her, looking timid—like he doesn't like the storm any more than she does.

I hop out, jog through the downpour, and grab her duffle.

She ushers Beef out into the pouring rain, and he hops up into the truck.

Inside my place, Beef charges in, and Andi steps tentatively inside, looking around. The storm still rages outside, causing a ruckus, with the low hum of the generator in the background.

"Welcome to civilization," I say, locking the door behind us.

She peels off her soaked hoodie, leaving her in just the tank, rain-speckled and irritated. "You live like this?"

"Prepared? Yeah."

She shakes her head, brushing wet strands from her face. "Show off."

I installed the generator a couple of years ago after a particularly brutal storm—the remnants of a hurricane left my mom and me without power for days.

I toss her bag onto the couch. "Hungry?"

She eyes the kitchen. It's small but clean. "No, I'm good."

We settle onto the couch, with Beef at our feet, while the storm continues outside. I've got candles on the coffee table and a couple more by the TV, casting everything in a soft, golden glow.

"Should we watch a movie?" I suggest.

"That depends. If you pick something stupid, I'm leaving."

"What kind of movies do you like? I don't take you for a rom-com kind of girl."

She laughs. "Not into rom-coms. And nothing with animals either. That sob-fest with the dog last year wrecked me."

"I gotchu." I scroll through the options until I

find something.

*"The Conjuring?"*

Her head snaps toward me. "No."

"Yes."

She glares, but her voice wavers. "Fine. But if I die, I'm haunting you."

"Noted."

Half an hour in, she's tucked under the blanket we're sharing, clutching a pillow like her life depends on it.

"Seriously?" she hisses as the music swells.

I chuckle, sliding a hand over the back of the couch, close—but not touching.

"You okay?"

"Shut up."

Thunder rattles the windows, and she jumps.

I raise an eyebrow. "You sure?"

She punches my arm, but her knuckles are white against the pillow.

I give it ten more minutes before she's practically in my lap.

"Alright," I murmur, pulling her closer. "Come here."

She hesitates, but then she exhales, sagging into me. Her head rests against my chest, and I wrap the blanket tighter around us, both of us breathing just a little easier.

The movie plays on, but I'm not watching it anymore.

I'm too busy memorizing this—her warmth, the way her fingers toy with the hem of my T-shirt. It's distracting as hell.

"You okay?" I ask again, softer.

She looks up at me, eyes wide in the candle-light. "Yeah."

"You sure?"

She nods, barely.

"I've got you," I whisper.

And she stays right there. Even when the credits end and the screen fades to black.

"You survived," I say.

"Barely," she breathes.

The storm fades, but we don't move.

We talk. Quiet and easy.

First about nothing—worst dates, our favorite pizza toppings, weird childhood fears.

But then it shifts.

She tells me about her dad teaching her how to ride a bike, how he used to call her "Bug" when she was little. About her mom's peach pie—how no matter how many times she's tried, it never came out right.

And I just listen. Soaking up every word.

"You don't talk about them much," I say after a while.

Her head is on my chest.

I'm playing with her hair.

"Hurts less when I don't," she murmurs.

I nod. "Still. I like hearing about them."

She turns to look up at me, something unmistakably soft in her gaze. "Why are you like this?"

"Like what?"

"Good."

I snort. "You don't know me that well."

"I know enough."

She shifts, facing me more, one leg bent under her.

"This scares me," she says, voice barely above a whisper.

"What does?"

"You. This. Needing someone."

My throat tightens. "I'm not going anywhere."

She leans in, mouth brushing mine. "Don't make promises."

"I'm not."

Her hand finds mine under the blanket, and she laces our fingers together.

"Okay," she says, so quiet I almost miss it.

And right there, in the soft light and fading storm, I know.

I'm in deep.

And I don't want out.

# 25
## THE SITUATION

*Andi*

The movie has ended, and the storm has died down, but we're still cuddled together on the couch.

I'm curled against him, one leg draped lazily over his, my head resting on his chest.

His heartbeat is steady under my ear, his warmth seeping into my skin, and everything feels... safe. Too safe. Safe enough that my mind wanders, my body restless, making it really, really hard to pretend I'm not thinking about how good he smells, how close his mouth is, or how badly I want to taste it.

His fingers play with my hair—slow, absently, like he doesn't even realize he's doing it. He twirls a strand of lavender between his fingers, as if touching me is second nature.

"Hey," he murmurs, his voice low and lazy. "What's your real hair color?"

I blink, pulling back just enough to glance up at him. "What?"

He grins, still playing with my hair. "Your real color. Before the purple."

I roll my eyes, but my lips twitch. "Dark blonde. Boring."

"I like it like this," he says, without hesitation. "It suits you."

"Messy?"

"Wild." His smile softens, his thumb brushing lightly against my temple. "Different."

I don't know what makes me do it.

Maybe it's the storm, the darkness, or the flickering candlelight.

Maybe it's the way he looks at me like I'm not something to be fixed or figured out.

I tilt my chin up and kiss him.

No warning, no hesitation. I just lift my face and press my mouth to his like it's the most obvious next step.

And he doesn't even flinch. Doesn't miss a beat. Our lips meet, slow and tentative. Warmth and pleasure zing through me.

His hand slides to the back of my head, pulling me closer, deeper, and suddenly I'm not just halfway in his lap—I'm fully there, straddling him, his hands on my waist, my knees bracketing his hips.

The kiss turns hot, fast, like we've been waiting for this all night.

He groans, low in his throat, and it vibrates through me. I fist my hands in his shirt, needing more, needing him.

Then he moves.

In one fluid motion, he stands, lifting me like I weigh nothing, and I gasp, my arms wrapping around his shoulders.

"Cole—"

But he's already walking, carrying me through the dim hallway, straight into his bedroom.

And whatever I was about to say?

Gone.

Just like me.

Once we reach his room, he lowers me to my feet.

His mouth is on mine, and I don't know how we got here—but I don't care.

I can't think. Can't breathe. All that exists is the way his hands grip me, the way his mouth moves over mine, the way every nerve ending screams for more.

But he slows. Pulls back, just enough to rest his forehead against mine.

"You good?" His voice is low, rough, steady, and calming.

I nod, fighting to catch my breath. "Yeah."

His thumb brushes my cheek, tracing a slow

line to my jaw. Something shifts in his eyes.

"Okay," he murmurs, kissing me again—deeper now, but still controlled. Measured. Like he's savoring every second.

I kind of love it.

I slide my hands under his shirt, feel the heat of his skin, the tension in his muscles. Need coils tight inside me.

"You're wearing too many clothes," I murmur against his lips.

He grins and peels his shirt off over his head. I stare, shameless. His chest is solid, defined, and unfairly hot. My hands roam, greedy, hungry.

Then it's a blur—my sweatshirt on the floor, his jeans halfway undone—until—

"Beef!" I yelp as one hundred and forty pounds of fluff cannonballs onto the bed, tail wagging like we're all just here for a group hangout.

Cole's laughing, shoulders shaking as he tries to regain control of the situation. "Guess he's not a fan of foreplay."

"I swear to—" I start, but I'm laughing too, burying my face in my hands as Beef noses his way between us, clueless and delighted.

Cole, slightly breathless and still grinning, gently pushes Beef off the bed. "Sorry, bud. Not tonight."

Beef huffs dramatically but trots out, and Cole closes the door behind him.

When he turns back, his eyes are darker, his grin softer. "Still good?"

I nod.

Then he's lifting my chin, his lips finding mine like he never left. His hands trace over my skin, slow, reverent, like he's memorizing me. He pushes my leggings down over my hips, and I shimmy out of them.

His jeans and boxers are next. My gaze lowers.

"Andi?" he sounds breathless, but I can't focus. Not at all.

Seeing him naked for the first time? Overwhelming. They should've issued a warning. Or a helmet. Or both.

So, fun fact—he's gargantuan. I've seen skyscrapers smaller than this man.

He guides us to the bed, and I follow, my brain still buffering—because naked Cole is... *a lot*. In the best, most holy-shit kind of way possible.

"Talk to me. You okay?"

I manage a shaky laugh, my eyes still locked on the situation.

That's what I'm calling it now. The Situation. Capital T. Capital S.

"I'm fine. Just... recalibrating."

His mouth curves into a lazy grin, but he waits. His thumb brushes my cheek, gentle and patient, like he has all the time in the world for me to catch up. "Recalibrating?"

"Yeah, I just need a second to adjust to... all of that." I wave my hand in its general vicinity.

He chuckles, moving us closer on the bed.

"Does it come with a manual, or what are we talking here?"

His mouth lowers, and he kisses me around a smile. Then I feel his hand take mine, placing it around The Situation.

Oh.

*Ohh.*

Okay.

Warm. Smooth. Hard enough to make my thighs clench.

I can work with this.

A rough breath punches out of him when my hand moves.

We kiss for a long time—hot and unhurried—until I'm aching. Restless. His tongue slides against mine, and I swear I forget my own name.

Then he fumbles briefly in the drawer, comes back with protection, and I feel my pulse race.

He doesn't rush.

Doesn't push.

He just... waits.

I reach for him, pulling him back onto me. "Put that on," I murmur between kisses.

"Yes ma'am," he groans. Once he's suited up, he shifts, sitting back and pulling me with him.

"Here," he says, his voice low, hands steady on

my hips. "I want to see you. Want to watch you take me."

My breath catches as I straddle him, his hands running up my sides, his mouth brushing over my collarbone.

"You're beautiful, Andi."

I can't respond—not with words.

So I move.

And he follows.

The first inch steals the air from my lungs. His hands grip my hips, holding me steady as I sink down.

"That's it," he breathes, eyes locked on mine. "Take your time. I've got you."

It's slow at first. Careful. Like he's stitching pieces of me back together. Like this moment means something to him.

His hands on my back, his lips at my neck, the way he looks at me—like I'm everything—it's too much.

And not enough.

I move faster, deeper, chasing that edge. The pressure builds, coiling tight in my core.

"Not gonna last if you keep moving like that," he groans, gripping me tighter, meeting me every time.

It's perfect.

His thumb finds where we're joined, circling. "You feel—*damn*, Andi. You feel perfect." His breath hitches, and I feel him pulse inside me.

Soon I'm right on the edge.

My name falls from his lips like a prayer, and I'm lost.

Gone.

Shattered into a thousand pieces that only he can put back together.

But not alone.

Because he's right there, holding me through it.

Steady. Sure. Never letting me go.

And when we collapse together, tangled and breathless, he kisses my temple. "Damn, Andi."

My mouth lifts in a smile, and something in my chest grows tight.

I lie draped across his chest, breath still uneven, his heartbeat steady beneath my ear—a quiet rhythm that grounds me as he traces lazy circles on my skin. He feels unshakable, like if the world fell apart, I could still hold on here.

Like a rock to cling to in a storm.

I'm so used to fighting to stay afloat, I almost forgot what it felt like to be held steady.

# 26

## ENEMIES TO LOVERS

*Andi*

**W**ork sucks today.

And not because it's unusually chaotic or gross—although, let's be honest, it always kind of is. It sucks because I'm distracted.

Hopelessly and ridiculously distracted.

I can't stop thinking about last night. About Cole. About his hands, his mouth, the way he looked at me like I was something he wanted to keep. Something worth holding onto.

I haven't stopped thinking about it since I left his place this morning, hair still a mess and my body sore in the best way, I've been trying to focus on paperwork and patient charts, but all I can think about is how he made me feel.

Warm. Safe. Wanted.

I swallow.

My mind betrays me, flashing back to all the hot things he whispered last night.

"Tell me what you want, Andi." Not a demand, but an invitation—to tell him what I liked, what I needed. Like he needed it too. Needed to know how to make me feel good.

Later, as his breath caught and his hands gripped my hips, he'd whispered, "I'm not gonna last if you keep moving like that." He sounded playful yet wrecked, as if I was the one undoing him instead of the other way around.

"Hey, Callahan."

I blink, looking up from my screen to find Mikey leaning against the doorway, arms crossed, that smug little grin of his front and center.

"What?"

He shrugs. "Heard you slayed at the bachelorette auction."

I huff. "I survived."

I try to focus but fail miserably.

"You okay?"

"Yeah," I lie. "Why?"

"You've read the same line in that chart three times."

"So?"

"So... you're distracted. And not in a 'my dog's sick' kind of way. More like an 'I've been thoroughly ruined by a man' kind of way."

My face heats instantly. "Shut up."

"Ah-ha!" He points, grinning wider. "It's true."

"It's not."

"It is." He walks in and sits on the edge of the desk. "You're practically glowing. Don't think I didn't notice you floating in here this morning."

"Are you done?"

He gives me a look. "You're terrible at this."

I groan, leaning back in my chair. "Don't you have something to do?"

"I'm making sure my friend's okay. And clearly, you're more than okay. So I'll leave you to... whatever's going on in that head of yours." He stands, still smirking. "Tell lover boy I said hi."

I flip him off as he walks out, but I'm smiling.

"Ow!"

Shay side-eyes me. "What now?"

"The tech just tried to take my whole toe off."

"You're such a baby."

I glare at her, but it's half-hearted. She's grinning like she knows exactly why I'm jumpy—and yeah, she probably does.

The little nail salon is quiet tonight—just us, a bored technician scrolling her phone at the front desk, and some muted reality show playing in the background. Shay's reclined in one of those ridiculous massage chairs, her toes freshly painted in a dangerously red shade that only she could pull off.

Me? I'm trying not to kick the poor girl filing my nails like she has a personal vendetta.

"So..." Shay says, dragging it out like she's been waiting all day to pounce. "You gonna tell me why you're glowing, or do I have to guess?"

I roll my eyes, but it's no use.

"I'm not glowing."

"You are."

"It's the bad lighting."

"It's Cole."

I freeze for just a second, but she catches it.

"Ha! I knew it." She leans over, smacking my arm. "You slept with him, didn't you? Oh my gosh, you totally did."

I groan, covering my face. "Shay, please."

"Don't you dare pull that shy act with me now. Spill. Was it good? No—was it life-changing?"

I peek at her through my fingers. "Shay."

"Don't 'Shay' me. This is what friends are for."

There's no way I can tell her about The Situation.

I drop my hands, sighing. "It was... yeah. It was good."

She gasps. "Good? That's all I get?"

I bite my lip, a smile tugging at the corners. "It was really good. Like... I didn't know it could be like that."

Her eyes go wide. "Holy shit."

"I know."

She grabs my hand, practically bouncing. "Okay, but wait. Details. How did it happen? When? Where? Did he undress you slow? Fast? Tell me everything."

I look down at the nail technician, who I'm pretty sure is now fully invested in this conversation. "You're relentless."

"And you love it. Now talk."

I cave because, honestly? I need to talk about it. About him. About how I can't stop replaying every single second in my head.

So I do.

I tell her about the storm, the candles, the way he looked at me. How gentle he was, how he checked in, how he carried me to his bed like I weighed nothing, and then worshipped every inch of me like he couldn't believe I was real.

Shay is silent, which is rare, but her face says it all.

"Damn," she finally breathes. "You're gone."

"I am not."

"You are so gone. Done for. Obliterated."

I laugh, but it's half-hearted. Because maybe I am. Maybe I'm in deeper than I meant to be.

And Shay sees it.

"So what now?" she asks, quieter now. "Is this... are you guys a thing?"

I draw a slow breath and shrug. "I don't know.

We didn't really talk about it. He said he wasn't going anywhere, but I just... I'm scared."

"Scared of what?"

I pause, looking down at my hands.

"Of needing him."

Shay softens, reaching over to squeeze my knee.

"You've been through hell, Andi. But not every guy's gonna leave you there. Maybe it's okay to let someone help you out."

I nod, swallowing hard. She sounds like my therapist. "I'm trying."

She grins, leaning back. "Good. And if you need me to vet him again, just say the word."

I laugh, grateful and more than a little terrified.

But also... maybe ready.

# 27

## CAN'T SAVE EVERYONE

*Andi*

**I**'m curled up on the couch, half-watching some reality show that's rotting my brain, half-staring at my phone.

Cole usually checks in by now. Sometimes it's something dumb like "Tell Beef I said hi" or "How's the world's bossiest person today?" Sometimes it's just a photo—like the one he sent yesterday, him in his turnout gear, face smudged, grinning like an idiot with some little kid wearing a plastic fireman's hat. He's not subtle, but I like it.

I like *him*.

Which is probably why this weird silence feels like a missing limb.

I glance at the time—almost eight. He said he was working today, but still. He usually texts me something by now. I type out a text and erase it three times before settling on:

*You alive?*

Simple. Non-needy. Fine.

I toss the phone on the coffee table and go back to pretending to care about which rich housewife is fighting now. A minute passes. Then two. The phone buzzes.

**Cole: Yeah. Just got home.**

That's it? My eyebrows scrunch. No dumb joke. No asking what I'm up to.

**Me: Everything okay?**

Three dots appear. Then vanish.
Then, finally, a reply.

**Cole: Bad day at work. Not
really in the mood to talk
right now. Raincheck on
hanging out?**

I sit up straighter. Raincheck?

My stomach twists. He's never... distant. Not with me. Not like this. I stare at the screen for a second, trying to decide if I'm being dramatic or if I should push.

I push.

**Me: Did something happen?**

It takes longer this time.

Crap. That's brutal.

I deal with the aftermath—cold, clinical, and already over. But Cole? His job is personal. He's the one kicking down doors, running into bedrooms, looking people in the eye while they beg him to save someone they love. He's the one trying to bring them back. And when he can't… he's the one left carrying it.

Something inside me twists.

And I grab my car keys.

Fifteen minutes later, I'm standing outside his house with a pint of cookie dough ice cream and no real plan. Beef's leash is in my other hand because I figured if I showed up with emotional support and ice cream, it might be just the right combo.

I knock twice and wait.

Nothing.

I knock again, louder this time.

When he opens the door, his face is a mess. Not physically—he still looks like him. But his eyes are dark, hollowed out in a way that makes me want to cry and shake him at the same time.

"You didn't have to come," he says, voice low.

"I know."

I hold up the ice cream. "But I brought this. So."

He steps aside. "You're ridiculous."

"You love it."

Beef trots in like he owns the place, flopping down in Cole's living room like this is just any other night.

But it's not.

Cole drops onto the couch, elbows on his knees, head hanging. I shut the door and walk over slowly, like if I move too fast, he'll bolt. Even Beef seems to sense something's wrong. He lays practically on top of Cole's foot—right up against his leg.

"You don't have to talk," I say, sitting beside him. "I'm just here."

He doesn't answer, just leans back, running both hands over his face. I can see it now—the weight he's carrying, the way it's digging into his shoulders. I shift closer, gently reaching up to rub them. He tenses at first, then lets out a breath that sounds like it's been trapped inside him all day.

"He was sixteen," Cole says, voice rough. "We got there too late."

I keep my hands moving, slow circles. "I'm so sorry."

"I keep thinking... what if we'd gotten the call sooner? What if—"

"Cole." I slide in front of him now, kneeling between his legs, forcing him to look at me. "You did everything you could."

His jaw clenches, but he doesn't argue. He just

drops his forehead to mine, like he's barely holding on.

"I hate this part," he whispers.

"I know."

I pull him into a hug, wrapping my arms around his waist, holding tight. He holds me back like he's afraid I'll disappear.

"You can't save everyone," I murmur.

"I wanted to save him."

I press my cheek to his chest, feeling his heart beat like a drum. "It wasn't your fault."

For a long time, we just sit like that. No words. No noise except Beef snoring nearby and the sound of Cole's steady heartbeat.

Eventually, he pulls back just enough to look at me. "Thanks for coming."

I smile, even though it's sad. "Always."

I press a soft kiss to his lips, and he lets me.

"Want some ice cream?" I ask.

"Sure." He gives me a small, sad smile.

I rise to my feet and head to his kitchen. It takes me a few minutes, but I locate bowls and spoons by pulling open a bunch of cabinets and drawers. Eventually, I get it all sorted out.

I return with two bowls of ice cream, but his eyes are closed. His head is resting on the back of the couch, and I don't want to wake him. I go back to the kitchen and place his bowl of ice cream in the freezer and take mine to the other end of the couch. I eat it quietly while I watch him.

He never acted like his job took much of a toll on him—he's always all smiles and easygoing charm, so it's strange seeing him like this.

He looks like he's carrying the weight of it, and it's strange—unsettling—to see him this way.

Something inside my chest pinches. Beef looks up at me with sad eyes. I don't understand how dogs are so perceptive, they just are.

"I know," I say, patting his head.

After a moment, I get up and make a mug of tea. Not because he asked, but because it feels like something a person does. I bring it over, nudging his arm gently.

He stirs, groggy, and gives me a tired smile. "Thanks."

"Drink it, then get in the shower," I tell him. "Hot water helps."

I'm kind of making this up as I go along. Truthfully, I'm out of my element. I'm not used to having people who rely on me. Not to mention this is Cole, who's basically a real-life superhero. It's tough seeing him shaken, and I want to do anything I can to help. Hot showers usually calm me, so that's what I try to push on him.

He doesn't argue, just rises slowly and disappears into the bathroom.

I clean up what little there is to do, tidy the kitchen, and try to pretend like this is normal. Like people do this kind of thing for each other all the time. It's weird, being needed. I'm used to being the one people avoid until they need something clinical and sterile. That's where I'm in my element.

But this? This is something else.

He emerges a little while later, hair damp, face flushed from the heat of the water, wearing a T-shirt and sweatpants.

I'm sitting on the edge of his bed when he walks in, and he doesn't say anything—just crawls in beside me, pulling the blankets up and tugging me close like he needs me here.

He wraps one big arm around me, and my head finds his chest.

"Stay," he murmurs.

My throat tightens. I nod. "Okay."

And I do.

# 28

## QUARANTINE AND CHILL

*Cole*

**I** rack the barbell, chest heaving, arms burning in the best way. Brennan's already circling behind me like a vulture, towel around his neck, water bottle in hand.

"That's six sets," I pant. "You trying to kill me?"

"You're the one who said 'one more.' Like, four more ago." He grins, clearly not suffering nearly as much as I am.

I flop back onto the bench and reach for my phone, mostly to stall. Two new texts blink at me—one from the department group chat, the other from Andi.

My thumb skips straight to hers. She finally replied to me from hours ago when I asked what she was doing on her day off.

Andi: On my death bed. Nice knowing you.

I sit up straighter, wiping my face with my shirt. She never texts dramatically unless she's being funny—or actually dying.

Me: Are you sick? Want me to come over and make you feel better?

I add the little smirking emoji because I'm being slightly inappropriate. But also because I'd drop everything in a second if she said yes.

Brennan sees the look on my face and groans. "Good grief. Are you flirting again?"

"Not flirting," I say, smirking at my phone. "Checking on a friend."

"She's not your 'friend.'" He does air quotes. "You've been soft for this girl for a month but won't admit it out loud. It's getting annoying."

I toss my towel at him.

Andi: No. Save yourself. I'm quarantining. You don't want this plague.

Too bad. Like hell I'm letting her suffer alone.

Me: Too late. Be there soon. I'll bring soup and a hazmat suit.

She doesn't reply right away, which I'm choosing to interpret as silent approval. She took care of me after my crappy day at work. There's no way I'm letting her suffer alone.

Brennan isn't too happy, but I call it good and hit the showers.

Twenty minutes later, I'm knocking on her front door with a bag of groceries in one hand and a bottle of cold medicine in the other. Beef barks on the other side, and I hear a groan that might be human.

"Andi?" I call out.

"Go away," comes the pitiful response.

I open the door anyway.

She's under a pile of blankets on the couch, face barely visible beneath a nest of tissues and a hoodie that's swallowing her whole. Her hair's a mess. Her nose is red. She glares at me like I just showed up with a camera crew.

"You're not supposed to be here," she croaks.

"Too bad. You used the words 'death bed.' That overrides all protocols."

She tries to sit up and fails. I cross the room in three strides and help her shift upright, fluffing a pillow behind her back while she fights me the whole time.

"You're ridiculous," she mutters.

"And you look like you fought a raccoon and lost."

She tries to swat me but misses a little.

I unload the bag—canned soup, ginger ale, cough drops, those neon green sports drinks she likes, and a box of saltines. She watches me like I'm a hallucination.

"Why are you like this?" she mumbles.

"Charming? Generous? Unreasonably good-looking?"

Her eyes narrow.

"You were there for me," I say, quieter now. "Last week. After that call. You just... showed up. No questions. So yeah, I'm gonna take care of you now. No use fighting it. It's happening, Callahan."

She snorts and immediately regrets it, clutching her head. "Ow."

"See? Should've just said thank you."

I get her settled with a bowl of soup and some meds, then plop down on the opposite end of the couch. Beef immediately claims the spot between us, his giant head flopping down on my thigh like I'm an acceptable substitute for his actual human.

We flip through bad movie options until she grunts something vaguely approving at one of the '90s rom-coms I suggested.

"You sure this isn't too stimulating?" I tease.

"Shut up and pass the tissues."

"Yes, ma'am."

I hand her the box, then glance over. She looks miserable. And tiny. And unfairly cute for someone who sounds like she gargled gravel.

"You doing okay?" I ask after a while.

She shrugs. "It's just a cold. Or the flu. Or a slow-moving plague. Hard to say."

"Well, you're stuck with me until you're back to full strength."

"God help me."

I grin and drape a second blanket over her just to be annoying. "You're welcome."

By the second movie, she's curled against my side, legs tucked under the blanket, head on my shoulder. I don't move. Even when my arm goes numb.

She's breathing evenly now, finally asleep, and I just sit there listening to it. The steady rhythm of someone letting themselves rest, letting themselves be taken care of.

She was the only one who didn't flinch last week when I came apart a little. She didn't try to fix me. Didn't rush me. Just stayed.

And now, it's my turn.

Brennan's voice echoes in my head from earlier—something about how I was screwed, how I was already gone for her. And yeah, he's not wrong. I'm falling for her. *Hard.*

I watch the slow rise and fall of her chest, the way her face softens in sleep. She's all edges when she's awake, but like this? Peaceful. Vulnerable. It undoes something in me.

And it scares the hell out of me.

Because I know what I want—I want her. All in. No games. But she's built walls around herself so high I don't know if she'll ever let me in. What if I'm already too far gone and she never meets me there? What if I love her, and she can't let herself love me back?

I shift just enough to press a kiss to the top of her head. "Sleep tight, Andi."

# 29

## FORE-PLAY AND FEELINGS

*Cole*

The moment she slides into the passenger seat of my truck, I know I'm in trouble.

Andi's wearing jeans and a red tank top that dips just enough to make it hard to think. Her hair's twisted up in some messy thing that still somehow looks perfect, and her lips are glossy in a way that makes me want to forget our plans entirely.

She eyes me like she knows it.

"So," she says, buckling up, "where are you taking me, firefighter? And if it involves anything with the word 'artisanal' in the name, I'm out."

I laugh, pulling out of her driveway. "No artisanal anything. I promise. But you might still judge me."

She raises an eyebrow. "Now I'm intrigued."

"Mini golf."

She snorts. "What are we, twelve?"

"No," I say, shooting her a grin. "We're two very competitive adults with questionable hand-eye coordination and a tendency to talk trash."

She leans back in her seat, lips twitching. "Okay. I'm listening."

The course is just outside of town, all glowing neon dinosaurs and bad '80s music piping through the speakers. A complete tourist trap. It's ridiculous. It's perfect.

Andi looks around like she's trying not to smile. "This place is aggressively ridiculous."

"So, you love it."

She shrugs. "We'll see. If there's a windmill hole, I might take that as a personal attack."

I eye her.

"A personal attack against my coordination," she continues.

"Got it. Windmills scare you."

We pay, grab our clubs, and head to the first hole. She insists on going second so she can "observe my technique and mock it appropriately." I tease her that she just wants a look at my butt. Andi pokes me with her club.

I sink my first putt in two strokes. Not bad.

She eyes me. "Beginner's luck."

She takes her shot. Misses entirely. Stands there, blinking. "Okay. The ball is obviously defective.”

I laugh and help her line up her next shot.

Halfway through the game, she’s winning, and I’m not even mad about it. Every time she sinks a shot, she does this little victory wiggle that makes her earrings swing and her top ride up just a little, and I have to look away before I combust.

She catches me looking. Of course she does.

“Eyes on your own putter, Hartley.”

I hold up my hands. “Just admiring the form.”

Her eyes narrow, but she’s smiling now. Full on, no hiding it. It hits me like a punch to the chest.

After the last hole, we grab ice cream from the shack by the parking lot. She gets chocolate with sprinkles. I get vanilla because I’m a simple man with simple needs. She steals a bite anyway.

“You’re not gonna make a move, are you?” she asks casually, licking her spoon.

I nearly drop mine. “What?”

“You heard me. You’ve been mooning over me for nine holes and half a cone. Are we gonna kiss or what?”

I blink. She’s serious. Teasing, but serious.

“You want me to kiss you in the mini golf parking lot?”

She shrugs. “Romance is where you find it.”

So I lean in. One hand on her jaw, one still holding my melting ice cream. She tastes like chocolate and summer and every dream I never let myself have.

When we pull back, she looks stunned. And just a little breathless.

"Okay," she says softly. "That... might have been worth the windmill hole."

We walk back to the truck slowly, our fingers brushing, then intertwining.

And somewhere deep in my chest, something settles.

She's letting me in.

God help me, I think I'm already in love with her.

"Come back to my place?" I ask, feeling hopeful.

Her lips lift in a secret smile. "Sounds good."

# 30

## WORLDS COLLIDE

*Andi*

One minute we were arguing over who had the better mini golf score and trying to keep our ice cream from melting down our wrists.

The next thing I know, he's unlocking the passenger side door of his truck and asking if I want to come back to his place.

My brain short-circuits, flashes to The Situation—not the guy from Jersey Shore, the one in his pants—and yeah, I blurted out *yes* so fast it probably counted as foreplay.

I know. I'm not proud. But I'm also not sorry.

And now we're driving through his neighborhood, the late summer sun just beginning to dip below the trees, casting everything in that golden, dangerous kind of light that makes everything seem okay. Like I'm not going to wind up falling for the wrong person only to have my shell of a heart shattered again.

Not that Cole is the wrong person. Probably. Maybe. God, I don't know.

He glances at me as he turns into his driveway. "You're quiet."

"I'm processing," I say.

He lifts an eyebrow. "That sounds serious."

"Don't flatter yourself." I smirk, even though my heart's hammering like I just ran a mile. "I just realized I forgot to feed my sourdough starter. Again."

He grins. "Wait, you bake bread?"

"I've made bread," I clarify. "Once. It went… okay."

"Was it edible?"

"That's a strong word."

He laughs as he shifts the truck into park. "Well, good news is I've got actual food inside. I'll keep you alive."

We step out and I follow Cole toward the staircase to his garage apartment when I hear footsteps.

I glance to my left and stop suddenly.

"Jack?"

He's holding a bottle of wine in one hand and a bouquet of flowers in the other. He stops dead when he sees us. His eyes narrow. "Andi?"

Cole stiffens beside me. "What the hell are you

doing here?"

Jack's mouth flattens. "I could ask you the same thing."

My eyebrows fly up. "Wait. You two know each other?"

"Unfortunately," Jack says flatly, still glaring at Cole like he personally insulted his entire bloodline.

Cole turns to me in disbelief. "How do *you two* know each other?"

And that's when the door opens and a woman steps out. Blonde hair, kind eyes, completely unaware she just walked into a minefield. "Jack, what's taking so—" Her eyes land on me. Then on Cole. "Oh."

I blink. This must be Cole's mom.

Wait. She's the one Jack's been seeing? I glance between them, stunned. "You're dating Cole's mom?"

Cole turns to me, confusion all over his features. He's clearly trying to work out how it is that I know Jack.

She hesitates. Shifts her weight. "Cole?"

"Hey, Mom," he says, still frowning. "Andi… this is my mom, Kate."

Kate stares at me. "How do you—"

Jack clears his throat. "Andi's a family friend. She's... close with me."

Cole scrubs a hand over his face.

There's a beat of stunned silence.

Kate blinks. "And you and Jack know each other?" she asks Cole.

"From work," Cole says.

I sense that there's history there, but no one's jumping in to offer it.

Jack exhales like he needs a drink, fast. "Well. This is a hell of a reveal."

Cole throws up his hands. "Awesome. Love this for us."

"No one warned me I was walking into a rom-com plot twist," I mutter.

Kate lets out a startled laugh. "Okay, I feel like I need flashcards."

Jack looks between me and Cole. "So… want to come in for a glass of wine?"

I glance at Cole. "Should we?"

He gives me a look like he's weighing his options. Kate takes my elbow, guiding me toward the main house. "Yes, please come in. I've made dinner too. It's nice to meet you."

I glance back, a little stunned. Cole gives Jack a long look before following.

He's watching me like I'm the only thing grounding him in the middle of this weird tornado.

So yeah. I guess we're doing this.

The inside of the house is warm and low-lit, scented faintly with vanilla candles. Whatever Kate had planned for their evening probably didn't entail our walking soap opera entrance.

"Wine?" Jack asks, already heading to the kitchen.

"Please," I say before anyone else can answer. Alcohol might be the only thing that gets me through this night without stress hives.

Kate gestures toward the couch. "Make yourselves comfortable." She sounds pleasant—sweet even—but there's a slight wobble in her voice like she's still buffering all the revelations.

I sit, perching on the edge like a guest at a funeral. Cole drops down beside me, noticeably closer than necessary, like he wants to make a point. His arm brushes mine, and the tension that's been humming in the air spikes again when Jack returns with four glasses of red wine.

He hands one to Kate, one to me, and gives Cole's a second of extra eye contact before passing it over.

Cole raises an eyebrow. "You poison this?"

Jack smiles without humor. "Thought about it."

Kate claps her hands once, too brightly. "Okay! So." She turns to me. "Andi, is it? What do you do?"

I nod, clutching my wine glass. "I'm a morgue tech at the hospital."

"Oh, wow. That sounds… intense."

I shrug. "You get used to the dead bodies. It's the living coworkers that are the problem."

Kate laughs, delighted. "Well, I suppose that means you're not squeamish."

"Not about blood," I say, then glance toward Cole. "Feelings, on the other hand…"

He smirks. "Working on that."

Kate looks between us, visibly trying to decide if this is cute or mildly alarming.

"What about your family?" she asks gently. "Are you from around here?"

My grip on the wine glass tightens, and Cole shifts beside me like he feels it.

"I grew up nearby," I say. "My parents passed away a few years back. It's just me and Beef now."

Kate's eyes soften. "I'm so sorry. That must've been hard."

I nod. "It was. But I'm okay."

Kate tilts her head, a curious smile playing on her lips. "Did you say Beef?" she asks, eyes widening slightly.

I chuckle. "Yes, Beef. He's my dog."

Kate's eyebrows arch in amusement. "That's quite a name. Any particular reason?"

I grin. "Well, he's a rescue—a big, goofy mutt with a heart of gold. When I first brought him home, he had this habit of stealing steaks off the counter. After the third time, I figured the name was fitting."

Kate laughs, the tension in the room easing a bit. "Sounds like he keeps you on your toes."

"Always. But he's also the best cuddle buddy

after a long day at the hospital."

There's a pause. Then Jack, trying and failing to sound casual, jumps in, "So how long have you two been… whatever this is?"

"Dating," Cole says flatly, before I can hedge.

My eyebrows shoot up. We haven't exactly had that conversation yet.

Jack notices. "Didn't realize it was official."

Cole leans forward. "You got a problem with it?"

Kate's head swings between them. "Boys."

I cut in quickly. "So! Dinner?"

Kate blinks. "Oh. Yes! I—I made way too much pasta. You're both welcome to stay."

Jack sets down his wine. "I'll help you plate it."

As they disappear into the kitchen, I turn to Cole. "You okay?"

He sighs through his nose. "I don't like him."

"I sensed that."

He glances at me. "You?"

"I don't know. He's basically family. He was my dad's best friend. And after they passed, he's stuck around—been there for me when I needed it."

Cole watches me, still quiet. I can't help but wonder about what kind of run-ins they've had at work. Jack does search and rescue for the county. I guess their paths have crossed. I always sensed Cole was the type to befriend anyone and everyone—but there's something he doesn't like about Jack.

Kate calls from the kitchen. "You like garlic bread, Andi?"

"Love it," I call back.

Cole leans in close and murmurs, "Let's survive this dinner. Then I get you alone."

"Deal," I whisper, my heart doing something stupid. "I guess I'll have to deal with The Situation later."

"What?" Cole asks, blinking.

I freeze. Shit. Did I say that out loud?

My whole face floods with heat. I lean in like I'm about to confess state secrets, cupping a hand over his ear. "I, um… gave your, *you know*, unmentionable a nickname."

There's a beat of silence. Then his body actually jerks a little, like I just zapped him. He pulls back to look at me, eyes wide, lips twitching.

"You named it?" he says, voice low and incredulous. "Like—what kind of nickname are we talking here?"

I straighten my spine, shameless now. "The Situation. Capital S. Deserving of its own area code."

He stares at me like he's not sure whether to laugh or throw me over his shoulder and haul me straight to bed. "You're insane."

"And yet," I say with a smirk, "you're still sitting here."

He shakes his head slowly, like he's trying to regain use of his brain cells. Then he brings one hand up to softly stroke my cheek with his thumb. "I don't think anyone's ever flirted with me like this before."

"Well," I say, rising to my feet, "you should've led with The Situation. It's a crowd-pleaser."

He groans into his hands, but when he peeks up at me again, he's grinning—cheeks pink, eyes warm, completely wrecked in the best way.

We head into the kitchen, and for a moment—just one—this almost feels like normal chaos.

Like a real family dinner.

A weird, wildly dysfunctional one.

But maybe not the worst.

The table's already set when we sit down, big bowls of pasta in the center and a salad that looks like it belongs in a cookbook. Jack passes the serving spoons with the brisk efficiency that I'd expect from him. Kate, on the other hand, has taken her seat beside me and is already folding her napkin with practiced ease.

"This looks amazing," I say, eyeing the pasta like it might solve world peace.

Kate beams. "Thanks. It's an old family recipe. Cole used to love it growing up."

Beside me, Cole gives a brief, noncommittal shrug. Jack's jaw tightens.

I glance at Kate. "So... what's it like raising a

human like this one?" I tip my head toward Cole and dig my fork into a pile of linguine.

She laughs. "Well, he didn't come with an instruction manual, but he was a pretty good kid. A little too serious sometimes. Always trying to keep the peace."

Cole makes a quiet sound like he disagrees but doesn't argue.

"Any fun stories?" I prod, twirling my pasta. "Weird memories? Embarrassing childhood obsessions? Got anything like that?"

Kate smiles like she's more than game. "There was a period when he insisted on sleeping in his snow boots. Just in case there was a blizzard and he needed to be ready to shovel."

I chuckle.

Cole's gaze snaps to his mother. "I was ten. And we'd had a storm warning."

"Better safe than sorry," I mutter, smirking behind my glass.

Cole glares at her, but there's no real heat in it.

Kate reaches for the salad bowl and passes it to me. "He used to organize all his Halloween candy by type, then trade based on a complex points system. It was very serious business."

"He's still like that," I say, grinning. "I saw his fridge. Labeled shelves."

Jack snorts. "Of course he does. God forbid anyone reach for the wrong yogurt."

The air shifts again—just a little tighter, a little tenser. Cole's smile fades.

Kate glances between them, the way moms do when they're counting how close they are to needing a fire extinguisher.

I clear my throat and gesture toward Cole. "Okay, but in fairness, he did make me soup when I was sick. And watched three whole movies with me. One of them had zombies. That deserves a medal."

Kate smiles again, this time warmer. "He's got a good heart. Even when he's being stubborn."

Cole nudges my foot under the table, subtle. I nudge back, just as soft.

The rest of the meal plays out in a strange balance—Kate and I swapping stories and easy conversation while Cole and Jack mostly circle each other in silence. Every now and then Jack chimes in with a dig, and every time, Cole swallows it down like he's trying like hell to keep the peace.

Eventually, dessert is brought up, and Kate rises to go cut something from the kitchen.

When she's out of earshot, I look between the two men and raise my eyebrows. "So. You two always this fun?"

Neither of them answers.

But Jack finally mutters, "It's been a long week."

Cole doesn't argue.

Just takes another sip of wine.

After dessert—which is a lovely lemon tart—Cole rises to his feet and reaches for my hand. "I'm sorry we can't stay longer, but we've got a situation to tend to," he says, eyes darkening on mine.

My heart rate ratchets up.

"Situation?" his mom asks.

My knees almost give out. "Yeah. It's this whole *big* thing, but I can handle it."

Kate blinks. "Is it… urgent?"

Cole bites back a grin. "Very."

Jack lets out a low snort like he's heard enough.

Kate watches us like she's doing mental calculus and almost decides to ask a follow-up question—but then just sips her wine and raises one eyebrow. "Well. Be safe, I guess."

I grab Cole's hand, cheeks blazing. He treats me to a look that says you started it.

As we head for the door, I whisper, "You're going to get us in trouble."

He leans in, voice rough near my ear. "You love it."

And we're out the door before I can say something wildly inappropriate in front of his mom.

# 31

## NAMING RIGHTS

*Cole*

We step outside into the cooling evening air, and I'm still grinning like an idiot over "The Situation" when Jack's voice cuts through the dark.

"Hey, Cole, wait up."

I stop, turning halfway. Andi's a step ahead of me on the walk, pausing when she realizes I'm not behind her.

"I'll just…" She motions toward the staircase leading up to my apartment, shooting me a look that says don't take too long.

Jack stands just outside the door, arms crossed, posture casual but eyes sharp.

"I know we got off on the wrong foot," he says, voice lower now. Not angry—just real. "But I really like your mom. So maybe we try being civil."

It's not an apology. But it's something. And I know what it costs him to even say that.

"Yeah," I say, nodding once. "Okay."

He studies me a second longer, then adds, "So you and Andi, huh?"

I nod, shoving one hand in my pocket. "It's new-ish. But yeah."

He looks me over again. "She's tough. She doesn't let people in easy."

I nod again. I know that better than anyone.

"But it's obvious she likes you," he says. "A lot. So I'll just say this once—if you hurt her, if you break her? You deal with me."

The words aren't a threat. They're a promise.

And even though my gut tightens, I respect the hell out of it. I'd say the same if the roles were reversed.

"I'm not gonna hurt her," I say quietly. "I'm not built that way."

He looks at me like he's deciding whether or not he believes it. Then he nods and steps back, still looking at me like we're two men who don't quite like each other but might be learning to tolerate our new proximity.

I head toward the staircase and take them two at a time. I find Andi waiting for me in the living room, standing by the sofa. From her vantage point, I can tell she'd been watching out the window.

She looks me over as I approach. "Is everything okay?"

I don't answer. Just close the distance between us and kiss her—soft at first, then firmer when she makes that little sound in the back of her throat that wrecks me every time.

She pulls back just enough to ask, "Do you think your mom likes me?"

I kiss the corner of her mouth. "She adores you."

Another kiss. "Are you and Jack okay now?"

I kiss her again, slower this time. "Working on it."

"Did he threaten you?"

I pause, considering it. "...Mildly."

She laughs and tugs me closer by placing her arms around my waist. "You gonna tell me what he said?"

"Nope."

She kisses me again, warm and wicked. "You're being cagey."

I kiss her back. "You're being distracting."

And honestly? I don't even care what we're talking about anymore.

Because all I can think about—and I truly mean *all* I can think about—is the fact that she gave my manhood a nickname.

She named it.

Game over.

I'm gone for this girl.

Hopeless.

Utterly, irreversibly gone.

Done for.

I should've stayed to help my mom clean up. She cooked for me—for us—and I always stay to help when she cooks for me. Always load the dishwasher, scrub the pots, ask where she keeps the weird Tupperware lids. That's our thing.

But tonight threw me off my game.

Introducing Andi? Not what I'd planned.

Meeting Jack wasn't in the script either.

And then finding out they know each other—well?

Yeah, that was the part that really knocked the wind out of me. Seeing that they have a relationship—a warm, joking, comfortable one made me see Jack in a new light. I still don't know if he's good enough for my mom, but if Andi can vouch for him, I guess I'll give him a chance.

I move closer and bring my hands around Andi's waist as I drop a kiss to her bare shoulder.

"Can you stay?"

She turns her head slightly, lips brushing my cheek. "I can't. I've gotta go home tonight. Let Beef out before he eats the drywall."

I groan into her skin. "I'll buy you new drywall."

She laughs, soft and breathless. "Tempting."

I run my hands along the straps of her tank top,

fingers grazing the warm skin of her shoulders. "How long do I have you?"

She pretends to think, like she's comparing options or waiting on a better offer. "Give or take thirty minutes."

"I can work with that," I say—and I mean it.

I catch her mouth in a kiss that starts slow—just lips and hands and heat—but it turns greedy fast. Because I miss her before she's even left. Because I'm not done being wrapped up in her.

She gasps when I lift her, both arms under her thighs like she weighs nothing, like this is the most obvious thing in the world. She clings to me instinctively, laughing against my neck, and I don't stop kissing her even as I walk us straight to my bedroom.

Her fingers knot in my hair. Her mouth curves against mine.

Thirty minutes.

That's all she's giving me.

So I'm gonna make every second count.

I drop her onto the bed with a bounce and crawl in after her, caging her in with my arms and this big, stupid grin I can't seem to shake.

She's still laughing when I nuzzle into her neck, but it turns into a squeak when I murmur, "So… The Situation, huh?"

Her whole body tenses. "I knew you were gonna bring that up."

I pull back just enough to see her face—bright red, adorably horrified.

"I'm sorry, I just need a little clarity here," I say, settling in beside her and propping my head up on one hand. "Is it like a title, or more of a code name?"

"I'm never speaking again."

"Because if it's a title, I feel like I should start capitalizing it in texts. Maybe add a trademark."

"Good grief."

I kiss her jaw, her neck, the place behind her ear that makes her shiver.

"You know you can't just say something like that and expect me to be normal about it," I murmur.

She makes a strangled sound. "I wasn't trying to say it out loud!"

I grin against her skin. "But you did. And now I'm haunted."

"Cole."

"Like… The Situation? Really?"

Her eyes go wide. "We are *not* discussing this."

"I just have questions, babe."

She groans, already pulling a pillow over her face. "I hate myself."

"Oh no. I love you. This is the highlight of my life." I chuckle. "Did you consider other options? The Crisis? The Phenomenon? The Event?"

"I'm begging you," she says, voice muffled under the pillow.

I pull the pillow from her face and kiss her flushed cheek. "Does it have a backstory?" I ask, mock-serious now. "Did it earn the name through a series of heroic deeds? Is there a plaque?"

She lets out a muffled, strangled noise. "You are such a troublemaker."

"I just think he deserves to know," I say, brushing hair from her face. "You can't name a man's junk and not tell him why."

She groans. "Can you not say junk right now?"

"Sorry. The Situation."

"I hate you."

"You don't." I lean down, pressing my lips to her cheek. "And you're blushing."

"No, I'm not."

"You so are." I grin against her jaw. "You realize this opens up so many possibilities," I say, unbuttoning her jeans.

She blinks. "Like what?"

"Custom boxers. A license plate. Maybe a podcast."

She throws her head back with a laugh. "You're unhinged."

I kiss the hollow of her throat. "You made me this way. I was normal before you."

"Liar." She smiles.

"You named my d—"

She slaps a hand over my mouth. "Finish that

sentence and I'm walking home."

I laugh, catching her hand and pressing a kiss to her wrist instead. "Fine. I'll behave."

"You're incapable."

"Not true. I just have very specific triggers. Like finding out my girlfriend secretly assigned my anatomy a formal title."

She softens immediately. "Girlfriend?"

The word hangs between us like a live wire. My pulse kicks up—stupid, really, considering everything we've already done—but this feels bigger somehow. More real.

I pause, feeling the shift in the air. Her eyes search mine, and I catch the tiny hitch in her breathing, the way her fingers curl slightly against my shirt. And my throat goes dry.

All that cocky confidence from thirty seconds ago? Yeah, that's taking a real nice vacation right about now.

"Yeah," I say, and my voice comes out rougher than I meant it to. "That okay?"

For a second—just a second—her whole face goes soft in this way that makes my chest tight. Like maybe she's been waiting for this. Like maybe she wants it as much as I do.

She doesn't answer—just slides her hand up to the back of my neck, fingers threading through my hair, and pulls me down into a kiss that tastes like a yes.

# 32

## COFFEE, DOG FOOD, AND DANGER-OUS FEELINGS



I only came in for dog food and coffee.

That's it. Two things. Five minutes, max.

But now I'm in the cereal aisle, parked in front of a wall of boxes as if I've forgotten how food works. I'm holding a bag of Beef's kibble in one arm and a can of cold brew in the other, and somewhere between Frosted Flakes and Cinnamon Life, my brain just… left.

Last week, I was here with Cole. We shopped, flirted, and drove home like a normal couple. He carried my groceries inside with one arm like it was nothing. Casually reached for my keys, unlocked the door, and set everything down before I even had the chance to dig for the bag of frozen peas that was burning through my fingers. Then he kissed me. Right there, next to a carton of eggs and a bag of baby carrots, like it was the most obvious thing in the world. No build-up. No hesitation. Just leaned in and kissed me like he'd done it a hundred times before.

And now I'm standing here, completely useless, smiling at a shelf of cereal like I'm being personally romanced by Tony the Tiger.

I blink, snap out of it, and shake my head as if I'm trying to clear a fog.

I'm that girl now.

A quiet voice pulls me from my daze.

"You thinking about someone sweet, or are the Lucky Charms just hitting differently today?"

I turn to see an older woman with silver hair and a denim jacket pushing a cart beside me. She has a half-smirk and kind eyes, like she's been catching people in grocery store love comas for years.

I laugh, my cheeks burning. "Uh… guilty."

She winks. "Don't worry. That look doesn't go away, honey. Enjoy it."

She pats my arm like a co-conspirator and rolls on down the aisle.

I stare after her for a beat, then look back at the cereal as if it might offer answers.

Maybe this is what it feels like.

Not fireworks. Not dramatic declarations. Just this weird, unexpected lightness. Smiling at nothing. Getting teased by strangers. Feeling like something inside me has shifted without my permission.

I grab a box of Honey Nut Cheerios, toss it in the basket, and head for checkout before I start doodling his name in the condensation on the freezer doors.

Sheesh.

As I unload my basket onto the conveyor belt, my brain latches onto something. Maybe this is what my parents felt. The easy happiness. The type that lives in the quiet moments—unloading groceries, making small talk, touching without thinking.

The quiet before everything turns. I wonder if there was a moment, right before it all went sideways, when they looked at each other and thought, yeah... this is it. We're safe.

I exhale and nod a greeting at the checkout clerk.

I know better than anyone how something good can vanish before you get the chance to hold onto it.

And it's possibly the most terrifying thought of all.

I pop the trunk of Shay's car and hoist a crate of boxed hair dye into my arms, trying not to let it crush me.

"Why do you order in bulk like you're preparing for the apocalypse?" I call over my shoulder.

Shay leans in the doorway of the salon, chewing gum and doing absolutely zero heavy lifting. "Because unlike some people, I plan ahead. And also, I was hoping your tiny goblin body would carry everything inside for me."

"You're a problem."

"I'm a visionary."

I nudge the door open with my hip and shuffle inside, the crate thudding on the nearest counter. It's warm in here, the familiar smell of coconut shampoo and the faint scent of chemicals clinging to the air. It's comforting in its weird way.

Shay's already sorting boxes into piles—platinum blondes, chestnuts, reds. I fall into step beside her, popping lids and checking expiration dates. We work in an easy rhythm. We've done this a hundred times before, usually with music blasting and both of us complaining about exes, landlords, or the price of iced coffee.

But today I'm quiet. Distracted.

And apparently, not subtle about it.

"You're awfully glowy for someone elbow-deep in boxes of developer," Shay says after a minute, side-eyeing me.

"I'm not glowy."

"You are. You've got that dazed, post-sex, maybe-I-like-him glow. It's disgusting. I'm filing a formal complaint."

I snort, but my ears go hot.

"I'm just… thinking."

"Uh-huh. Thinking about how a certain paramedic could probably carry two crates of hair dye at once? Maybe shirtless?"

I throw an empty box at her head. "Shut up."

She grins, completely unfazed. "No, seriously. What's going on with you? You're like… softer. Less fighty."

I pretend to be very interested in a row of auburn tubes. "I met his mom."

Shay's eyebrows shoot up. "Oh shit. That's big."

"I didn't know it was going to happen. But she made us pasta, and she was… warm. Sweet."

"And?"

"And he met Jack."

Her jaw drops. "Wait—"

"I know. Long story. It was awkward and weird, and Jack did that silent glare thing like he was trying to set Cole on fire with his mind, but… it happened."

"*How* did it happen? *Why* did it happen?" She looks as confused as I felt at the time.

"In the strangest coincidence ever, Jack and Kate are dating."

Shay's expression melts. "Okay, that's adorable."

I nod. It kind of is. Jack deserves someone good

in his life. Someone who makes him smile the way Kate does.

"And you survived?" she asks.

"Barely. But yeah. Cole is…" I shrug, trying to play it cool even though my chest feels like someone's squeezing it. "He's just… good. With me. For me."

The scary part? I actually believe it. Like when he looks at me, I'm not a project to fix or a puzzle to solve. I'm just... me. And somehow that's enough.

Shay bumps my shoulder with hers. "You're falling for him."

"I don't—"

"You so are."

I sigh, feeling my defenses crumble. "Maybe."

"Maybe?" She snorts. "Babe, you've got that look."

"What look?"

"Oh babe." She gestures to my face. "That's the face of someone who's been emotionally steamrolled by a man who knows exactly what he's doing inside the bedroom and out of it."

My stomach does this stupid flutter thing. Because yeah, he does know what he's doing. With his hands. With his words. With the way he looks at me like I hung the moon when all I did was make a snappy remark.

It's going so well it terrifies me. Like I'm standing on the edge of something massive, and one wrong step sends me tumbling. My therapist would call it catastrophizing—planning for disaster just because things feel safe.

But still... part of me keeps flinching for impact. It's hard not to brace for the crash when you've lived through the wreckage.

She grins. "Told you you'd fold eventually."

"I haven't folded," I mutter, reaching for another box of dye.

"Oh honey." She gestures at my face. "That smile says otherwise."

I try not to grin.

I fail spectacularly.

# 33

## ADRENALINE AND AFTERMATH

*Cole*

The kitchen smells like burnt toast and over-confidence.

Brennan's standing by the toaster, shirt half untucked, smirking like he didn't just absolutely butcher breakfast.

"I told you it was on the wrong setting," I say, flipping through the morning log with one hand and pointing at the blackened bread with the other.

He shrugs. "I like it with a little crunch."

"That's not crunch. That's ash."

Trey walks in with a mug of coffee and snorts. "Are we toasting bread or Brennan's culinary skills again?"

"Same thing," I mutter.

"Both," Brennan says, holding up the toast like it's a trophy. "And I stand by it."

Trey slides into a chair across from me, kicks his feet up on the bench. "You planning on cooking for your date Friday? Or are you just gonna hand her a smoke detector and pray?"

"Please," Brennan says, tossing the burnt toast into the trash. "I'm not wasting moves on date one. That's rookie behavior."

"You are a rookie," I say.

"I'm a gift." He shoots me a grin. "A rare and precious gift, and you're just mad I've got better hair and a more compelling origin story."

Trey chokes on his coffee. "What is this, Marvel?"

Brennan shrugs again, totally unbothered. "Tell me I don't give off golden retriever energy with a tragic backstory."

I roll my eyes, but I'm grinning. This is how most mornings go—banter, trash talk, and someone forgetting how a toaster works. It's easy. Good. Like muscle memory.

We're halfway into a debate about whether or not Brennan could survive one week in the woods with only a pocket knife and a granola bar when the tone sounds overhead.

Dispatch crackles through the speaker. "Engine 4, respond to multi-vehicle accident—possible entrapment, Highway 42 at mile marker 18. Hazmat possible. Tanker truck involved. Repeat—tanker truck involved."

Everything shifts in an instant.

Trey's already on his feet. Brennan tosses his half-full water bottle in the trash and grabs his coat without a word. I slide the logbook closed and follow them out to the truck.

No more jokes. No more toast.

Now it's just go time.

Luckily, I was born for this. It's like second nature.

We gear up and climb in the truck—radios on, helmets buckled, oxygen tanks prepped. I glance over at Brennan, who's seated across from me, tugging on his gloves.

He catches my eye and gives me a quick nod.

I nod back.

We don't need to say anything. We've done this a hundred times.

But something in my chest goes tight anyway.

Because sometimes, it's the days that start normal—the ones where you laugh too loud and think you're untouchable—that blindside you hardest.

We pull up fast, lights flashing against the thick haze of smoke already curling into the sky. The smell hits before we're even out of the rig—gasoline, burnt rubber, something sharp and chemical that makes the back of my throat go tight.

I hop down from the truck and take it in.

It's bad.

The pileup stretches across three lanes of highway—cars crumpled like soda cans, some flipped, one pushed clear off the shoulder into a shallow ditch. In the center of it all is the tanker truck, jack-knifed and tilted at an angle that screams unstable.

Flames lick along the asphalt near its rear wheels. Not full-on engulfed yet, but close. Too close.

I hear sirens in the distance—backup en route—but for now, it's just us.

"Let's split it," I bark. "Trey, take the southbound side—check that sedan and the pickup. Bren, with me. We've got movement in that Toyota."

We move fast, practiced. Adrenaline sharpens everything—sound, smell, instinct. I barely register the heat baking off the pavement or the sweat already dripping down my back.

There's a woman trapped in the Toyota, dazed, bleeding from the scalp. I check her pulse. "Hey," I say, voice low but firm. "Can you hear me?"

She nods faintly. I call for stabilization and extraction gear, and Bren's already there, tossing me the hydraulic cutters like we've rehearsed this a thousand times. Because we have. Good training will save your life.

We get her out together—clean, efficient. She's loaded into the back of the ambulance within minutes.

It's chaos all around—metal groaning, glass crunching under boots, radios squawking, someone crying nearby—but we're locked in. Focused.

I barely look at Brennan as we move on to the next vehicle, but I can feel him at my shoulder, matching my pace, reading my mind. This is our rhythm. This is the job at its best—knowing that people are going to walk away because we showed up.

We get to a minivan next. Driver's out. Backseat's crumpled in on itself. I squeeze inside to double-check for kids. Empty. Thank God.

"You good?" Brennan calls out.

"Yeah," I say, already climbing back out. "Your turn. Check the hatchback over by the guardrail—I saw someone moving."

We switch spots.

I'm halfway to the next vehicle when it happens.

A low, vibrating boom that doesn't sound like anything at first—just pressure, a hum in the air—and then everything erupts.

The sound. The heat. The force.

I don't even have time to turn around.

Just a flash of light.

And then—

Nothing.

Just black.

Like the world I knew no longer exists.

# 34

## THE WAITING ROOM

*Kate*

The phone rings at 9:13 a.m.

I almost don't answer—I'm at school, halfway through grading essays during my planning period—but the number's local, and something inside me tells me to answer it.

"Hello?"

"Ma'am, this is Dispatch. We're calling about your son, Cole. Is this Kate Hartley?"

Something inside me twists. "Yes, it is."

"Ma'am, there's been an incident on a call. Your son was involved, and he's been transported to Memorial General."

That's all it takes.

The words don't even finish echoing before I'm on my feet, my chair screeching back, my hand shaking so hard I can barely hold the phone.

"What happened?" I ask, heart in my throat. "Is he okay?"

"I don't have medical details, ma'am. I'm just the call operator. I'm very sorry."

I hang up without saying thank you. Without saying anything. I just move.

I don't remember grabbing my bag. I don't remember leaving the school. I barely remember dialing Jack's number, but I must've, because his voice is suddenly in my ear.

"Kate? Everything okay?"

"No," I breathe. "It's Cole. There was an accident. They took him to Memorial."

A pause. Just a beat.

"I'm on my way," he says, instantly. "Do you want me to come get you?"

"No—I'm already in the car."

I hang up again, fingers clenched so tight around the steering wheel they ache. I run every red light. I don't even feel my hands go numb until I'm pulling into the ER lot and almost forget to throw it in park.

Inside, the hospital smells like disinfectant and fear.

I steady my palms on the front desk. "My son—Cole Hartley." My voice cracks and I have to draw a breath before I can get the rest out. "He was brought in. He's a firefighter."

The nurse behind the desk flinches but taps

her keyboard fast. "They're working on him now. That's all I know."

*Working on him?* Those words alone nearly knock me flat.

"Is he—was he—conscious?"

"I'm sorry," she says gently. "You can wait just down the hall. There's a waiting area for families."

My throat threatens to close.

I walk stiffly down the hall, following the signs until I round the corner—and stop.

Half the fire department is here. That's not good.

Some are sitting, some are standing, all are still in uniform. Like they rushed straight here. Boots scuffed, faces drawn tight. I recognize almost all of them. Trey. The captain. Even a few of the younger guys who barely know Cole but showed up anyway.

A show of support. Brotherhood.

But I don't need a show of support. I don't need sympathy.

I need someone to tell me my son is alive.

Trey sees me first and stands up quickly. "Kate."

I walk straight up to him. "Is he okay?"

"They won't tell us much yet. Just that he's here. And it was bad."

My stomach flips.

I look around. "Brennan?"

Trey hesitates.

And that's when I know.

He's not here in the waiting room—he must be back here. Involved in whatever this is.

I sink into the nearest chair, legs barely holding me up. My hands won't stop shaking.

Someone brings me a bottle of water. Another firefighter I don't know says something kind. I nod, thank them, but it's like my ears are full of static. None of it matters.

I just want someone in scrubs to come through those doors and tell me my son's going to be okay.

And I want him to walk out behind them with his trademark smile and tell me he's fine and not to worry so much, Ma.

But that doesn't happen.

A few minutes later, I hear my name and nearly jump out of my seat.

"Kate."

Jack's voice.

I look up and he's already crossing the room—eyes scanning, face pale but steady. The second I see him, my whole body gives out. I stand, or try to, but my knees buckle and he catches me fast, arms locking around me like a shield.

I collapse into him, fingers fisting his shirt.

"Oh God, Jack—"

He holds me tighter. "I've got you. I've got you."

He guides me gently back down into a chair,

never letting go, his voice calm even as mine is falling apart.

"What happened?" he asks, brushing hair back from my face. "What kind of accident was it?"

I blink at him, breath catching. "I don't—" I shake my head. "I don't know. They didn't say. Just that they were bringing him here and now they're working on him. That's all I know."

Jack's mouth tightens, but before he can say anything, a man steps forward. Fire Captain Monroe. Cole's commanding officer. His face is drawn, his uniform stained with smoke and grit.

He kneels beside me, hands resting on his knees.

"It was a bad one, Kate. A highway pile-up. A tanker truck jackknifed; there were cars everywhere. Cole was working the scene." His voice tightens up, but he draws a breath and continues. "The fire spread fast. Hazmat situation. We're still getting updates from the scene. I'm sorry I don't know more."

My heart races, hammering against my ribs like it's trying to escape.

Monroe's voice softens. "I'm not going to lie to you. There are going to be fatalities. It was… one of the worst I've seen."

I stare at him. My ears ring. Fatalities.

Jack lowers me carefully into the seat again when I start to sway, like I might go down for good.

His hand finds mine, strong and steady, holding tight. But it doesn't help.

My son.

My only child.

Fatalities.

My breath catches, then breaks, and I cover my face with both hands as the sob rips out of me. Raw. Shaking.

"I can't do this," I choke. "Jack—I can't—he's, he's my whole world."

He wraps both arms around me and pulls me in like he can hold the pieces together by sheer force. I don't care that people are watching. I don't care that I'm gasping for air between sobs.

I just want my son back.

I just want him to be okay.

I don't know how long I cry.

Jack never lets go. One hand grips mine, the other rubs small circles across my back like I used to when Cole was a baby and I couldn't get him to stop crying at 3 a.m. Like if I just kept moving, we'd both stay afloat.

Eventually, the sobs taper into silence. But the ache doesn't.

My body feels hollowed out.

Jack clears his throat, voice rough. "I should call Andi."

I blink, disoriented. "What?"

"She should know. She'd want to be here."

I nod slowly. The name barely registers through the fog. "Yes. Yes, you're right." Andi, who Cole had never told me about—but who I'd met last weekend. She was so pretty—unexpected with her purple hair and her genuine adoration for Cole.

Jack pulls out his phone and steps a few feet away. I can hear the low murmur of his voice as he talks, but not the words. Then a pause. A quiet, pained exhale. He hangs up.

"She's on her way," he says when he returns. "She was at work."

I nod again.

The waiting room shifts around us—nurses coming and going, doors swinging open and closed. The clock ticks so loud it feels like a countdown. Still no answers. Still no doctor. Still no him.

Then the doors at the end of the hall burst open.

Andi rushes in, nearly tripping over herself. She's in scrubs under a wrinkled lab coat, hair pulled back in a messy ponytail. There's a smear of dried blood on the sleeve of her jacket—someone else's, probably, not hers—and her eyes are wide and wild and wrecked.

The second she sees me, she stumbles forward.

"Kate—oh my gosh—"

I don't even hesitate.

We crash into each other like waves, arms around shoulders and backs, and it's not graceful or quiet or pretty. It's broken and raw and desperate.

She's crying now, too. Shaking like she ran the whole way here.

"What happened?" she gasps, clutching me tighter. "Is he—do we know anything?"

I pull back just far enough to look at her, my own voice thin. "They won't tell us anything. I'm still waiting to hear."

Andi presses a hand to her mouth.

Jack steps beside us, quiet. Solid. "It was bad. A pile-up. Tanker truck. Explosion."

She nods once. But her eyes stay on me. "He's strong, Kate. He's so strong."

I nod, too. Because I want to believe it.

But no one has any answers.

Not yet.

So we hold each other and wait.

And pray that the next person through those doors has a reason to let us breathe again.

# 35

## WHEN THINGS FALL APART

*Andi*

The clock won't stop ticking.

Every second punches through the silence like a countdown, but to what, no one can say. I'm sitting in the same seat I sank into twenty minutes ago, or maybe two hours ago—I don't know anymore. Time feels elastic. Unreal. Like it's only moving to keep my body vibrating with dread.

My knee bounces uncontrollably. I dig my nails into my palm to make it stop. It doesn't help.

I keep thinking about how this is exactly what it felt like when my parents died.

The phone call. The rushing. The white walls and that smell—sanitized, like even grief has to follow hospital protocol. The waiting room. Time seeming to slow. And even Jack.

He was there that day too.

Standing off to the side, quiet and serious. Same as now.

I hate it.

I glance at him across the room, where he's talking softly to Kate. She hasn't moved in over an hour. I don't think she's blinked in twenty minutes. Her hands are clenched in her lap like she's holding her own heart together.

I can't do this again.

Not like this.

Not with Cole.

A surge of emotion rises hard and fast in my throat. Anger. Terror. That helpless, frantic energy that makes you want to punch through drywall just to feel like you're in control of something.

I bite down on the inside of my cheek until I taste blood.

Trey sits down a few seats over and leans forward, elbows on his knees. "Hey. I'm heading to the cafeteria. Want anything?"

I shake my head. "No. Thanks."

"You sure? Coffee, water—something to throw at a wall?"

I try to smile. It doesn't land. "I'm good."

He nods and stands, then gives me a look that says I'll check in later.

The second he's gone, Jack moves toward me, slow and deliberate, like he's giving me space to bolt if I want to.

"I was thinking we could take a walk," he says. "Just for a few minutes. There's something I want to say."

I shake my head before he finishes. "No. I can't leave."

"We won't go far."

"I can't leave. What if they come out? What if something happens?"

"I'll have someone come get us the second they do," he says gently. "I promise."

My heart slams hard against my ribs. I hate this. I hate being asked to move when all I want is for time to stop until I know Cole is okay. Until someone says the words I need to hear.

But there's something in Jack's eyes—something calm and quietly determined—that unsettles me just enough.

I nod, even though it feels impossible.

"Okay," I whisper. "But not far."

He places a hand on my shoulder, a reassuring squeeze.

"We'll stay close."

We walk to the exit and the glass doors slide apart for us. The air outside is more humid than I expected.

I draw a breath, hoping to clear my head—but there's no such thing in the emergency bay. I wrap my arms around myself as Jack leads me toward the edge of the overhang, near the ambulance zone. It's mostly empty now. Just a couple of units parked, engines off, doors shut. Waiting, like the rest of us.

The fluorescent lights buzz overhead. A discarded latex glove flutters across the pavement like a ghost.

Jack stands beside me with his hands in his pockets, gaze fixed on the horizon like there's something out there to anchor to.

He doesn't speak right away. I don't either. Because honestly, what is there to say?

My heart's still racing. My stomach's doing somersaults. My thoughts are tangled and sharp, a mess of what-ifs and memories I've tried for years to bury.

He finally breaks the silence. "You okay?"

It's so gently asked, I almost don't answer.

Then I laugh, humorless. "I'm freaking out."

"That's what I figured."

I press a hand to my chest, like I can force it to stop vibrating. "It's like… I keep waiting to hear the worst. Because that's what happened last time. I waited, and then—" My voice catches. "Then I didn't have parents anymore."

Jack nods, quiet. "That's what I was worried about. You're back in that headspace."

"I never really left it," I admit. "I just got better at living with it."

He lets that settle between us for a beat.

"I remember everything about that day," he says quietly. "When the doctor came out and told you. When they said there was nothing they could do."

I nod, throat tight.

"I remember how you looked. And how still you went. Like the world stopped spinning for you, and you weren't sure it was ever going to start again."

I blink fast. "Feels like that right now."

He turns to face me. "But this time, it's different."

"How?" My voice cracks. "How is it different?"

"Because Cole's not gone. He's in there. And until someone tells us otherwise, he's still fighting. Which means we hold the line."

I exhale a shaky breath.

"Sometimes the waiting is the worst part," Jack continues. "But you're not alone in it, Andi. And you're stronger than you think."

"I don't feel strong."

"You don't have to. You just have to stay standing."

I'll try.

His voice softens. "I know it feels like you're right back in the wreckage. But this isn't then. It's not over."

I swallow hard, eyes burning. "I want to believe that."

"I know." He steps forward and pulls me into a hug. Strong arms, warm and steady. The kind of hug you don't realize you need until you're in it.

"I'm not going anywhere," he says. "No matter what happens. You're not going to be alone in this."

I close my eyes and let myself lean into it, just for a second. Just until I can breathe again.

Even if nothing feels okay, I believe that.

He's not going anywhere.

The waiting room feels colder when I step back inside.

Kate's still in the same chair, staring straight ahead, unmoving. Trey's across from her, scrolling through his phone with a blank expression that I know too well—the I-need-to-distract-myself-or-I'll-lose-it expression.

I ease back into my seat and fish my phone from my pocket with shaking hands. It takes me a second to type.

> Me: Something happened. It's bad. Cole's in the hospital.

> Me: Please don't freak out. I just needed to tell someone.

> Me: I'll text again when I know more.

I stare at the screen, thumb hovering over send. Then I hit it before I can change my mind.

Shay responds almost immediately.

Shay: WHAT.

Shay: ANDI. WTF.

Shay: I'm on my way.

I don't text back.

Because now it's just me and this seat and the wall clock and the echoing nothingness of waiting. Again.

I lean my head back and close my eyes.

Cole's face flashes behind my eyelids—stupid handsome and way too cocky. That grin he gets when he knows I'm trying not to laugh. The way he looks at me. Holds me…

I think about that night in his bed. My face pressed against his chest. His voice, low and certain: I've got you.

I want to believe it still.

I want him to keep having me.

I want there to be a next time.

The door opens.

"Kate Hartley?"

The name is like a shot through the room.

I shoot to my feet before I realize I've moved, heart leaping into my throat.

Kate stands too—slow, like her body's forgotten how—but I'm already halfway to the nurse, hands clenched at my sides, pulse roaring in my ears.

Please, please, please.

Just let him be okay.

The doctor approaches. Mid-forties, scrubs beneath a surgical gown, mask pulled down around his neck. He looks tired. Focused. Like someone who's walked into too many rooms like this and still doesn't know how to soften the blow.

Kate steps forward slowly, her posture stiff, like her whole body's bracing for impact. I hover just behind her, my hand ghosting near hers in case she needs it.

"I'm Dr. Sen," he says. "I'm the attending trauma surgeon overseeing Cole's case."

Case. Like he's a file. A name on a chart. Not him.

Kate's voice is barely audible. "How is he?"

"He made it through the first part of surgery. He sustained multiple blunt force injuries from the blast—broken ribs, a lacerated spleen, and a puncture to the liver. There was internal bleeding, but we've controlled it for now."

For now. My stomach twists.

"We've stabilized his vitals," Dr. Sen continues. "But he's not out of the woods yet. It's still touch and go."

Kate nods slowly, eyes locked on his.

"He's young," the doctor says, softer now. "Strong. That's on his side."

Kate sways, just slightly, and I step closer. My hand finds hers and she grips it like a lifeline.

"We'll keep updating you as things progress," he finishes. "We're doing everything we can."

She nods again, her mouth moving but no sound coming out.

"Thank you," I say for her.

Dr. Sen gives a quick nod and walks off down the hallway, leaving silence in his wake.

Kate turns toward me, eyes glassy and wide, and I don't even think. I wrap my arms around her and hold her tight, tighter than I ever have before. She clutches me right back.

"He's alive," I whisper. "He's still fighting."

But before we can even take a breath—before the weight of it settles—a second set of doors opens.

Another doctor steps out, this one slower. Shoulders slumped.

Across the room, I see Brennan's mom and dad stand up. They'd arrived while I was outside with Jack, someone said. They're holding hands.

"I'm so sorry," the doctor says gently. "We did everything we could. He didn't make it."

The cry Brennan's mother lets out cuts straight through me.

Like something breaking in real time.

Her knees give, and his father catches her, just barely. Around us, the entire room goes still—no one moves, no one speaks. Trey presses a fist to his mouth and turns away. One of the younger firefighters sits down hard and drops his head between his hands.

Kate's hand finds mine again and squeezes. I squeeze back, hard.

The pain is too big for the room. It spills out everywhere—into the sterile air, into our chests, into the spaces between words.

Cole's still alive.

But Brennan isn't.

Brennan—who cracked jokes and teased me endlessly—but who always held the door for me.

I didn't know him well. Not really.

But I remember his laugh. I remember how much Cole trusted him. I remember watching them at O'Malley's—shoulders pressed together, joking over beers—and thinking, they're lucky to have that kind of friendship.

And now he's just… gone.

Like someone snapped their fingers and erased him from the world.

I feel it like a whiplash. Hope and heartbreak colliding so fast I can't tell one from the other.

The sliding doors hiss open again, and this time it's Shay.

She moves fast, eyes sweeping the room like she's ready to throw hands if someone doesn't point her toward me immediately. Her hair's pulled up in a messy twist, oversized sunglasses pushed to the top of her head, and she's still wearing her work apron over leggings and boots like she left in the middle of a blowout.

When she spots me, she doesn't say a word—just beelines straight over and drops to her knees in front of my chair.

"What happened?" she whispers. "Tell me everything."

I try.

I open my mouth, and the words just... get stuck.

"He's—he's in surgery," I say finally. "There was an explosion. Tanker truck. Highway pile-up. Internal bleeding. Something with his liver or his spleen, I don't—"

My voice catches. Everything blurs again.

"I should know this," I whisper. "I work in a hospital. I should be able to say it right. Remember everything the surgeon said."

Shay grabs my hands, squeezes hard. "Stop. That's not your job right now."

"But I—"

"No." Her voice is firm, like she's anchoring

me. "Your job is to breathe. Sit. Hold Kate's hand. Let them work. That's it."

I shake my head, blinking too fast. "He said it was touch and go. That they stopped the internal bleeding but…"

Shay pulls me into a hug so tight I can't even move.

"You don't have to be strong right now," she murmurs. "You just have to let the people who love you keep you standing."

And I do.

I let her hold me. I let myself shake. I let the tears come again, and I don't bother wiping them away this time.

And I know—no matter what happens next—none of us walk out of here the same.

# 36

## BACK FROM THE EDGE

*Cole*

It starts with a beeping.

Soft. Rhythmic. Annoying.

Then pressure. Something in my side—tight, pulling. My chest feels like someone sat on it. My mouth is dry as hell. Everything hurts in a dull, faraway kind of way, like my body's trying to keep secrets from my brain.

I blink.

White ceiling. Fluorescent lights. IV pole.

Shit. Hospital.

A figure leans over me—blurry at first, then clearer. A woman in scrubs, hair pulled back in a tight bun, a pen tucked behind her ear.

"Hey there," she says gently, brushing something—maybe a monitor wire—from my chest. "Welcome back, Cole."

I try to swallow. It takes too much effort.

"Where…" My voice is gravel. "What happened?"

"You were in an explosion," she says calmly. "Tanker truck on the highway. Your crew brought you in fast. You've been in surgery."

Surgery? For what?

I blink again. Try to sit up. Instantly regret it.

"Hey, no—don't move," she says, pressing a hand to my shoulder. "You've got broken ribs, and we had to operate on your abdomen. Lacerated spleen, punctured liver. But you're stable now. We stopped the internal bleeding."

That's… a lot.

I sink back against the pillow, heart pounding too fast for a body that feels this slow.

"Is Brennan okay?" I ask before I can think.

The nurse pauses. Just for a second.

"I'm not sure," she says softly. "Someone else will talk to you about that soon, okay?"

I nod, but something tightens in my chest.

*I try to remember*—what was the last thing I saw?

He was heading for the hatchback. I'd just told him to check it out. He waved me off, said *I've got it,* and then—

The explosion.

That blast of light. The heat. The sound of it deafening.

I don't remember seeing him after that. I don't remember anything after that.

"Your mom's in the waiting room," she adds after a moment. "She's been here all day."

Of course she has.

"Do you want me to bring her in?"

I nod—just barely. "Yeah. Please."

My throat burns. Not from the breathing tube. Not from the meds.

From the fact that I know what I'm about to see in her face when she walks through that door.

And I almost made her live through losing me.

The door opens slowly.

And then there she is.

My mom.

Her eyes are red and tired, and she looks like she's been through hell.

"Hey, Ma," I say, my voice still scratchy, trying to lift one side of my mouth in a smile. "Guess I really know how to make an entrance, huh?"

She lets out a sound—somewhere between a sob and a laugh—and rushes to my side.

"Oh, baby," she whispers, her hands fluttering uselessly over me before finally landing gently on my arm. "Look at you. Look at all this. I—I thought—"

"I'm okay," I lie, even as everything inside me throbs.

"You're not okay, Cole," she says, her voice

cracking as she pulls a tissue from her pocket and wipes at her eyes. "But you're *alive*. And I'll take that. I'll take that any day."

She's crying again before she finishes the sentence. I reach out slowly—everything hurts—and squeeze her hand.

"I'm sorry I scared you," I say, softer now.

The door opens again.

A doctor steps in, clipboard in hand, and gives my mom a polite nod. "Good to see you awake, Cole."

He pulls a chair up to the foot of the bed and settles in with a practiced calm. "I'm Dr. Sen. I just wanted to give you a clearer picture now that you're awake and stable."

"Okay," I say cautiously.

"First, the good news," he says. "You've got no head trauma. No spinal damage. Your lungs are clear, no signs of inhalation injury. No burns. That's huge."

I nod slowly. "Okay."

"But," he continues, "you did sustain serious blunt force trauma to your torso. You had a lacerated spleen and a puncture in your liver. We stopped the bleeding, but we had to remove part of the spleen. You'll need to be very careful for the next few weeks."

"How careful?" I ask.

"No lifting. No exertion. No work for at least

six to eight weeks, minimum. More if there are complications. You also have three broken ribs, which will take time to heal on their own. You'll be sore. Easily fatigued. It'll be frustrating, but you have to take it seriously."

I feel my mom flinch beside me.

The weight of it sinks in slowly, like fog filling a room. No work. No firehouse. No *anything*.

Just pain and waiting.

"And Brennan?" I ask again.

Dr. Sen gives me that same pause. "Someone will be in to talk to you about that soon."

I nod once. Jaw tight. Maybe he's still in surgery too. *Damn, I hate this.*

He glances at my mom. "He's lucky, ma'am. He's very lucky."

She swallows hard, brushes the hair back from my forehead with shaking fingers.

"I know," she whispers. "But I'd rather be lucky and yelling at him than—"

She cuts herself off, can't finish. Doesn't need to.

Because we both know how close it was.

As soon as the doctor leaves, the room feels too quiet.

Too still.

I shift slightly—just enough to make my ribs scream—and glance around, suddenly remembering something important.

"Where's my phone?" I ask, wincing. "I need to call Andi."

My mom, still hovering near the bed, gives me a soft look. "She's here," she says. "She's been here all day. Since this morning. Jack called her."

That hits me harder than I expect.

She's *here*.

"I'll go get her," Mom says. "She's just down the hall."

I nod, and she leans in to kiss the top of my head before quietly slipping out of the room.

I try to sit up a little straighter, swearing under my breath at how every movement feels like a knife. My chest aches, my side is on fire, and my heart's doing something I don't recognize—something tight and unsteady.

And then she's there.

Andi. With her lavender hair and her blue eyes. She looks like she's barely holding it together—and the second she sees me, her mouth crumples.

She doesn't say anything.

Just crosses the room in three quick steps and falls into my arms.

I grunt at the impact, biting back a groan, but I don't let go. I can't. She's clinging to me like she thought I might disappear, and my body may be broken, but my heart remembers exactly how to hold her.

We stay like that for a long time.

No words. Just breathing.

When she finally pulls back, her hand cups my cheek like she's trying to convince herself I'm real.

"You scared the hell out of me," she says, voice shaking.

"Yeah," I rasp. "I scared the hell out of myself too."

She leans down and kisses me—carefully, softly—but I still wince when her arm brushes my ribs.

"Oh—shit, sorry—" She pulls back instantly, eyes wide with guilt.

"It's fine," I say, breath hitching. "Totally worth it."

But I can't help noticing the look in her eyes. That terror, still lurking behind her relief. Like if she lets herself exhale too deeply, I'll vanish.

"Cole," she says around a sob. Her face is still streaked with tears.

"Hey," I say softly, trying for a smile that probably looks more like a grimace. "I'm okay. See? All in one piece. Well, mostly."

A sad, broken smile touches her lips. She presses them to my forehead.

"Andi…"

She looks up.

"Where's Brennan?" I say quietly. "Tell me. Please."

Her face folds before she can even speak. A breath. A pause. "Cole." Her voice breaks. "I'm so sorry."

The words hit like a hammer to the chest.

"No," I say, shaking my head. "No—he was right behind me. He was—he said he had it."

She nods, tears spilling fast now. "I know. I know."

"Is he still in surgery? Is it bad?"

She presses her hand to her lips and shakes her head. "His injuries were too severe. He's…gone, Cole."

My stomach turns. My lungs squeeze tight. My brain flashes—stupid shenanigans in the firehouse, Brennan singing off-key in the truck, stealing my fries when he thought I wasn't looking, talking big about poker nights and girls he'd never call back.

*Just* being there.

Always there.

And now he's not.

"But he can't—" My throat closes up. "We were just... yesterday we made plans to… He can't just be□—"

Gone. The word I can't say. Because saying it makes it real, and this can't be real. This is some morphine nightmare, some twisted dream where everything goes wrong.

Except Andi's climbing carefully onto the bed beside me, and her arms are real, and her tears soaking through my hospital gown are real, and the hole opening up in my chest is so real I can't breathe around it.

Andi wraps her arms around me like she can hold the loss at bay.

But it's already here.

And I feel it breaking me open from the inside out.

# 37

## EMOTIONAL DAMAGE AND PINOT GRIGIO

*Andi*

Cole's apartment smells like disinfectant and the overly floral candle Kate lit to make it feel less like a hospital. She's fluffing pillows like her life depends on it, while Cole mutters from the couch, already done with being fussed over.

"Do you want another blanket?" she asks, already draping one over his legs.

"I'm good, Mom," he mutters, shifting just enough to wince. "Damn that thing weighs a hundred pounds."

"It's weighted. It's supposed to calm you."

"I'm already calm."

"You're cranky."

"I'm injured."

Kate rolls her eyes and turns toward the kitchen. "I'm making you tea."

Cole looks at me like he's being held hostage.

"You're really thriving here," I say, forcing a smile.

"I was a great patient in the hospital," he insists, shifting again. "Now I'm just a prisoner in my own home."

"You're lucky you have people who love you," I say, grabbing my purse off the counter.

"Wait—where are you going?" he asks, frowning as I slide my keys into my coat pocket.

I hesitate. "Home."

His brows draw together. "You're not staying?"

"No," I say lightly. Too lightly. "Figured you were in good hands. You've got tea and supervision and approximately four dozen throw pillows on your lap."

He blinks. "But… we could hang out. Watch reality TV. Order that awful Thai you pretended to hate but devoured last time."

I smile at him. It hurts. "Not tonight."

He doesn't say anything right away. Just looks at me. And I hate the way his face softens. The way he tilts his head a little, searching me.

"You okay?" he asks.

"Yeah," I lie.

I kiss his cheek—quick, too fast—and walk out before I can hear him say anything else.

The door closes behind me with a soft click.

I barely make it to my car before I'm sobbing.

My hands shake as I grip the steering wheel, keys still dangling from the ignition, my breath catching on the edge of panic.

Because everything's changed.

I almost lost him. And it broke something inside of me.

I don't know how to love someone like this again.

I can't stop thinking about the way Cole looked at me—hopeful. Hurt. Like he didn't understand why I was leaving when everything was *finally* okay.

Except it's not.

I don't even realize I'm calling Shay until her voice comes through the speaker.

"Hey, what's up?"

My throat tightens. "Can you come over?"

She doesn't even hesitate. "Of course. I'll grab a bottle of wine and head that way."

Twenty minutes later, we're on my couch, two wine glasses on the coffee table and my legs tucked under a blanket. Shay's kicked off her boots and settled in beside me, but her eyes haven't left me once.

"Okay," she says finally. "What's going on?"

I run a hand through my hair and stare at the ceiling. "I think I'm going to break up with him."

She blinks. "Okay. I'm gonna need a little more info than that."

I grab my wine glass and take a fortifying sip of pinot grigio. "Because I can't handle this. I can't go through losing someone again."

"You didn't lose him."

"I *almost* did. And that was enough of a wake up call."

She exhales. "You're allowed to be scared, Andi. But walking away from someone you love just so you don't have to feel scared? That's not protecting yourself. That's punishing both of you."

I don't even argue with her about using the L-word, I just wipe my eyes with the sleeve of my hoodie. "I don't know how to do this, Shay."

Shay leans forward and sets her wine down. "You don't have to have it all figured out. But you don't get to run just because it's hard."

"Brennan's funeral is in a few days," I say quietly. "And I keep thinking… what if it had been Cole? What if it *is* one day?"

Shay reaches for my hand. "Then you love him while you can. You don't pre-break your own heart to save yourself the trouble later."

I cry harder then—shoulders shaking, wine forgotten, words stuck.

And she just squeezes my knee and lets me fall apart.

Because that's what Shay does.

She shows up.

Even when I don't know what I need.

My phone buzzes.

It's Cole.

**You okay?** it says.

I stare at the screen.

I don't answer.

Not because I don't want to.

But because I don't trust myself not to answer everything he isn't asking.

He's healing. Slowly. He's still in pain, still sleeping more than he's awake most days, still flinching when he laughs too hard.

But I can't let myself think about him just yet. I have to think about me—about what my heart can take and what it can't.

Beef hops up onto the couch beside me and noses his head under my hand, like he knows something's wrong.

I press my cheek to his soft fur and close my eyes.

# 38

## THE GOODBYE I DIDN'T EXPECT

*Cole*

The church is full, but it doesn't feel crowded. Just heavy. The air feels thick, almost suffocating.

I sit in the second row with my mom, dressed in my Class A uniform—black coat, badge polished, tie perfectly knotted. It's stiff, formal, too hot under the collar. My ribs still ache when I breathe too deep, and my arm's in a sling because my shoulder won't stop protesting every time I move. But none of that hurts as much as the emptiness inside me.

Brennan's parents are just ahead, sitting together but looking like they're on separate islands. His mom's shoulders shake silently. His dad stares straight ahead, like maybe if he doesn't blink, none of this is real.

People keep filing in. Fellow firefighters in

dress blues. Some of the guys from dispatch. Old friends from the academy.

I glance toward the back.

I keep doing that.

Waiting to see her.

Andi said she'd be here.

Every time the door opens, I flinch. Every time it's not her, something tightens in my chest.

The priest starts speaking. The music plays. A slideshow of photos clicks past on the projector screen—Brennan as a kid, Brennan at the station, Brennan grinning with his arm slung around someone else's shoulders. Always smiling. Always in motion.

It feels unreal. Like any second he's going to burst through the back doors, late and loud, offering some dumb excuse about why he's late this time.

Instead, they call my name.

I wasn't sure I could do this. The captain asked if I wanted to speak, and I said yes before my brain caught up. Now I'm here, my legs stiff and trembling as I rise to my feet.

My mom squeezes my good hand before I step past her.

The walk to the podium feels a hundred miles long. I grip the edges when I get there, just to stay steady.

"Uh, hey." My voice comes out rough, shaky.

I clear my throat. "Most of you knew Brennan the same way I did. Loud. Loyal. And impossible to shut up."

There's a soft ripple of laughter. I press on.

"We were partners. In the truck, on calls, in life. He was the guy who always had my back. Who made every shift feel lighter. Who could be knee-deep in something awful and still crack a joke that made you want to throw something at him."

I pause, trying to steady my breath. It doesn't work because my heart's beating way too fast. I press on.

"I don't remember the first day we met. Not really. I just remember that one day he wasn't there, and the next day he was—and then it was like he'd always been. Like he was a permanent fixture. A given. The idea that he's not anymore… I still can't make sense of it."

The room goes still.

A lump rises in my throat. I swallow hard.

"I've run into a lot of fires. A lot of wreckage. But nothing prepared me for this. Nothing prepares you to lose the person who knew all your tells, who filled the silences without asking, who made the job—and life—more bearable."

I glance down. My hands are shaking.

"I don't know how to live in a world where Brennan doesn't exist. But I do know he wouldn't want me to sit in that pain forever. He'd want me to laugh again. To show up. To live.”

I look up. My eyes scan the crowd.

And then I see her.

Back row, near the aisle.

Andi.

She's in a black dress, her hair's pulled back, and her hands are twisted in her lap. Her eyes are locked on me, wide and wet, and for a second—just one—I forget everything else. Because she came.

I close the speech the best I can. I don't remember the words. I just remember walking back to my seat on shaking legs, and my mom reaching for me.

The service continues. I hear almost none of it.

I keep thinking about Andi. How she waited until I was already up there to come in. How she hasn't come over.

After the final prayer, everyone stands. People start moving toward the front to pay their respects to Brennan's family. Hushed voices. Tears. Hugs that don't fix anything.

I glance back again.

Andi's still there.

I break away from my mom with a soft squeeze of her shoulder and make my way to the back of the room.

She sees me coming and stands, brushing her hands down her sides like she's trying to smooth out her nerves.

“Hey,” I say softly.

"Hey."

"I wasn't sure you were coming."

"I wasn't either."

Her voice is so quiet I almost miss it.

I study her face. Something's off. Her eyes are distant, like she's here but not *really* here.

"You want to come back with me?" I ask. "Sit for a bit? We can go get food after. Or go home and crash. I'm not picky. Just… don't leave yet."

She hesitates. Then shakes her head.

"I can't."

The breath leaves my chest like a punch.

"What do you mean?"

"I mean I can't do this, Cole. I can't pretend I'm not terrified every second. That I didn't sit in that hospital waiting room wondering if you'd ever wake up again."

I take a step closer, jaw tight. "I *did* wake up."

"I know. But next time? What if you don't?" Her voice breaks. "I love you. I didn't mean to, but I do. And it hurts. It hurts so much I feel like I'm back in that hospital waiting to hear they're gone. My parents. You. I can't do it again."

She presses a hand to her mouth, like she's trying to stop the words. Or the sob.

I'm frozen.

"Andi…"

"I'm sorry," she whispers. "But it's easier to let go now than keep falling deeper and wait for it to all come crashing down."

She lifts up on her toes and kisses my cheek, the same way she did the day she left my apartment.

Then she walks past me, out the doors, into the gray afternoon.

And I just stand there.

Destroyed.

All over again.

A few hours later, I'm at O'Malley's with a half-empty glass of whiskey and a group of guys who don't know what to do with their grief except drink it down in slow sips.

Trey's telling a story about Brennan climbing out a second-story window at a bachelor party because he didn't want to pay the tab.

"Swore he was being 'fiscally responsible,'" Trey says, raising his glass. "Idiot still left his jacket inside with his wallet."

We all laugh—loud and sudden.

It's good to be here. Loud voices. Glasses clinking. Distraction. I'm surrounded by guys who get it. We've all lost something and there's a strange sense of comfort in that. Like sharing it makes it easier somehow.

We continue swapping stories. Brennan and the donut contest. Brennan doing karaoke after two beers. Brennan sneaking glitter into the captain's boots for a prank that backfired.

And I let myself laugh. Let myself be here.

Because I can't think about Andi right now.

I can't.

If I let myself feel *that* grief on top of this one, I might not get back up.

So I raise my glass with the rest of them, and I toast Brennan, and I keep my smile steady.

Even if everything inside me is breaking apart.

# 39

## AVOIDANCE 101

*Andi*

I'm already picking at the seam of the couch cushion by the time Dr. Reyes closes the door and settles into her usual chair. She's in her mid-forties, always in muted colors and soft cardigans, with eyes that miss nothing and a calm that unnerves me more than it should.

I've been coming here off and on since college—long enough that she knows about my parents, my panic spirals, and exactly how to ask a question that makes me want to flip the coffee table. We don't do surface-level. We don't do small talk. Not anymore.

She opens her notebook, crosses one leg over the other, and studies me for a moment.

"Tell me what's been going on," she says.

I hesitate. I grab a throw pillow and hug it to

my lap. "I met someone."

She doesn't react, just waits.

"And I fell for him. Harder than I meant to."

Still waiting.

"He makes me laugh even when I'm dead tired. And he's got this ridiculous, lopsided smile he uses when he knows he's annoying me on purpose. He talks to my dog like he's a person, and he's just… nice. Sweet, a good person," I say, my voice going soft.

"That's nice, Andi," she says gently.

"He's a firefighter," I add. "And last week there was an accident. He almost died. He's still healing. And I couldn't handle it, so I… left."

Dr. Reyes doesn't flinch. She just nods. "Tell me more."

"He was getting better, and I was getting worse. Every time I looked at him, I saw a hospital bed. I saw a funeral."

She stays silent, letting the words hang.

"And I don't think it was just me spiraling either—his coworker *did* die in this accident. Brennan. It was awful."

"I'm sorry to hear that; that must have been very hard," Dr. Reyes says.

I nod. "I kept picturing what it would feel like if it happened again. If Cole was the one I lost this time. And it… it broke something in me."

She leans forward slightly. "And what did you

do when that fear showed up?"

"I panicked."

"And after that?"

"I… left."

Her eyes soften, but her voice doesn't. "Did leaving make it easier?"

"No," I whisper.

"Did it make you feel safer?"

I shake my head.

"So let's call that what it is. Avoidance."

I let out a sharp breath. "I didn't know what else to do."

"And instead of telling him all this, you ran?"

"Sorta. But I did tell him, told him I couldn't live through that kind of loss again."

There's silence between us for a minute. Not heavy. Just… full.

"And now?"

I shrug. "And now I'm here."

"Which tells me you don't want to keep running."

I lean back, still hugging the pillow in my lap. "I don't know what I want. I just know I can't keep feeling like this."

"Do you think he'd ever give up his job? Move to something with less inherent risks?"

I cross one leg over the other, shifting uncomfortably. "I don't think so. He loves it. And he's good at it. I would never ask him to do that. I mean…I don't think I would. What do you think I should do?"

She leans forward slightly. "Andi, your brain is trying to protect you from something it thinks will break you."

I release a slow breath.

"Do you agree?" she asks.

I nod, but it feels mechanical. Her words make sense, but this doesn't feel like something I can control.

"Fear is a survival instinct. But love isn't something you survive—it's something you show up for. Over and over. Even when it's terrifying. Because it's worth it."

My throat tightens. I don't have an answer.

But I'm here. And that's something.

Even if it hurts like hell.

At first, I just stare at the blank piece of paper.

It's stupid. That's what I tell myself as I drag a pen across the page like I'm writing to someone who can actually read it. Someone who might somehow *know* what's going on in my life.

But Dr. Reyes said to try it. To write to them like I would if they were still here. Like they were waiting for a phone call I never made. Like I hadn't shut that whole part of my life into a box and left it in the back of my closet.

So I write.

> *Hey,*
>
> *So... I met someone.*

The words feel like too much and not enough all at once.

> *His name's Cole. He's a firefighter. And before you roll your eyes— yeah, I know what that means. I know it's risky and messy and sometimes terrifying. But he's also steady. And kind. And stupidly handsome. And he makes me laugh even when I don't want to. He never pushes when I shut down, and he never flinches when I push back.*

I pause, chewing the end of the pen.

> *I think you'd like him. Mom, he's sort of old-fashioned—insists on holding open doors and paying for dates. Dad, he rebuilt the porch at his mom's house because he wanted to make sure it was done right.*

The tears sneak up on me. One minute I'm writing, and the next, I'm wiping my face on the sleeve of my sweatshirt.

I finish the letter without thinking too much. Without reading it over. Then I fold it in half and carry it to my bedroom.

The box is still in the same place. Top shelf of the closet, behind a stack of old textbooks I'll never touch again.

I set it on the bed and lift the lid.

Inside are photos. Movie ticket stubs. A charm bracelet. A birthday card with my dad's messy handwriting. A pressed flower from my mom's old garden. I lift it to my nose and inhale.

I slide the letter in on top. Let it settle.

Then I sit there, cross-legged and quiet, letting the weight of it all wrap around me.

They're gone.

But I'm not.

I'm here, and I have no idea what comes next.

# 40

## HEARTBREAK PROTOCOL

*Cole*

My apartment is quiet for once. No Netflix humming in the background. No visitors coming in and out with casseroles or check-ins I didn't ask for. Just me, a heating pad, and my mom rearranging my bookshelf for the third time this week.

"I liked the hockey books on the top shelf," I say without looking up.

"I like them where I can reach," she says, not missing a beat.

My ribs still ache, but not as sharp as they did last week. I'm off the heavy meds, walking more, breathing easier. But everything still hurts in that weird, slow, under-the-skin way. Like my body's made of bruises and scar tissue and quiet landmines.

And under all of it? The ache for Brennan hasn't dulled at all. And the space where Andi used to be? That feels just as raw.

I glance at the photo on the coffee table—one of the crew from last year's station holiday party. Brennan's in the middle, holding a cookie shaped like a fire hydrant, grinning like an idiot.

I swallow hard.

Mom finally sits, mug in hand, eyes on me. "How's your pain level today?"

"Manageable," I lie.

She gives me a look.

"Fine. It sucks. But less than it did."

"Progress," she says. "And the other thing?"

"What other thing?"

She raises an eyebrow. "Don't be dense, Cole. The girl."

I lean my head back against the couch. "I don't know."

"Have you called her?"

"She left."

"That doesn't answer my question."

"No, I haven't called her." I scrub a hand over my face. "I texted a few times. But I don't want to beg someone to stay when I'm still trying to remember how to keep standing."

She takes a slow sip of her tea. "Sometimes people run because they're scared, not because they don't care."

"She is scared," I say quietly. "And I get it. Hell, I scared myself. But it doesn't make it hurt less."

"No," she says. "It doesn't."

I nod. "And it's not like I can promise her nothing bad will ever happen. Maybe she can't handle it—who the hell knows."

We sit there for a minute. Just breathing. The kind of silence you can only share with family.

"I miss him," I say finally, nodding toward the photo. "I keep waiting for a dumb text or him to show up with that awful gas station candy he loved. And every time he doesn't… it's like losing him all over again."

She reaches over and squeezes my knee.

"I know you do. I'm so sorry, Cole."

I nod, blinking faster than I want to.

"Let yourself grieve. It's okay. Healing's going to take time, and you don't have to figure it all out today."

"I know." I pause. "But I really thought she'd be part of the figuring-it-out."

Mom smiles, sad and fond. "Then maybe she still will be."

# 41

## BOX WINE AND BOMBSHELLS

*Kate*

It's barely 5 p.m. and Margot's already pouring wine like she's hosting a bachelorette party instead of a Tuesday evening catch-up in my kitchen.

"I brought the good bottle," she says, wiggling it at me before twisting off the cap. "By which I mean it was on sale and has a fancy font."

Helen snorts as she drops into a chair. "As long as it's not the boxed stuff again."

"That was one time," Margot says, already handing her a glass. "And we both know you didn't hate it."

I lean against the counter, smiling as I watch them settle into their usual chaos. I'd cleaned the house this morning before leaving for work because we had plans—Margot insisted on a proper catch-up, and Helen and I both quickly agreed. We all needed this.

Helen kicks off her shoes and fixes me with a look. "Alright, spill it. How's Cole?"

I sigh and reach for my own glass. "Healing. Slow, but steady. He's walking without the cane now, only using it when he's tired. Eating like a horse again. Back to being a pain in the ass."

"So," Margot says, "normal."

"Normal-ish," I say. "He's quieter lately. I know he's dealing with some stuff. But he's getting there."

I hesitate, not wanting to overshare Cole's personal business.

"What is it?" Helen asks.

I frown and pick a piece of lint off my shirt. "On top of everything else, his girlfriend broke up with him."

Margot groans, shaking her head. "That's awful."

I nod. "I know. He really liked her too. I've been trying to stay out of it."

Margot takes a sip, then points at me. "He's lucky to have you. You know that, right?"

I roll my eyes. "He's also lucky I haven't smothered him with a pillow for refusing to rest properly."

Helen laughs. "I mean, that's love."

Margot leans back in her chair, eyeing me over

the rim of her glass. "And speaking of love…"

"No," I say immediately.

"Yes," Margot counters. "We've been patient. We've given you *weeks*. But we need Jack updates. I need details. I need adjectives."

Helen, ever the quiet instigator, just sips her wine and nods. "It's true. We've let you grieve and cope and mom your way through this, but now it's time for a little gossip."

I groan and cover my face with one hand. "Why do I even let you in my house?"

"Because we bring wine and we know too much," Margot says sweetly. "Now. Was it good? Was it... memorable?"

"It was... fine," I mumble.

Margot gasps. "Fine? You don't sneak off with a tall, broody literal GI Joe and call it *fine*. Try again."

I set my glass down with a sigh. "Okay, fine. It was *really* good. There. Are you happy?"

Helen grins. "See? That wasn't so hard."

Margot fans herself with a napkin. "You realize I'm going to picture this for at least the next twenty-four hours, right?"

"Please don't."

"Too late."

We all burst into laughter, it's too loud for the kitchen but just right for the moment. For a little while, we forget the heaviness of the last few weeks. The grief, the worry, the quiet that had settled over everything like dust.

And instead, we drink cheap wine, tell inappropriate stories, and let ourselves be women again—not just mothers or caretakers or worriers.

Just us.

And honestly? It's exactly what I needed.

Margot tops off our glasses and leans in like she's settling in for round two. "So. Are you seeing him again, or was that a one-time field trip to the land of orgasms?"

"Margot," Helen hisses, laughing.

I shake my head, cheeks warm. "We've seen each other a few times since. Coffee. A walk.

A casual dinner that involved takeout containers."

Helen raises her brows. "Sounds serious."

"Well, it's not *not* serious," I admit. "He's easy to be around. Solid. Quiet, but not in a way that makes me work for it. Just… steady."

Margot clutches her chest. "You're falling for him. Oh my gosh, first guy you met on a dating app and boom!"

"I am not," I say quickly. Then, after a beat, "Okay maybe."

Helen grins into her wine glass. "You deserve good, Kate."

I shrug. "It's been a long time since good didn't come with caveats. I'm not sure I know how to trust it yet."

"You'll get there," Helen says gently.

Margot raises her glass. "To healing, hot men, and highly inappropriate friends."

We clink our glasses and drink. And in that moment, surrounded by the women who know every version of me, I let myself hope that maybe, just maybe, it's not too late for something good.

# 42

## BACK ON DUTY (SORT OF)

*Cole*

It's weird how something as simple as walking into a building can make my heart pound like I'm gearing up for a rescue call.

But it does.

The second I step back into the station, I can feel it in my chest. The mix of nerves and nostalgia, the smell of coffee, sweat, and whatever weird air freshener someone keeps plugging in near the dorms. The familiar clang of metal lockers and the scrape of chairs on linoleum. I'm home.

"Look who it is!" Trey bellows from the kitchen. "Looking good, lover boy."

"You can't get rid of me that easily," I shoot back, stepping in slowly, careful but steady on my feet.

The guys all crowd around—clapping me on

the back, pretending not to notice the slight wince when one of them gets too enthusiastic. There's a cake on the counter, lopsided with bright blue frosting that says *Welcome Back, HFN* in painfully uneven letters.

I raise an eyebrow. "HFN?"

Trey shrugs. "It was supposed to say 'Hot Nurse Magnet,' but we ran out of space."

"You guys are idiots," I say, laughing.

It's stupid and loud and absolutely perfect. For a few minutes, it's easy to laugh. Easy to fall back into step with the rhythm of the place.

But then my eyes land on Brennan's locker.

Still closed. Still labeled. Still there.

The ache hits sharp and fast. Like it always does.

I swallow hard and force my gaze away before I spiral.

"Hey," Trey says more quietly, nudging me with his elbow. "You okay?"

I nod. "I guess so. It's just… weird being here without him."

He doesn't push. Just nods. We all feel it.

They give me a quick tour of the recent changes—new coffee maker, different turnout gear storage, some reorganized cubbies. I half-listen, letting their voices carry me through it.

And then something shifts in the room.

I look up.

Andi.

She's standing just inside the bay doors, not saying a word. Hair pulled back, hands tucked into the pockets of her ripped jeans. Her eyes lock on mine like maybe she's been staring at me this whole time.

Everything else goes quiet.

She doesn't move.

Neither do I.

But something in me exhales.

She came.

Later, when the cake is cut and the attention has shifted and no one's watching, I find her standing off to the side by the gear racks.

I stop a few feet away. Let the silence settle.

"You came," I say quietly.

She just nods, her eyes glassy. "Yeah."

And that's all it takes.

Because she's here.

"Your mom texted me," she says next. "We've kept in touch a little."

I nod. That's… interesting.

She takes a step closer. "I thought seeing you back here again would wreck me. But instead all I feel is proud."

I don't say anything. I can't yet.

"I was scared," she adds, voice trembling. "Honestly, I still am. But I'd rather be terrified with you than safe without you."

I step forward and pull her into a hug. Her arms slide around my waist, careful but sure, and I bury my face in her shoulder like I've been holding my breath since she left.

"I missed you," I murmur. "So much."

She squeezes me tighter.

And for the first time in weeks, the ache in my chest starts to lift.

A second later, Trey rounds the corner with a half-eaten slice of cake in hand. He stops short when he sees us, then grins like he just walked into a rom-com.

"Well, well, well," he says, taking a dramatic bite of frosting. "Look who's back—and brought his better half."

Andi laughs, cheeks pink but smiling. "Hi, Trey."

He gives her a quick once-over and nods approvingly. "You two are good together. Don't mess it up, kid," he says to me before sauntering off.

I don't plan on it. But it's anyone's guess if Andi's really going to let me back in.

Later, when it's just the two of us walking out to the parking lot, Andi turns to me and says, "Alright, you've got me for the rest of the day. What do you want to do?"

I don't even hesitate. "I want to see Beef."

She stops in her tracks. "Seriously?"

I nod.

"Of all the things we could do right now—" she gestures between us, eyebrow raised, mouth twitching into a smirk, "you want to go see my dog?"

"Yeah," I say, deadpan. "Beef and I have unfinished business."

She shakes her head like I'm ridiculous, but the smile stays. "Alright, fine. Let's go."

We drive to her place, and as soon as the front door opens, Beef barrels toward me like a golden wrecking ball of love and fur. I crouch—carefully—and let him bury his massive head into my chest while his tail thumps like a drumline behind him.

"I think he missed you more than I did," Andi says, laughing softly.

"I doubt that," I murmur, running a hand through Beef's thick coat.

The dog whines and licks my jaw, then promptly flops onto his back with all four paws in the air.

Andi watches from the doorway, arms crossed, expression soft as I treat the world's most ridiculous dog to a belly rub.

I lean over him like we're old friends catching up. "Was she nice to you while I was gone? Did she buy more of those salmon dog treats you like? Or did she go back to the boring peanut butter ones?"

Beef rolls to his side, panting.

"He likes the peanut butter ones too," Andi

chimes in.

I pat his head, grinning. "Be honest, buddy. Did she have any other guys over while I was out?"

Beef lets out a happy bark.

Andi groans from the doorway. "Don't encourage him."

I look over my shoulder, grinning. "Sounds like a confession to me."

"There was never anyone else, Cole. Only you." Her voice is softer now, her eyes locked on mine.

I rise slowly to my feet.

And then I pull her in.

One arm around her waist, the other curling behind her neck as I lower my mouth to hers.

The kiss is slow and deep—more gravity than fire at first—but it doesn't take long to turn molten. It's not rushed, not frantic. It's everything I've wanted to say since the second I saw her in the station earlier.

She melts into it with a quiet sound in the back of her throat that sends something surging through me. Her fingers tangle in the front of my shirt.

When we finally break apart, I rest my forehead against hers.

"Definitely missed you more," I murmur.

She laughs softly. "Yeah. Same."

We stand there for another breath, just long enough for the air to shift. Then she tugs gently on the front of my shirt and says, "Come on."

I follow her down the hall, trying not to smirk like a teenager.

Her room is simple. Warm. A little chaotic in the corners—like she threw her clothes on a chair with the intent of folding them later and then forgot—but it feels like her. Fierce, messy, unfiltered. Real.

I stand in the doorway for a second, just looking.

She turns, watching me watch her. "You gonna stand there all night or—"

I cross the room in two steps.

This time, the kiss isn't slow.

Then she pulls away to look up at me. "Just… before we do anything, I have to ask. Are you, um—medically cleared to, you know." She makes a vague motion with her hand.

My eyebrows lift, amused. "Are you asking if I'm cleared for… adult recreational activities?"

Her face goes crimson. "I was trying not to be obvious."

I grin, stepping closer. "Yes. I'm cleared. But I had to promise two different doctors I'd take it slow."

At this, she smiles.

Then she tugs off my shirt like she's been waiting, and I let her. Her hands pause when she sees the scar—pale and angry-looking across my side.

She reaches out, fingers brushing gently over it.

For a second, we both go quiet.

Her touch is soft, reverent.

I want to make a joke. Something about battle scars or how chicks dig wounded warriors. But the words die in my throat because she's looking at me like I'm breakable.

"I thought—" Her voice catches. "When Jack called, I thought—"

"Hey." I tip her chin up. "I'm here. I'm okay."

She nods, but her eyes are glassy. Then, before I can say anything else, she leans in and presses her lips to the scar. Just once. Soft as a promise.

"It's part of you," she whispers against my skin. "That makes it perfect."

I pull her against me, burying my face in her hair. She smells like vanilla and home.

"You scare the hell out of me," I admit into the curve of her neck.

She exhales like she's been holding that same truth. "You terrify me too."

We don't say anything after that.

We don't need to.

We just kiss for a long time, like we're making up for every second we spent apart.

When Andi finally pulls back, I force a breath into my lungs and try to get myself under control.

"How's the Situation?"

My lips twitch. "Extremely neglected, but otherwise holding up."

She laughs.

"He's been asking about you," I add casually. "Feel free to say hi—or, you know, properly greet him."

She arches a brow. "Hi?"

I smirk. "Preferably with your mouth."

She steps closer, and something shifts in her eyes—that look that makes my pulse kick up like I'm sixteen again. She gently nudges me toward the bed.

"Sit," she murmurs, voice low enough to wreck me.

I do—heart hammering against my ribs, breath uneven—not from nerves, but from the way she's looking at me. Like I'm the only thing in her universe right now. Like she's been thinking about this as much as I have.

She lowers herself slowly between my knees, and holy hell, the sight of her there—lavender hair falling forward, bottom lip caught between her teeth—is going to be permanently etched in my brain.

Her hands hover at my waistband for a second. "Still okay?"

"More than," I manage, voice rougher than I meant it to be.

She smiles—this small, private thing that's just for me—and her fingers get to work on my jeans.

Every movement is deliberate, like she's unwrapping something important. Something she's been waiting for.

I reach down and tangle my fingers in her hair, the strands silk-soft against my palm.

"You're beautiful," I say, because it's the truest thing I know right now.

Her cheeks flush pink, but she doesn't look away. Doesn't deflect or make a joke. Just lets the moment be what it is. One hand grips my thigh while the other moves with sure, steady confidence. But it's the way she's looking at me that undoes me—not just want, but something deeper. Something that terrifies me as much as it thrills me.

"Andi," I breathe, and her name comes out like a prayer.

She leans in, her breath warm against me, and I swear time stops. Everything narrows down to this—to her, to us, to the way she makes me feel like I'm coming apart and being put back together all at once.

"I've got you," she whispers, and then her lips are on me, and everything inside me pulls tight and warm and alive.

The past few weeks—all the fear, the grief, the space between us—start to fall away, piece by piece, under the feel of her hand and the soft warmth of her mouth. And for the first time since waking up in that hospital, I feel whole.

# 43

## A SEAT AT THE TABLE

*Andi*

The warm, spicy aroma of sizzling fajitas and freshly baked tortillas envelops us as we step into El Camino, the local Mexican joint known for its vibrant atmosphere and killer margaritas. The hostess leads us to a cozy booth near the back, where the hum of laughter and clinking glasses creates a lively backdrop.

Kate slides in first, followed by Jack, who offers a polite nod in my direction. Cole and I settle across from them, his hand finding mine under the table—it's a small gesture, but it sends a comforting warmth through me.

As we peruse the menus, Kate leans over, her eyes twinkling. "Andi, you have to try their guacamole. It's life-changing."

I grin. "I'm always up for a culinary revelation."

Kate picks up her menu, skimming it with a little hum of approval. "They've updated the menu since we were last here," she says, lifting her brows at Jack. "The shrimp tacos look tempting."

Jack leans back in the booth, arms stretched out like he owns the place. "As long as they haven't messed with the margarita recipe, I'm good."

Cole smirks beside me, then glances over. "Remember the last time we were here?" he says, his elbow brushing mine. "You dared me to try the ghost pepper salsa."

I let out a snort, the memory bubbling up fast. "Your face turned a shade of red I didn't know was medically possible."

Kate laughs, the sound light and genuine, like she's just happy to be here. "Sounds like you two have some spicy memories here."

Before I can fire back with a witty retort, the waiter arrives to take our order. Drinks are delivered quickly—margaritas all around, except for Cole, who opts for a beer with a wink in my direction. When we clink glasses, the moment feels easy, like we've all done this before.

Cole rests his arm behind me along the back of the booth, his thumb absently stroking the back of my hand under the table. It's subtle, almost unconscious, but grounding—like he's reminding me I'm not alone here.

I catch myself smiling more than I expected.

Our food arrives in a colorful, sizzling parade—fajitas, tacos, the scent of lime and cilantro making my mouth water. I'm halfway into a chip when Kate tilts her head at me, smiling like she's been sitting on this question all night.

"So, Andi," she says innocently, "any embarrassing stories about Cole you'd like to share?"

Cole groans beside me. "Or you could, you know, *not*."

I grin, already picturing it. "Well… there *was* that time he tried to cook dinner to impress me and set off the smoke alarm."

Kate's eyes sparkle. "Oh, do tell."

"He lit the oil on fire," I say, deadpan. "Trying to 'sear' something. There was a lot of smoke. A *lot*."

"In my defense," Cole mutters, his cheeks pink, "the recipe was misleading. It was very unclear about the part where I wasn't supposed to *dump* the oil in all at once."

Jack chuckles, shaking his head. There's been progress between them.

"Excuse me, Mom," Cole snorts. "You once burned Jell-O."

"Jell-O can be temperamental!"

The laughter around the table is easy now, flowing like the tequila. For a while, it feels like the world outside the booth doesn't exist—just four people, good food, better drinks, and easy conversation.

Even Jack, who had been stiff when we first sat down, seems to relax. His shoulders no longer look like they're bracing for an ambush, and he's not avoiding Cole's gaze as much.

By the time the plates are cleared and the last round of drinks is being nursed, I lean into Cole's side, warm, full, and just a little sleepy from the food.

He turns his head and murmurs, "Thanks for coming tonight. It means a lot."

I look up at him and smile, fingers tightening around his. "I'm glad we did."

His thumb brushes over my knuckles again, slow and deliberate.

And under the soft hum of the restaurant and the fading buzz of conversation, I let myself hope that this—whatever *this* is—might just work.

I glance up from my desk when I hear the door creak open.

It's Cole.

He's still in his uniform, his hair is messy, and there's fatigue around his eyes, but his smile—when it hits—still knocks the air from my lungs.

He crosses to me and props a hip against the

metal counter. "Busy night?"

"Not really. Quiet. I got stuck with the paperwork because Mikey bailed early. Again."

He winces in sympathy. "Want me to rough him up?"

"Please do. Just don't get blood on my tables. I'm already behind on disinfecting."

We stand there for a moment—me scribbling something on a chart, him watching me like I'm doing something fascinating instead of just marking liver temps.

"You're quiet," I say finally, not looking at him. "Everything okay?"

"Yeah," he says. "I just like watching you work."

I glance up, skeptical. "You're watching me weigh a gallbladder."

His eyes soften. "Still counts."

I snort and go back to the chart, trying to act like my heart isn't doing the Macarena in my chest.

He doesn't speak again for a while, just stays where he is, close but not crowding. There's comfort in it. In *him*. I've gotten used to that—his presence, his steadiness, his stupid jokes, soft touches, and the way he always seems to know when I need him.

Too used to it.

Which is maybe why, when I finally set the clipboard down and glance up again, I blurt out, "I don't want to get used to you if you're not planning on sticking around."

His eyes meet mine instantly. "What?"

I swallow. "I mean, you keep showing up. And I keep... letting you. And I know I'm not exactly easy. I say the wrong thing, or shut down, or make jokes at wildly inappropriate times—"

"You mean like right now?" he says, his voice gentle.

I laugh, nervous and dry. "Yeah. Like now."

There's a long pause. I look down at my hands. I *hate* this feeling—raw, exposed, too honest—but I can't stop.

"I think I'm in love with you," I say very quietly. "Actually, no. Not think. I *am* in love with you."

Cole exhales like he's been holding his breath for days.

He pushes off the counter and closes the space between us, hands settling lightly on my waist.

"I've been waiting for you to say that," he murmurs, "so I wouldn't screw it up by saying it first."

I blink up at him. "You—"

"I love you, too," he says, firm and sure. "Have for a while."

His hands slide up my back, and he leans in, forehead against mine. I breathe him in—soap, hand sanitizer, and something that's just *him*—and I feel it everywhere.

The morgue hums around us. The smell of antiseptic. The buzz of old lights. The quiet weight of everything I thought I couldn't have.

And somehow, this—*this*—is the place I fall in love.

Leave it to me.

I pull back an inch. "You just told me you love me in a room with three dead bodies."

He grins. "And you told me *you* love *me* while holding a gallbladder."

We both laugh, and somehow, it feels like the most romantic thing that's ever happened.

# 44

## CODE RED AT TARGET

*Andi*

"We need to talk about your grocery shopping habits."

Cole looks up from where he's examining a box of cereal like it holds the secrets of the universe. "What's wrong with my grocery shopping habits?"

"You've been staring at that box of Lucky Charms for five minutes."

"I'm reading the nutritional information."

"No, you're not." I lean against the cart, watching him. "You're trying to figure out if the marshmallows have gotten smaller since you were a kid."

His mouth twitches. "They definitely have."

"Cole."

"Corporate shrinkflation is a real problem, Andi."

I grab the box and toss it in the cart. "You're twenty-six years old."

"And?" He follows me down the aisle, hands in his pockets. "Age doesn't diminish my appreciation for magically delicious breakfast foods."

We turn the corner and nearly collide with another cart. The woman pushing it looks up, and her face brightens like its Christmas morning.

"Cole?"

I watch as recognition dawns on his face, followed immediately by what I can only describe as mild panic.

"Stephanie. Hey."

She's pretty in that yoga-instructor-who-actually-does-yoga way. Blonde ponytail, Lululemon everything, one of those giant reusable water bottles.

"Oh my gosh, it's been forever!" She touches his arm, and I have the sudden urge to hit something. Mostly her. "How are you? Still fighting fires?"

"Yeah, still at it." He steps back slightly, closer to me. "Uh, Stephanie, this is Andi. My girlfriend."

Stephanie's smile falters for exactly one second before she recovers. "Oh! Hi! So nice to meet you."

She doesn't mean it. I can tell by the way her eyes do this quick scan of me—taking in my faded band tee, ripped jeans, the fact that I'm buying generic cereal while she's got a cart full of organic everything.

"Likewise," I say, not bothering to match her fake enthusiasm.

"So how long have you two been together?" she asks, still looking at Cole like I might disappear if she ignores me hard enough.

"Six months," he says, sliding his arm around my waist. "Best six months."

The possessive gesture shouldn't make my stomach flutter. But it does.

"That's... great." Stephanie's voice goes up at the end like it's a question. "You know, I always wondered what happened with us. We had such a good thing going."

Oh. Hell. No.

"Did you?" I ask sweetly. "Because from what Cole's told me, you had a habit of 'forgetting' to mention your other boyfriend."

Cole coughs. Stephanie's face goes red.

"That was—I mean—it was complicated."

"Cheating usually is," I agree, still smiling like we're discussing the weather.

Cole's hand tightens on my hip. I can't tell if he's trying to hold me back or hold himself back from laughing.

"Well." Stephanie straightens her perfect ponytail. "I should go. Brad's waiting in the car."

"Brad?" Cole asks. "The personal trainer?"

"Investment banker," she corrects quickly. "It's new, actually."

"Congratulations," I say. "I hope he knows about all of you."

She shoots me a look that could peel paint, then turns back to Cole with this tragic expression. "It was really good seeing you, Cole. You look... happy."

"I am," he says simply.

She wheels her cart away like she's fleeing a crime scene. The second she rounds the corner, Cole turns to me.

"Did you just—"

"Defend your honor? Yes."

"That was—"

"Petty? Also yes." I grin.

He stares at me for a beat, then crushes his mouth to mine right there in the cereal aisle. When he pulls back, we're both breathing hard.

"That," he says against my lips, "was the hottest thing I've ever seen."

"Really? Because I have follow-up questions about the personal trainer."

He groans. "Can we not?"

"Was his name actually Brad? Because that feels too on the nose."

"Andi."

"Did he wear those tiny tank tops? The ones with the aggressive arm holes?"

"I'm going to kiss you again to make you stop talking."

"That's not really a deterr—"

He makes good on his threat, backing me against the shelf of Frosted Flakes. This kiss is different. Deeper. His hand slides into my hair, and I forget we're in public until—

"Excuse me."

We break apart to find an elderly woman glaring at us over her glasses.

"Some of us are trying to shop," she says pointedly.

"Sorry," Cole says, not looking sorry at all. "We were just—"

"I can see what you were doing." She sniffs. "In my day, we kept that sort of thing private."

"Ma'am," I say seriously, "in your day, people were doing it in the backs of Buicks. At least we kept our clothes on."

Her mouth opens and closes like a fish. Cole makes this choking sound that might be horror or laughter.

"Well, I never—"

"Clearly," I mutter.

Cole grabs my hand and the cart, steering us away before I can cause more scandal. We make it two aisles over before he loses it completely, laughing so hard he has to lean against the freezer section.

"You just—that poor woman—"

"She started it."

"You told an old woman she wasn't getting laid enough."

"I *implied* it. There's a difference."

He pulls me against him, still shaking with laughter. "You're a troublemaker."

"You love it."

"I do." He kisses my forehead. "I really, really do."

"Good. Now can we talk about how your ex shops in the bougie Target? Because that feels like information you should've shared."

"Can we talk about how you went full territorial?"

"I did not—" I stop. "Okay, maybe a little."

"A little?" He grins. "Babe, you practically peed on me to mark your territory."

"That's gross."

"And accurate."

I shove him, but he just catches my hands and pulls me closer.

"For the record," he murmurs, "I liked it."

"Yeah?"

"Yeah." He glances down the aisle, then back at me with this look that makes my knees weak. "You know what? Let's go."

"We haven't finished shopping."

"Don't care." He's already pushing the cart toward checkout. "I need to get you home."

"Cole, we need actual food—"

"Lucky Charms count as food."

"No, they don't."

"They're fortified with vitamins. Says so on the box."

"You're impossible."

"And you're hot when you're jealous." He stops walking, turns to face me. "Like, seriously hot. I'm having thoughts."

"In Target?"

"Especially in Target."

I roll my eyes, but I'm smiling. "Fine. But we're coming back tomorrow for real groceries."

"Deal." He leans down, lips brushing my ear. "But right now, I need to show you exactly how much I appreciate you putting my ex in her place."

My whole body goes warm. "That's... acceptable."

"Just acceptable?"

"Take me home and we'll upgrade it to enthusiastic."

He practically sprints to the checkout.

The teenage cashier looks at our pathetic haul—Lucky Charms, milk, and the emergency bottle of wine I grabbed—and smirks. "Big dinner plans?"

"The biggest," Cole says seriously.

I elbow him. The cashier's smirk widens.

"Would you like bags?"

"Definitely bags," I say quickly. "All the bags. Speed is good."

Cole's hand finds the small of my back, thumb stroking in a way that's definitely not helping my composure. The cashier takes his sweet time, because apparently the universe hates me.

"You guys have a rewards card?"

"No," we say in unison.

"Would you like to sign up? You get—"

"We're good," Cole interrupts. "Really good. Just the cereal. And the wine. Mostly the wine."

The kid finally gets the hint and finishes ringing us up. Cole throws cash at him, grabs our bag, and practically drags me out of the store.

"Smooth," I say as we hit the parking lot. "Real subtle."

"Says the woman who just verbally destroyed my ex in the cereal aisle."

"She had it coming."

"She did." He opens my door, caging me against the car for a moment. "And now, so do you."

"That was terrible."

"You love my terrible lines."

I do. Heaven help me, I really do.

"Home," I say. "Now."

"Yes, ma'am."

He kisses me once more—quick and hard and full of promise—then rounds the car.

As we pull out of the parking lot, I catch sight of Stephanie loading her organic groceries into a Tesla. She sees us too, and her expression could curdle milk.

I might wave.

Just a little.

Cole catches me and laughs. "Troublemaker."

"Your troublemaker," I correct.

"Yeah," he says, reaching over to lace our fingers together. "Mine."

And somehow, in the Target parking lot with a box of Lucky Charms in the back and my lipstick probably smeared everywhere, that word feels like everything.

# 45

## BROKEN PARTS

*Andi*

I wake up at 3:17 a.m. to find Cole's side of the bed empty and cold.

My hand automatically reaches across the sheets, searching for him even though I already know he's not there. The bathroom light is off. The hallway is dark. But I can see a sliver of light coming from under the door of what we've been calling the spare room—though we both know what it'll eventually become.

Rising from the bed, I pad along in the dark.

I find him sitting on the floor, back against the wall, staring at a paint sample card in his hand. Beef is curled beside him, massive head resting on Cole's thigh.

"Hey," I whisper, sliding down to sit next to him.

He doesn't look at me. "Did I wake you?"

"No." I lean into his shoulder, studying his profile in the dim light from the streetlamp outside. "Bad dream?"

He's quiet for so long I think he won't answer. Then, he shakes his head. "I keep seeing him."

Brennan. It's been almost a year, but grief doesn't follow calendars.

"In my dreams, he's always just out of reach," Cole continues, voice rough. "I'm trying to get to him, trying to pull him clear, but I can't move fast enough. And then I wake up and remember that I'll never be fast enough because he's already gone."

I take his hand, lacing our fingers together. His are cold.

"I thought moving in together would make it better," he says. "Like having you here all the time would chase away the ghosts. But sometimes..." He trails off, jaw working.

"Sometimes it makes it scarier," I finish softly. "Because now you have more to lose."

He turns to look at me then, eyes glossy in the low light. "Yeah."

I understand. Possibly better than anyone. Every happy moment carries the shadow of what could go wrong. Every time he leaves for a shift, every time I watch him put on that uniform, there's a voice in my head calculating odds, measuring risks, preparing for impact. I hate it, but it comes with the territory of loving someone this much.

"I think about kids," he says suddenly. "About this room. About painting it yellow or green or whatever color you tell me to paint it. And then I think about them growing up without me. Or you having to explain why Daddy's not coming home."

My throat tightens. "Cole—"

"I know." He squeezes my hand. "I know we can't live like that. But knowing and feeling are different things."

We sit in silence for a moment. Outside, a car passes, headlights sweeping across the wall. The paint sample in his hand is a soft blue called "Dream Dust."

"You know what I think about?" I ask finally.

He makes a questioning sound.

"I think about Sunday mornings when you make pancakes and get batter everywhere. I think about you teaching our kids to ride bikes in the driveway. I think about growing old with you, arguing about what to watch on TV when we're seventy."

"Andi—"

"I think about all the life we get to live," I continue, turning to face him fully. "All the ordinary, beautiful moments. And yeah, I'm terrified. Every single day. But the fear means something. It means what we have is worth being afraid for."

He drops the paint sample and pulls me into his lap, burying his face in my neck. I feel him shake slightly—not quite crying, but close.

"I love you so much it scares me," he whispers against my skin.

"I know." I hold him tighter. "Me too."

We stay like that for a long time, just breathing together in the dark of our maybe-someday-nursery. The weight of loving someone this much—it's not easy. It's not simple. But it's real.

"We could paint it yellow," I say eventually. "Sunshine yellow."

He pulls back to look at me. "Yeah?"

"Yeah. But not yet. Not until we're ready."

"Okay." He nods slowly, some of the tension leaving his shoulders. "Can we go back to bed?"

Beef stretches and yawns, then wedges himself more firmly between us, like he's trying to absorb whatever sadness is in the air. He's good at that.

"Come on."

He follows me down the hall, our fingers still intertwined. When we crawl back under the covers, he pulls me close, my back to his chest, his arm heavy and protective around my waist.

"Thank you," he murmurs into my hair.

"For what?"

"For getting it. For being here. For not trying to fix it."

I turn in his arms so we're face to face. "We're both broken in places," I whisper. "But I think maybe our broken parts fit together."

He kisses me then, soft and lingering, tasting like gratitude and grief and love all mixed together.

# 46

## MARRIED LIFE, BUT MAKE IT ICELANDIC

*Cole*

**One Year Later**

The sky outside is still bright even though it's almost midnight. Iceland's weird like that—it's messing with my internal clock, but I don't care—because my wife is naked in a hot spring and keeps making dolphin noises every time she kicks her foot through the steam.

The air smells faintly of sulfur and wild moss. Somewhere nearby, the sound of water trickles over stone, and the sky casts everything in silver-blue light. It feels like we're at the end of the world— with nothing but time and each other.

"You know this is probably sacred Viking water or something," I say, sinking deeper beside her, arms spread along the stone edge. "We're probably breaking like ten different laws."

"Please. If Vikings had access to a natural spa like this, they'd be in it naked too." She raises her brows, daring me to argue.

It doesn't get much better than this. So far, our week has been spent in steaming saunas, leisurely hikes, and a private cabin tucked so far into the middle of nowhere I'm not convinced we aren't technically squatters. We picked Iceland because it was weird and wild and beautiful—kind of like her.

I reach over and flick water at her.

"How you doing over there, big guy?" she asks, eyeing me.

"I'm fan-freaking-tastic." And it's true. This is the happiest I've ever been.

She tips her head back against the rock, steam curling around her shoulders. "This is the best honeymoon spot. Ten out of ten. Hot, quiet, isolated. Minimal murder vibes."

"Yeah," I say, trailing my fingers through the water. "All we're missing is a commemorative plaque. Here lies *The Situation, fully appreciated Iceland, July 3rd, 9:42 p.m.*"

She snorts. "Dude, you're still calling it that?"

"You named it!"

"And I regret it every day."

I lean in, voice low and mock-serious. "Which is why I think it's only fair I name *yours*."

She blinks. "Nope."

"Come on. Equal opportunity."

She lifts her chin, considering it. "Fine. But I get full veto power."

"Obviously."

I rub my hands together like a cartoon villain. "Alright. First suggestion: *The Chamber of Secrets*."

She gags. "Immediate no."

"Why? Mysterious. Magical. Very... restricted access."

"You are *so* lucky you're hot."

I grin. "Okay, okay. What about *Mount Pleasuremore*?"

She squints. "That one's so bad I think I got a cramp just hearing it."

"You're a tough crowd."

She slides closer, wrapping her legs around my waist under the water like she's planning to drown me if I keep going. "Try again before I revoke naming privileges permanently."

I press my lips together, dramatically thoughtful. "Hmm... *Andi's Inferno*?"

She stares at me. "That's the best you got?"

"No, but it's currently leading the pack."

I'm quiet for a minute, just watching her. The way the light hits her collarbone, her flushed skin, the damp tendrils of lavender hair escaping her braid... She's beautiful. And somehow mine.

I don't think I'll ever get tired of that word.

"Don't tell me you're out of ideas already," she says, goading me.

"What about... *Snuggles McDangerZone?*"

She side-eyes me. "Absolutely not."

"*AndiLand.* Population: Very lucky me."

She bursts into laughter. "You're insane."

She kisses me, and I get momentarily distracted.

Then I pull back with a smug grin. "Okay, I've got it. *The Situation's Nemesis.* Because she's the only one who can destroy him."

She sighs and leans her head on my shoulder. "You are the dumbest man I've ever loved."

"I'll take that as confirmation that you *do*, in fact, love me."

"Unfortunately, yes. Very much."

We sit like that for a while, the water hot and the air cool, steam curling around us. In the distance, there's a strange bird sound that Andi claims is a puffin but could honestly be a malfunctioning goat for all I know.

The steam rises in lazy coils. Her fingers draw soft patterns on my chest, and for a second, I forget the rest of the world exists. It's just us. And warmth. And a weird bird.

I shift slightly, burying my nose in her damp hair. "This is the best thing I've ever done, by the way."

"Name my vajayjay?"

"Marry you."

She goes quiet, fingers tracing lazy patterns on my chest. "Yeah. Same."

Did I picture myself getting married at twenty-six? No. But I never imagined meeting someone like Andi. She stormed her way into my life, and everything finally made sense. Actually, that's not true; she didn't storm her way in. In fact, she tried to flee from me every chance she got. Good thing I'm stubborn and finally wore her down.

I press a kiss to her temple. "But also yes, I will eventually find the perfect nickname."

"I swear to you, Cole—"

*"Andi's Arc?"*

She dunks me.

# EPILOGUE

## AndiLand

*Andi*

"**C**ole!" I yell, balancing the world's squirmiest baby on my hip while trying not to get pureed banana in my hair. "This one is yours. I did the last blowout. I'm officially on a diaper strike."

Across the yard, Cole looks up from the grill—shirtless, tongs in hand, baseball cap on backwards, grinning like a man who has no idea his daughter just redecorated her onesie with something suspiciously green and gelatinous.

"Happy to take my turn," he calls back, voice all sunshine and smugness. "That's how parenting works, babe."

"Not when she's leaking *that*."

Kate snorts from her lounge chair, sipping iced tea like she's watching a comedy special. "Oh, honey. You think it gets better once they're potty trained, but then they just start peeing *on purpose*."

Jack's beside her, flipping through a dog-eared paperback, the baby monitor from their house somehow clipped to his belt like he's the new sheriff in town. They're newly married and disgustingly cute about it—he calls her 'darlin'' now like he was born in a Hallmark movie.

"Well," Jack says without looking up, "at least Beef's housebroken."

Beef, the thousand-pound fluff monster, is currently curled up under the picnic table with our two-year-old daughter asleep across his back like a tiny, drooling queen on a furry throne. Her sippy cup is in one hand, half a graham cracker in the other, and I'm ninety percent sure she bribed him with food scraps to stay perfectly still.

"They're co-conspirators," Cole mutters as he approaches with a fresh diaper and his patented *I got this, babe* smirk. "I'm starting to think she speaks fluent dog."

"She does," I say. "That's her first language. English is her second."

Cole takes her gently from my arms, not even flinching as she gurgles and snorts and proceeds to smear banana across his shoulder.

"Hi, angel," he coos, kissing her cheek and pulling a face when he gets baby drool in his mouth. "Wow. Okay. That's... earthy."

"She's got your aim," I say, rubbing my temple. "And your weird love of chaos."

He beams. "High praise."

Kate waves a baby wipe in the air like a flag of surrender. "There are more in the bag under the stroller. And for the record? This is the *best* entertainment I've had in weeks."

"Glad we can be your sitcom," I grumble, plopping into the chair beside her.

She pats my leg. "You're a great mom, Andi."

I narrow my eyes. "Is that what you said after I cried over accidentally buying non-organic puffs?"

"You care," she says, simple and true. "That's the whole job."

Across the yard, Cole is narrating the diaper change like he's hosting a nature documentary.

"Here we have the elusive Wild Poop," he says, voice low and reverent. "It's cunning. It's fast. It's *everywhere*."

"Cole!" I bark, trying not to laugh.

He grins back at me over his shoulder. "You're the one who didn't want to do this round. You gave up naming rights."

I groan, burying my face in my hands.

"Don't worry," he adds. "I'll name it something classy. Like... Sir Stinks-a-Lot."

Kate leans over. "Still dreamy."

"I know, right?" I say, peeking at him. "Best dad ever. Total weirdo. I'm stuck for life."

Later, the baby's clean, the toddler's been bribed with cookies, and Beef has consumed five unauthorized mini hot dogs. We gather on the porch—Jack and Kate in their matching rockers, Cole and I tangled together on the swing, the baby asleep across both of our laps and our toddler digging in a potted plant with a stolen spatula.

I don't have the energy to stop her.

"She's gonna be just like you," Cole says, watching our daughter methodically destroy my begonias. "Stubborn. Determined. Completely unable to leave well enough alone."

"Good," I say. "Someone needs to keep you on your toes when I'm tired."

He chuckles.

The sun's slipping behind the trees, painting the sky with soft gold and cotton-candy pink. The air smells like charcoal, sunscreen, and baby shampoo. This messy, noisy, perfect little moment is everything I never knew I wanted.

I glance over at Cole, who's stroking the baby's hair with that soft look he gets when he thinks no one's watching.

"I love you," I whisper.

"Love you more." He doesn't look away from her. "Still can't believe you let me knock you up twice," he murmurs against my hair.

I elbow him gently. "Behave."

Kate sighs happily. "Alright. But next week,

it's *our* turn to host."

"Deal," Cole and I both say at the same time.

We stay like that until the stars come out, our weird, patched-together little family held together by hot dogs, baby wipes, and unconditional love.

Who knew that a meet-cute in a morgue could lead to this? To banana-covered chaos and stolen spatulas and a love so big it barely fits in our messy little yard.

Honestly?

It's perfect.

Thank you so much for reading Cole & Andi's story! I have another standalone you might love. Dean is incredibly grumpy and broken, and Poppy is his medicine. There's also a very naughty goat.

## THE GRUMP NEXT DOOR

# BONUS

## Into the Wild(erness)

*Andi*

**"A**bsolutely not."

Cole doesn't even look up from where he's loading the back of his truck. "You already said yes."

"That was before I knew what camping actually *entailed*."

"It's one nights, babe. Twenty-four hours. You can do anything for twenty-four hours."

"I've binged entire TV series in twenty-four hours. That doesn't mean I want to sleep on the ground." I hold up the solar shower bag I found in the camping supplies pile. "What is this?"

He glances over, grinning. "Solar shower. You hang it in the sun, it heats up, you rinse off."

"Rinse off *where*?" I lift one eyebrow.

"Outside."

"Outside?" My tone shifts to panic.

"Yeah. Behind a tree or whatever."

I stare at him. "You want me to shower. Outside. Behind a tree. Like a woodland creature."

"Or you could just not shower. It's one night, two days…"

"Cole Hartley, I swear to—"

"Babe." He crosses to me, taking the solar shower from my hands and setting it aside. His hands find my waist, and he's looking at me like I'm the most entertaining person alive. "You said you wanted to try things that scare you. Be more spontaneous."

"I was thinking, like, karaoke or learning to ski. Not *feral bathing*."

He laughs, pressing a kiss to my forehead. "It's camping. People have been doing it for thousands of years."

"Yes, and then they invented hotels. For a reason."

"Come on." His thumbs stroke my sides gently. "I've been wanting to take you camping since we met. You keep saying you want to understand why I love the outdoors so much. This is how."

I sigh, looking past him at the truck bed that's slowly filling with gear: tent, sleeping bags, cooler, lanterns, and about fifteen other things I don't recognize.

"Fine," I mutter. "But I'm bringing the solar

shower."

"Deal." He kisses me quickly, triumphant. "Now go get Beef. He's gonna lose his mind."

Beef does, in fact, lose his mind.

The second we pull into the campground—a sprawling, tree-dense paradise about two hours outside the city—he starts whining and pawing at the window like he's spotted the Promised Land.

"Down, bubs," I say, trying to keep him from climbing into the front seat. "You're going to give me a concussion."

Cole parks in our designated spot—a small clearing surrounded by towering pines—and Beef practically explodes out of the truck the second I open the door.

"He's never been camping before," I point out, watching him sprint in circles around a tree.

"Doesn't matter. It's in his DNA. Look at him—he's *thriving*."

Beef stops mid-sprint to sniff aggressively at a pinecone, his tail wagging so hard that his whole body wiggles.

"Okay, that's actually adorable," I admit.

Cole starts unloading gear, and I try to help, but honestly, I'm not sure what half of this stuff is for. There are poles, stakes, tarps, and bungee cords, and I'm starting to think we're building a small village instead of just sleeping outside for two nights.

"Where do we start?" I ask.

"Tent first. Then we'll set up camp."

"Aren't those the same thing?"

He grins. "You're cute when you're clueless."

"I'm going to murder you and leave you for the bears." I grin sweetly at him.

"There aren't any bears here."

"Then I'll import some."

Twenty minutes later, I'm rethinking every life choice that led me to this moment.

The tent is half-collapsed, the poles are in a nonsensical pile, and Cole is laughing so hard that he has to sit down.

"It's not funny," I snap, holding up two identical-looking poles. "How am I supposed to know which one goes where?"

"They're color-coded."

"They're both *gray*."

"Different shades of gray."

I throw one at him. He catches it, still laughing.

"Okay, okay. Come here." He stands, brushing dirt off his jeans, and guides me over to the tent frame. "This part goes here, see? And then you thread it through like this."

I watch him work, his hands steady and sure, and I'm hit with a wave of affection that's so strong it almost knocks me over. He's patient. He's not frustrated that I don't know what I'm doing. He's just... here. Teaching me. Making space for me in his world.

"Got it?" he asks, glancing at me.

"Yeah," I say softly. "I got it."

We finish setting up the tent together, and by the time we're done, I'm sweaty and covered in dirt, but there's something satisfying about it. Like we built something. Together. Even if that something is just temporary shelter.

Cole steps back, hands on his hips, surveying our work. "Not bad for your first time."

"It's lopsided."

"I prefer to think of it as *rustic*," he grins.

My phone buzzes in my pocket. I pull it out to find a text from Kate.

> Kate: How's the great out-
> doors? Do I need to send a
> search party?

I snap a picture of the tent and send it back.

> Me: Still alive. Barely.

> Kate: I'm proud of you, sweet-
> heart. Jack says to tell you to
> watch out for poison ivy.

> Me: There's POISON IVY?!

Kate: He's kidding. Probably.

I show Cole the texts, and he laughs.
Another buzz. This time, it's Shay.

Shay: Please tell me you're
not actually sleeping on the
GROUND like a cave person.

Me: Apparently I'm sleeping in
a tent like a very dignified cave
person.

Shay: I give it twelve hours
before you're back home crying into takeout.

Me: You have so little faith in
me.

Shay: I have a REALIS-
TIC amount of faith in you.
There's a difference.

I slip my phone back into my pocket, grinning
despite myself.

"What?" Cole asks.

"Shay thinks I'm going to bail."

"Are you?"

I look around—at the trees, the dappled sunlight, Beef rolling in something that definitely
smells like death. At Cole, standing there in his

flannel, worn jeans, and boots, looking at me like I'm the best thing that's ever happened to him.

"No," I say. "I'm not."

## Cole

She's trying so hard.

I can see it in the way she's carefully arranging our sleeping bags inside the tent, making sure they're perfectly aligned. In the way she's studying the camp stove like she wants to learn how it works. In the way she keeps glancing at me, as if she wants to make sure she's doing this right.

"Babe," I say gently, "you don't have to be perfect at this."

She looks up, startled. "I'm not trying to be perfect."

"You've adjusted those sleeping bags three times."

"They were crooked."

"They're sleeping bags. They're supposed to be a little chaotic."

She sits back on her heels, sighing. "I don't know how to do this. How to just... *be* without a plan."

I crawl into the tent beside her, sitting close enough that our knees touch. "That's kind of the point. Camping isn't about having everything figured out. It's about adapting. Rolling with it."

"Yeah, that sounds like a nightmare."

I laugh and reach for her hand. "I know it's hard for you, and I'm not asking you to be someone you're not. But maybe—just for this weekend—you could try letting go a little? See what happens?"

She's quiet for a moment, then nods slowly. "Okay. I'll try."

"That's all I'm asking."

We spend the afternoon exploring. Andi has never been hiking before, and watching her navigate the trail is equal parts endearing and hilarious. She stops every ten feet to identify plants on her phone. "This is a hemlock. Did you know hemlock is poisonous?" she says, and she keeps asking if we're lost, even though we're on a clearly marked path.

Beef is in heaven. He bounds ahead, circles back, and then bounds ahead again, as if he can't believe his luck.

"He's going to sleep for a week after this," Andi says, watching him chase a squirrel up a tree.

"Worth it."

We reach a clearing with a view of the valley below, and Andi stops to genuinely take it in.

"Okay," she admits. "This is pretty."

"Just pretty?"

"Fine. It's beautiful. Happy?"

"Very." I slide an arm around her waist, pulling her close. "Thanks for doing this. I know it's not your thing."

She leans into me, resting her head on my shoulder. "You do a lot of things that aren't your thing for me. I figured I should return the favor."

"Like what?"

"You watch true crime documentaries even though they freak you out. You let Beef sleep in our bed even though he takes up seventy percent of the mattress. You learned how to make peach pie just because I mentioned my mom used to make it."

My throat tightens. "Those things aren't hard."

"Neither is this." She tilts her head up to look at me. "Well, okay, this is a *little* hard, but I'm doing it anyway."

I kiss her then—slow and sweet—because I love her so much it feels like it might crack me open.

Dinner is an adventure. That's the word I decide to use.

Cole insists on cooking over the camp stove, which apparently requires a degree in engineering to operate. I watch as he fidgets with the propane, adjusts the flame, and curses under his breath when the pan nearly tips over.

"Need help?" I ask innocently.

"I've got it."

"You sure? Because it looks like you're about to burn down the forest."

"Have a little faith, Callahan."

Ten minutes later, we're eating slightly charred hot dogs and baked beans straight from the can, and honestly? It's kind of perfect.

"This is the best meal I've ever had," I say, deadpan.

"Liar."

"No, really. The dirt adds a certain... *je ne sais quoi.*"

He flicks a bean at me, laughing.

Beef, of course, is living his best life, snuffling around the campsite for dropped food and rolling in the dirt at every opportunity.

"He's going to need a bath when we get home," I say.

"Worth it. Look how happy he is."

As the sun starts to set, Cole builds a fire. I sit on a log nearby, wrapped in a blanket, watching the flames flicker and dance. There's something hypnotic about it—primal, almost. My phone buzzes again.

**Trey: Yo, heard you're camp-**

ing. Cole better not be making you pee in the woods.

I snort.

Me: Too late. Already violated
by nature.

Trey: RIP. You're braver than
most.

Me: Or dumber.

Trey: Nah. You're good for
him. Even if you're suffering.

Me: Not suffering. Surprisingly.

Trey: Look at you. Growing.

I smile, slipping my phone away.

Cole sits beside me, close enough that our thighs press together. "Who was that?"

"Trey. Checking in."

"Of course he is." He drapes an arm over my shoulders. "You doing okay?"

"Yeah." And I mean it. "I'm actually... kind of having fun?"

"Kind of?"

"Don't push it, Hartley."

He chuckles, pressing a kiss to my temple.

We sit in comfortable silence for a while, watching the fire. The woods are alive with sound—crickets, the rustle of leaves, and something that might be an owl in the distance. It's not quiet, exactly, but it's peaceful in a way I didn't expect.

"I've been thinking," Cole says after a while.

"Dangerous."

He ignores that. "About what you said the other night. In the nursery."

My chest tightens. "Yeah?"

"You were right. About the fear meaning something. About it being worth it." He shifts, turning to face me more fully. "I think I've been so scared of losing you—or losing what we have—that I forget to just... live in it. You know?"

I nod, my throat thick. "Yeah. I know."

"I don't want to spend our life together waiting for the other shoe to drop. I want to spend it actually living—making memories, building something."

"Even if it scares you?"

"*Especially* if it scares me." He takes my hand, lacing our fingers together. "Because if I've learned anything from losing Brennan, it's that time isn't guaranteed. So we might as well make the most of it."

I lean in, resting my forehead against his. "When did you get so wise?"

"I've always been wise. You just didn't notice

because you were too busy being difficult."

I laugh, though it comes out watery. "I love you."

"Love you more."

"Impossible."

We stay like that until the fire burns low and the stars come out—so many stars I lose count—and for the first time in a long time, I'm not thinking about what could go wrong.

I'm just here.

With him.

And it's enough.

## Cole

Later, when we're in the tent and Andi's curled against me in her sleeping bag, she whispers, "I'm sorry I'm not better at this."

I frown, stroking her hair. "Better at what?"

"Spontaneity. Adventure. Not needing a plan for everything."

"Hey." I tilt her chin up so she looks at me. "You're here, aren't you? That's all that matters."

"I almost bailed three times before we left."

"But you didn't."

"I wanted to."

"But you didn't," I repeat firmly. "You showed

up. You tried. That's what counts."

She's quiet for a moment, then says, "I used to think love meant not being scared. Like if you really loved someone, the fear would just... go away. But it doesn't, does it?"

"No," I admit. "It doesn't."

"So what do we do?"

"We love each other anyway." I press a kiss to her forehead. "We choose each other even when it's hard. Especially when it's hard."

She shifts closer, and I can feel her smiling against my chest.

Outside, Beef is snoring near the campfire, probably dreaming of squirrels. The wind rustles through the trees, and somewhere in the distance, I hear the hoot of an owl.

Andi's hand finds mine under the blanket, and she threads our fingers together like she's anchoring herself.

"Thank you," she whispers.

"For what?"

"For being patient with me. For not giving up when I wanted to run. For bringing me here."

"Always."

I wake up warm.

Physically warm—because Cole is basically a human furnace and has somehow wrapped himself around me like a very attractive octopus. But I'm also warm in that deep, settled way that has nothing to do with the temperature. I'm not ready to admit it out loud, but this is…nice.

Sunlight filters through the tent fabric, casting everything in a soft green glow. Cole is still asleep, his face relaxed, one heavy arm draped over my waist.

I should feel trapped. Uncomfortable. Desperate for coffee and a real bathroom.

But I don't.

I feel... content. *Huh*. Who knew? Camping's not so bad…at least not when I have a sexy, sleeping Cole by my side.

Beef starts barking outside—probably at a bird, a leaf, or his own shadow—and Cole stirs, groaning.

"What time is it?" he mumbles.

"Early."

"Too early."

"Beef disagrees."

He cracks one eye open, grinning. "Beef can wait."

His hand slides under my shirt, fingers tracing lazy patterns on my lower back, and suddenly I'm very awake.

"Cole," I warn.

"Hmm?"

"We're in a tent."

"I'm aware."

"In a campground."

"Very aware." His mouth finds my neck, and I shiver. "But we're also alone. And you're really warm. I've been thinking about this since we got here."

"We had sex last night."

"Yeah, and?" His hand moves higher, and my breath catches. "I'm a man of simple needs, Andi. You. Me. Alone time. It's a winning combination."

I laugh, but it turns into a gasp when his thumb brushes the underside of my breast. "Someone's going to hear."

"Then I guess you'll have to be quiet."

He rolls me onto my back, settling between my legs, and okay, maybe morning sex in a tent isn't the worst idea he's ever had.

"Wait," I say, even as my hands are already tugging at his shirt. "What about Beef?"

"He's fine. He's got the whole forest to entertain him."

"He might come back."

"He won't."

Famous last words.

We're mid-kiss—his hand halfway up my thigh, my fingers tangled in his hair—when we hear it.

The unmistakable sound of Beef's giant paws thundering toward the tent, followed by enthusiastic panting and the rustle of him flopping down right outside the entrance.

We freeze.

"You were saying?" I whisper.

Cole drops his forehead to my shoulder, groaning. "I hate him."

"No, you don't."

"Right now? I really do."

I'm laughing too hard to care, and after a second, Cole starts laughing too. We're just lying there in our sleeping bags, tangled together and cracking up like idiots.

"Okay," he says finally, rolling off me. "New plan. We'll bribe him with food and hope he wanders off."

"Solid strategy."

He unzips the tent and tosses a piece of jerky into the distance. Beef, predictably, sprints after it.

"Now," Cole says, turning back to me with that wolfish grin I know all too well, "where were we?"

An hour later, we emerge from the tent, looking thoroughly rumpled and extremely pleased with ourselves.

Beef gives us a judgmental look.

"Don't start," I tell him.

We pack up camp slowly, neither of us in a rush to leave. Cole teaches me how to properly fold the tent (apparently, my method was "creative but inefficient"), and I only threaten to break up with him twice.

As we load the last of the gear into the truck, my phone buzzes.

> **Kate: Still alive?**

> **Me: Barely. But yes.**

> **Kate: I'm so proud of you. Truly.**

> **Me: Thanks, Mama H.**

I send it before I can overthink it, and when she responds with a heart emoji, mine does this stupid flutter thing.

Cole catches my expression. "You good?"

"Yeah." I pocket my phone, smiling. "Really good."

We drive home with the windows down, Beef's head hanging out the back and my hand in Cole's.

"So," he says casually, "think you'd do it again?"

I pretend to consider. "Maybe. In like... five years."

"I'll take it."

"But next time, I'm bringing a toilet."

He laughs, squeezing my hand. "Deal."

As we pull onto the highway, the forest disappearing in the rearview mirror, I realize something: I'm not scared anymore. Or maybe I am, but I'm doing it anyway. And that feels like progress.

That feels like love.

# THE GRUMP NEXT DOOR

*One guest house. One week. One slow-burn disaster waiting to happen.*

Dean Whitaker has zero interest in weddings, fairy lights, or the perky woman currently turning his guest house into a scented-candle crime scene.

He's a divorce attorney. He thrives on prenups, logic, and *not* getting glitter on his suits.

Poppy Monroe is a wedding planner with a checklist for everything—except how to survive living next door to a hot, brooding, tightly wound lawyer—aka the groom's brother.

They're opposites in every way—except for the undeniable chemistry neither of them wants to talk about.

Their mission: survive one week of wedding chaos.

Her vibe: sunshine and glitter pens.
His vibe: whiskey and restraint.

Opposites attract. Then they combust.

# ACKNOWLEDGMENTS

To my husband, John, and my two wonderful sons—you're my heart. Thank you for loving me through the chaos, for putting up with my endless plotting, and for reminding me what truly matters. I adore you more than words.

To the best marketing guru an author could wish for, *thank you* to Alyssa Garcia for all the things! I'm so glad the dream team is back together!

To my besties — thank you for every lunch date, happy hour, girl's trip, and set of matching pajamas. I'm so lucky to have you in every chapter. You're my favorite side characters!

To my readers—thank you, thank you, *thank you!* You're the reason these stories exist, and I hope you loved quirky, unforgettable Andi as much as I did. Writing her was such a delight, and I had so much fun playing with this book. I've never written four point-of-view characters before, and the challenge stretched me in all the best ways.

I'm so grateful to every single one of you for joining me on this journey. Here's to more stories, more characters to fall for, and more books to share with you.

# ABOUT THE AUTHOR

Kendall Ryan is a *New York Times*, *Wall Street Journal*, and *USA Today* bestselling author of flirty, feel-good romance filled with heart, heat, and plenty of banter. An American author who has lived all over the world, her books have sold millions of copies and been translated into multiple languages. She writes swoony heroes, bold heroines, and stories that make you laugh, blush, and fall in love. When she's not dreaming up new plotlines, she is a proud mom to two amazing sons and the wife of her real-life hero.

# OTHER TITLES BY KENDALL RYAN

*Unravel Me*
*Make Me Yours*
*Filthy Beautiful Lies*
*The Room Mate*
*Dirty Little Secret*
*Dirty Little Promise*
*Baby Daddy*
*Love Machine*
*Flirting with Forever*
*Playing for Keeps*
*The Rebel*
*The Forever Formula*
*A Beginner's Guide to Forever*

For a complete list of Kendall's books, visit:
www.kendallryanbooks.com/books

www.ingramcontent.com/pod-product-compliance
Lightning Source LLC
Chambersburg PA
CBHW021229190726
48289CB00005B/1242